Nikola the Outlaw

»»»»»»»»» 《《《《《《《《《

Ivan Olbracht

Nikola the Outlaw

TRANSLATED FROM THE CZECH
BY MARIE K. HOLEČEK

NORTHWESTERN UNIVERSITY PRESS
EVANSTON, ILLINOIS

»»»»»»»»»» 《《《《《《《《《《

Northwestern University Press
Evanston, Illinois 60208-4210

Originally published in Czech under the title *Nikola Šuhaj loupenyžník*.
English translation copyright © 2001 by Northwestern University Press.
Published 2001. All rights reserved.

Printed in the United States of America

10 9 8 7 6 5 4 3 2 1

ISBN 0-8101-1827-0

Library of Congress Cataloging-in-Publication Data

Olbracht, Ivan, 1882–1952.
  [Nikola Šuhaj loupežník. English]
  Nikola the outlaw / Ivan Olbracht ; translated from the Czech
by Marie K. Holeček.
      p.   cm.
  ISBN 0-8101-1827-0
  1. Šuhaj, Nikola, d. 1921—Fiction. I. Holeček, Marie K. II. Title.
  PG5038.Z35 N513 2001
  891.8'6352—dc21

                                                                2001000907

»»» CONTENTS «««

Nikola the Outlaw

When the author of this narrative was collecting his data in the homeland of his hero, Nikola Šuhaj the Invulnerable, he heard the testimony of a great number of respectable and trustworthy citizens who had known Šuhaj personally. He had no reason to doubt their story: Šuhaj (who had robbed the rich and given to the poor, and who never, except in self-defense or out of just revenge, had killed a fellow man) had been rendered invulnerable by a green bough which he had waved about, warding off gendarmes' bullets as a farmer on a July day might shoo the swarming bees.

The author believed their explanation because this wooded country, creased with mountains as a piece of paper is crumpled before we throw it in the fire, can still produce weird events. We are wont to smile foolishly at such happenings, only because in our part of the state they have not been capable of occurring for centuries. In this land of hills upon hills and caverns within caverns, where streams are born and maples decay in the lasting shadows of primeval forests, there still exist enchanted places, from which neither deer, nor bear, nor human being, once lost, has ever yet succeeded in escaping. Bands of morning fog creeping wearily over the pine tops to the mountains might easily be processions of corpses; clouds drifting over the depressions are like evil dogs with wide open mouths who hide behind hills in order to do harm. And below, in the narrow ravines, in villages green with cornfields and yellow with sunflowers, live the werewolves. Clambering over a log after nightfall, they change from men to wolves and, toward morning, back from wolves into men. Here on moonlit nights, young enchantresses gallop on horses into which they have transformed their sleeping husbands. No need to look for witches in windswept valleys beyond seven mountains and seven rivers. The wicked ones may be met on the pastures as they sprinkle salt over three pieces of cow dung to make the cow's milk dry up. The kindly ones may be visited any day in their huts; they will leave their brakes to chant away the poisonous effects of a snakebite or bathe an ailing child in a brew made of nine herbs to make him strong.

God still lives here in the close silence of the forest—the ancient god of the earth who embraces mountains and valleys, plays with the bears in the thickets, pets the young cows who have run away from their herd, and loves the evening bugle of the shepherds. He breathes into the crowns of old trees, drinks from the brooks out of the palm of his hand, illuminates the night fires on the pastures, causes the cornstalks to rustle and the sunflowers to nod. He is a pagan god, master of forests and flocks, and he refuses to be identified with that proudly ostentatious god residing amidst gold and silks within the walls of icons on the one hand, and, on the other, with that disagreeable elderly personage hiding behind the shabby *paroches* shades in the synagogues.

But the story of Šuhaj's green bough is not true.

"No," the old cowherd of the high pasture on Holatýn told me, "that's what people say, but it happened very differently."

And as he roasted a mushroom stuck on a stick over the open fire, he described to me the fateful incident that determined the life of Nikola Šuhaj, the outlaw. What really happened is even more worth telling on winter evenings in huts in front of beech log fires than the tale of the green bough. More worth telling! Those are the only words properly to be applied, although the significant terms "marvel" and "miracle" necessarily present themselves. But these expressions have been taken from the Christian terminology and refer to an exceptional incident, one to be wondered at. Here, however, things do not happen by exception, and there is no need to be surprised at anything. It is as well known that good fairies live in the grain and evil spirits near muddy streams as that grain ripens in July and hemp in August. It is just as obvious that a logger will drown if he falls into the flooded Terebla as that he will lose his mind if he steps on the spot where a witch has poured the dregs of her filthy brew.

The cowherd of Holatýn began his account of Nikola Šuhaj before a group of cowherds, sitting in a circle around their evening fire. A drizzle, typical of early July, interrupted him, and he finished in the darkness of the shelter as his audience, resting on the hay, smoked their heavy-lidded pipes. Then they all went to sleep, and the only sounds were their measured breathing, the drumming of the rain, and an occasional faint tinkle from the other side of the wooden partition—a tinkle as faint, as gentle, as when a brook bounds over a pebble. It was made by the cattle sleeping there, when now and then an animal, in one or another corner, moved its head and caused the clapper of the bell on its neck to strike its metal sides. This odd sound gave color to the whole night, for it created the impression that somebody unseen was creeping from place to place, listening and acquiescing.

Here then is that Macbeth-like story of the invulnerable outlaw Nikola Šuhaj, who took from the rich and gave to the poor, and who never, except in self-defense or out of just revenge, killed a fellow man. These are virtues of outlaws the world over, in countries that can still love robbers and honor them as national heroes.

It happened during World War I in an unknown spot behind the front lines, the kind of place where deserters loitered for weeks. Here they hid from the field police and told men of the Fifty-second

Regiment that they were looking for the Twenty-sixth, and told those from the Twenty-sixth that they were looking for the Eighty-fifth, called the Balassagyarmatian. It was to this last that Šuhaj belonged together with his pal, a German machinist from Transylvania.

Both were hiding in the hut of an old Russian woman. The crone was ugly, and her hut, made of mud and with a tall straw roof, resembled a toadstool rising unexpectedly on a flat surface, or, even more, a hat all askew, covering a rotten egg from which nothing sound could ever hatch. She had two daughters, both of them stupid, hairy, and with flea-bitten legs. But the shack was isolated, and since soldiers devote themselves little to aesthetic meditation and much to the question of how best to amuse themselves between two explosions of gunshot, they got themselves involved with the girls. They went along with them to pasture the cows and get wood in the thicket, and at night, they followed them up the ladder to the attic.

"You, Ruthenian," said the hag to Nikola at supper one night, "you will become a famous man in your country, and armies and generals will tremble before you." As she spoke, she dipped into the family platter of fermented cucumber with onions. Her tone of voice was the same as though she were talking of the linchpin or the roof shingles. "I want you to marry my daughter Vasia."

"May she be struck blind," thought Šuhaj to himself. "So she knows all about it; this is unpleasant." Out loud he said, "Why not?" And then, reaching out for a last hope, "And what if they shoot me tomorrow?"

The old woman did not answer.

"And you, German," she swallowed a mouthful of pickle, "you will be the richest man in your country. I want you to marry my daughter Jevka."

"Well," replied the German, "if only I get out alive." He, too, showed plainly that he fancied such talk about as much as an awl in his eye.

Needless to say, the soldiers had no intention of marrying the daughters. Nikola at this time already loved Eržika and the German also had a sweetheart at home. They only wanted to get away with what they could and have as good a time as possible, and the hag was feeding them well.

The supper seemed suddenly repugnant to them, with Jevka crunching cucumber and onion and Vasia using the handle of her wooden spoon to scratch the nape of her neck, in pursuit of some louse or other under her plait.

"But if you've deceived me, three times seven kinds of woe unto you!" The curse was the uglier for the seemingly careless way in which it was spoken, the old woman's eyes fixed on the landing over the soldiers' heads.

"Why should we?" grunted the German, only because something of the sort was indicated.

But Šuhaj was strangely affected by the silence and the twilight. It was just as though far away in his homeland somebody had cut out a piece of the atmosphere and transplanted it here, over this hut with its high thatched roof. At home there remained a sphere of emptiness, an enchanted spot in the forest, where bears, deer, and men alike would get lost. He distinctly breathed the fragrance of forest decay and resin which entered the small windows together with the silence and the twilight.

"Let me have your mess kits!" commanded the hag. She went out with their tin dishes and brought them back filled with some sort of brew.

"Drink this!"

They obeyed. The stuff was neither bitter nor sweet, neither good nor nasty.

"Now no missile can hit you, whether shot from a revolver, a pistol, a machine gun, or a cannon."

It looked like a ceremony. Nikola shivered a little.

That night they went to bed early and did not climb up in the garret to see the girls. But before they went to sleep in the hay in the barn they talked and talked.

"What nonsense!" The German was provoked. Did she really think that she could fool them with such rot? Let her talk to crones as stupid as herself and to old soldiers. He was vexed with himself for having allowed her to take him unawares, for not having given her a piece of his mind, and finally for having drunk that slop at all. It must be said that he was really angry even though (or perhaps because) a troublesome inner voice kept insinuating how good it would be if, after all, the stuff worked.

"Let's get out of this!" said Šuhaj.

Good! In a few days they could take their leave. A lot they needed the hag!

The few days, however, stretched out. Here was peace and rest as though they lived a hundred miles and a hundred years away from a war. Nobody came around the whole time. They had no hankering to get in range of pounding Russian machine guns and exploding shrapnel. Their beautiful safety, the most precious of all possessions, was worth even an uneasy conscience. Again they helped the daughters graze the cattle and collect firewood in the alder grove.

Early one morning they were both out in the yard. Nikola was lopping off and whittling a pine branch for the old woman's rake; the German, seated on the ground with his back against the picket fence, was playing a mouth organ. The old woman came out of the house, leaned the ladder against the barn, and started up to the loft. Suddenly there came a gust of wind which blew under her skirts and exposed her. And here a very strange fact indeed was revealed: the hag's backbone was elongated and covered with fur like a goat's tail.

The German, the ignorant German, who knew only his machines and his computations, who knew nothing and believed in nothing, burst out laughing. But Šuhaj was taken aback, for he was from

Carpathian Ruthenia, where God still lived, from the province of Oleksa Dovbuš, the outlaw who for seven years had roamed the countryside with his seven hundred men, who had robbed the rich and given to the poor, and who could be wounded only by a silver bullet over which seven masses had been said as it lay hidden in the grains of spring wheat. Nikola Šuhaj knew at once that the woman on the ladder before him was a witch.

"She'll hurt us. Let's kill her!" he whispered.

"Why bother?" The German waved a hand.

But what do soldiers care about the life of one old woman more or less? Both of them had killed plenty of people and had seen all too many of their own comrades killed. Why not oblige a pal, the more so as they had not gotten even with the hag for her successful attack on their reason?

The next morning as the old woman was going out to the barn, they beat her to death with sticks and ran away. For a time, they wandered through the country. Then they returned to their regiment, the Eighty-fifth. Again they shot, again they carried the wounded to the field dressing station and the dead to pits, again they smelled the acrid stench of the trenches and their stomachs contracted with hunger. And again, like all normal soldiers, they longed for some good clean wound that would not harm them overmuch, but would send them home or at least behind the front lines for a few months. They had long since stopped remembering that there had ever been an old woman, a Jevka, and a Vasia.

It happened by chance one time that these very two were on patrol together in an old oak forest. It was three days after a hot fight, when the cannon had roared for a full four hours and everything had been in a white haze of smoke and whirling sand that had flashed fire. Three attacks by the Russian infantry and one counterattack, flesh by the carload! When it was over, they had no strength left to sigh in relief that they had come out of it whole.

Now, after three days of calm, the restlessness opposite and the preparations in the home trenches indicated that the show would start up again. Should they hide? Where? Run away? Not a chance! Let themselves be taken? Not for the world!

"You, Šuhaj," spoke the German as they were walking along among the sparse stumps. He stretched out his left hand, turned it palm upward and then swiftly downward again. "I'm fed up with all this. Won't you shoot me?"

Such a matter had to be entrusted to a comrade. He could hardly do it for himself, unless he shot through a loaf of bread to catch the grains of powder that would otherwise have burned the edges of the wound and have landed him before a court-martial.

"You want me to?"

"I do."

Šuhaj nodded without speaking. The German laid the back of his hand on the trunk of an oak, and his white palm looked like a paper target on which soldiers practiced in school.

Šuhaj stepped back a few paces, aimed, and fired.

"Baaaa . . ." roared the terrified oak grove. The trunks tossed each other the hot sound and threw it out to the plain, where it died. The soldiers stared at each other. What had happened. . . ? The shot had missed its mark.

"What are you doing?" The German was angry and perplexed. But Šuhaj made no answer, for at that moment something came over the earth, something nameless, for it was of another world. Everything around grew as quiet as though touched by death and lost color. Nikola Šuhaj was filled with a great fear.

"Once more! Come closer!"

What was it that had appeared to Šuhaj? Death? Fate? God?

"Are you crazy? Shoot!"

That voice seemed to come from under the earth, as though from the distant trenches. And the comrade's palm was like a paper target, so surprisingly white. So white that such fearful whiteness had never been heard of before. Šuhaj took aim as though in a daze. He was a good shot. A brigade usually has only one such, or two at the most. Once the major had thrown coins in the air for him to shoot.

He pressed the trigger.

Far away he heard a sound dying out, as though back home over the village of Koločava or over the mountains a storm had announced itself.

"What are you doing, numbskull?" stormed his comrade, examining his clean palm. "Don't you know how to shoot? Why, it'll be suspicious when they hear so many shots from this direction!"

Again Šuhaj did not reply. He threw the gun over his shoulder and went on. The German followed him, muttering curses. Then Šuhaj suddenly turned. He was pale, but his eyes shone and his voice carried a command.

"Now it's your turn!"

"Shoot you?" asked the German. "Well, for all of me!"

"But don't go far!"

"Where shall I hit you?"

"Stop, that's far enough. In the chest."

"Idiot!"

"Or no, not the chest. Aim at my head."

"Ass!"

Naturally, one does not shoot a pal in the chest, nor in the head, so the soldier aimed at the shoulder, aimed accurately and at twelve paces. As near as that, one could not miss.

The oaks again screamed with an explosion.

Šuhaj stood calmly by a large trunk and gazed somewhere over his comrade's head, as though all this did not concern him and he were thinking of something else.

"What is this?" asked the German, bewildered, and he, too, grew somewhat pale. He turned the weapon in his hands and examined the sight.

"Come, let's get going," said Šuhaj.

They walked on through the oak grove; the old trunks were far apart and between them there was much light, green underneath and blue from above. Strangely enough, it was a different woods than it had been a short time before. The sun was getting low, but the forest had grown brighter. The bark was lighter, the greenness of the foliage fresher. The men's feet sank into the moss as never before, and if they stepped on a limb, the crackle did not frighten them as it had so recently, but sounded gay and cheerful. The enemy was far away. But was there any enemy at all? And was there any war at all?

For a long hour they walked side by side in silence. Finally toward nightfall, down on the plain near the trenches, the German spoke: "Do you really believe in that nonsense?" He tried to make his voice sound rough, but it broke a little.

Šuhaj did not move an eyelash.

And then again for weeks on end they lived the hideous life of the trenches and the camp. While other soldiers (who dared think no further ahead) watched the falling grenades and thought, "If that grenade lands yonder in the big field back of the wild pear tree, I'll get out of the War alive . . . ," these two lived with the strange incident in their hearts. They never talked about it. Šuhaj did not feel the necessity of speech, and the German was afraid lest he should have to lie to himself and his friend.

Then they parted, and they never saw each other again. The German was put in the field telephone service; the company was replaced, sent back of the front line, and then took up a different position on it. That was the way things went in the War. People often lost track of each other.

But Šuhaj's wife, Eržika, his old father, Petr, and his father-in-law, Ivan Dráč, all of whom suffered considerable persecution, and all his friends (or those who after a lapse of eleven years are not still afraid to admit relations with Nikola) will tell you that Nikola often thought of the German and often expressed the desire to see him again.

Such was the shepherd's story. To be sure, he told it knowing the outcome of Šuhaj's life, but the story is no less instructive than the accounts of Achilles, Siegfried, Macbeth, Oleksa Dovbuš, and all the rest who were cheated by Fate, for excluding a far-fetched notion like Immortality, we all long to be invulnerable. But the devil always finds a chink to penetrate the armor even of Fate and Faith, and plays havoc with them.

1

Koločava

On either side of the narrow valley lie mountains, for in this region there is little else. Their strata of slate and graywacke have been crumpled like a scrap of waste paper, twisted, bent, kneaded, pressed into the clouds. Mountains, hills, and mountains. They are split by ravines and gorges, by valleys just wide enough to allow the passage of four soldiers marching abreast, with a thousand springs and dozens of streams that bubble over boulders and form pools as translucent as green jewels.

Here beneath the crumbling rocks the river Koločava fights its way to join the Terebla. Profiting from the ancient victory that made its bed a valley at least a hundred paces broad, it merely flows here, for it no longer needs to bubble and bound. It flows beneath the crumbling rocks; a highway twists under the opposite slope. Between them is a community, a village so long that the inexperienced traveler, making his way through the valley past huts and Jewish shops, past meadows and gardens, and again past rows of dwellings, becomes furious or resigned according to his nature, for after an hour, even after three or four hours of travel, he is still told that he is in Koločava—in Koločava-Negrovec or Koločava-Horb or Koločava-Lazy.

The name of Nikola Šuhaj is closely connected with Koločava-Lazy, so when we refer merely to Koločava, this is the one we have in mind. This village is the best built of the Koločavas and has a Greek Orthodox church. The highway running through it loses its likeness; bordered by fences on both sides and strewn with rubble and pebbles that crunch so pleasantly when people and cattle pass over them, it becomes a street. In some places the fences are made of poles, in others of wickerwork or pickets, but always they have gates and crude stiles which people can climb and dogs can jump, but over which the cattle cannot pass. Back of the fences are the courtyards and between these and the river Koločavka are the gardens. In summer these give Koločava its characteristic colors—green, red, and yellow—for the beds of potatoes and hemp are green, the blossoms of the climbing beans are like drops of blood, and the hundreds of sunflowers that border the beds and provide Lenten oil glow like gold. Yellow, too, are the black-eyed Susans. (Heaven only knows when and from what noble garden the plant got here, and who brought it!) They appear late in the summer, in clusters that tower above the fence tops and surround the strangely massive crossroad shrines, crucifixes with two horizontal beams and with the figure of Christ very crudely carved.

The inhabitants of this town are Ruthenian cowherds and woodcutters and Jewish artisans and shopkeepers; some of the Jews are poor, others a little richer; some of the Ruthenians are poor, and others are poorer still.

Through centuries of association the Jews and Ruthenians have become used to each other's peculiarities, and religious hatred is foreign to them. True, a Greek Orthodox Christian would not for the world consume a milk dish during the fast of Peter and Paul, and a Jew would rather perish than drink any wine that had been touched by a Gentile. But if the Ruthenian pokes fun at the Jew for not eating bacon, for sitting at home with his hat on, and for burning expensive candles to no purpose each Friday night, he laughs at him in all friendliness; and if the Jew scorns the Ruthenian for praying to a man who was put to death in such an unpleasant manner and for venerating a woman (mind you, a woman!) standing on a crescent, he scorns him only in the abstract. They see into each other's ritualistic mysteries and religious sorcery just as they see into each other's kitchens and rooms. Should a peasant come to a Jewish artisan, who at the moment happens to be conversing with his God, the workman calmly leaves his striped prayer shawl on his shoulders and his phylacteries on his forehead and his left wrist, bids his neighbor good morning, and negotiates at length for the price of repairing the peasant's wagon or putting a patch on his sandals or glass in his window. The Almighty is not in a hurry and will wait.

They are interdependent, they visit each other, they owe each other a little cornmeal or a few eggs, or the price of some fodder or the cost of mending a harness. But beware of casting a new idea in their midst, for then at once two types of mind and nervous system will reveal themselves, and the lightning of two clashing gods will flash.

Here we obviously refer only to the poor Jews: artisans, carters, peddlers, and those who live from unknown sources. Insofar as wealthy Jews are concerned—Abraham Beer, Hersh Wolf (not Hersh Leib Wolf, who must be excepted)—these are disliked by Ruthenians and Jews alike. The distaste borne by the Ruthenians is one of their several aversions, but the animosity of the poor Jews has been sharpened by jealousy into the bitterest hate.

Grain does not ripen here, for the shadow of the mountains retreats but slowly in the morning, and spring comes late. Aside from the gardens near the cabins there are only woods and pastures. But life has been possible. In spring the men used to put away their shaggy sheepskin coats, throw their axes over their shoulders, and with the melting snow descend into the valleys. They wound their way over paths still frozen, even as their ax blades gleamed in the full sunlight. They went to a Koločava agent who took them to Galicia, Transylvania, Bosnia, or Herzegovina to work in the woods. To be sure, an agent sometimes ran away with their wages and they never saw him again. An agent was always up to some graft with the contractor, he swindled them of part of their pay and overcharged them for fares and food (until finally they could stand such treatment no longer and would beat him up), but in any case they started for home in June with their belts filled with rustling banknotes.

Meanwhile, with the menfolk out in the world, the women gathered their flocks of sheep on a meadow grown sweet in May, and arranged the celebration of the intermingling of flocks. The girls behaved virtuously, mindful that they would have to prove their virginity on their wedding night, and the married women gaily drank and shouted and danced to the sounds of two fiddles and a Turkish drum. The herdsman and other experts estimated the approximate amount of milk that each ewe would give during the summer, before they led the large flock far up into the mountains. Then the women let the cattle loose on the mountain pastures, they hoed their gardens, and they waited for their husbands.

These came back by the beginning of July. When they had mowed their meadows (at least the lower slopes, where the grass was ready for mowing), each one threw over his shoulders a scythe (instead of an ax this time) and went to the Hungarian plains to work for every tenth sheaf. The harvest over, they all came back, accompanied by a Hungarian groom who brought their sacks of wheat and golden corn kernels to their very doors. Even in autumn and in winter they were not idle. They worked in sawmills, they hewed trees in the woods, they took whizzing rafts down the river Terebla to the Tisza and then to Hungary. They had enough to eat, and even had money left over to buy tobacco and brandy for themselves, and, for the women, fabrics to make red kerchiefs and black aprons, and even silk blouses, as well as glass beads to wear. The Jewish storekeeper, too, did well.

And then came the War. May it be accursed!

The men no longer carried axes or scythes, but guns. The women were left alone, as ever, but what kind of solitude was this? The days might be bright, and yet it seemed as though heavy, ashen-colored clouds were drifting over the valley, making it impossible to breathe deeply. The men sent no messages (for how many of them knew how to write?) and when a wife knelt in church before the miraculous icon of the Virgin Mary and prayed that her husband might be preserved, she never knew whether she might not be praying for the life of a man already dead and rotting.

This went on for months and for years, and then one day the old postman would come from town with a card that he would spell out for her. It would be a printed form with the name of her husband written in; it would have some words about the fatherland and the field of honor, and it would mean that her man was dead and would never return. But even that was better than if he should come home maimed or blind, which was just like having another child in the house, of whom, even so, there were all too many already, huddling back of the oven chimney, crawling down from their warm perch only to squeal and stretch out their hands for a piece of cornbread. And where was one to get it? The garden produce lasted barely till Christmas and nobody brought in sacks of corn and wheat anymore. And official gentlemen came in the company of gendarmes and rounded up the cattle from the pasture hills and led them away, depriving the people of their last resources, milk and cheese, for which they paid in worthless paper. The mountaineers were starving. The children grew potbellied and the mothers had no milk for the newborn, their only souvenirs of their husbands' furloughs. The people were so hungry that they felt like screaming and killing.

"When the king wins, he will reward his subjects for all their suffering," the Greek Orthodox priests would proclaim from their pulpits, and the women prayed for the king of Hungary, not just that he might win, but that he might win soon.

"The czar will free you," whispered the Russian Orthodox clerics, "he will give you peace and freedom."

"Oh, go to hell," thought the people, "everybody brings liberty and nobody a handful of cornmeal, and everybody promises peace, but only when he shall have won."

Nevertheless, they prayed for the czar too. But the czar was defeated, and the *honveds* (Hungarian soldiers) came and hanged people and dragged others away. Then the women came to rely only on higher powers. They consulted witches and followed their advice to collect newspaper pictures and postcard representations of the various rulers. The witches pronounced unintelligible curses over all those kings, czars, and emperors and pierced their heads and their hearts with pins, and then the women would hang the pictures up in their chimneys to be smoked. True, their combined efforts finally harassed Francis Joseph to death, but to what purpose? Against so many lords with countless unclean powers to help them, even the witches were powerless.

The women stopped believing and came to rely on nothing.

Formerly in such times as these, great outlaws had appeared. Black Lads. Just avengers, kind to the poor and without mercy for the lords. Thus it had been in the past, but was no longer. To be sure, the women shook their fists at the office of the notary who deprived them of their cattle and cheated them of their allotments. They shouted threats in Abraham Beer's store as the food rations were being divided: "Just wait until the men get back!" But they did not believe in their own words any longer. The men were cowards. Why had they done nothing when the authorities had taken away their families' last possessions? Why had they not grabbed their axes and gone out to murder when their own children were being murdered by starvation? They had let themselves be dragged out to war like a herd of cattle, they had cowered and obeyed and been afraid of inspections, and when they came home for their leave they lolled in bed and bragged about their heroic deeds and could not get their fill of laziness and of joy that nobody was shooting at them.

Or was there at least one who was unwilling to bear all those horrors in silence?

Nikola Šuhaj returned.

He deserted. He came home to his mountains, for they were the only ones worthy of homesickness.

Koločava! Koločava! How sweet a name, and how well it rolled off the tongue!

He stood on the highway at night and drew in the milky fragrance of Koločava. The darkness was like coal, the yellow lights in a few scattered windows like veins of fool's gold in it. The silence was broken by the hollow blows of the mill wheel that pounded down the wool for the home looms and was heard only at night. A little girl walked through the darkness from one hut to another, with glowing coals on a large shovel. Only her face and shoulders showed, the rest of her body was not visible.

Koločava! Koločava! It was surprising how he could identify himself with everything here: the air that he inhaled and exhaled, the golden-glimmered darkness of which he was part. Even the glowing child that appeared for only a moment seemed to belong, and the dull thuds from the mill came forth as though from his own breast.

He went home to the cabin of his father, Petr Šuhaj, which was located about an hour's walk up the river from the winding village there, where the Koločavka met the forests of Suchar Mountain. He knocked on the window, and his mother's face appeared against the pane. What might Nikola be doing there? She came out in her chemise and faced him on the threshold. Both were smiling a little and looking at each other. No need to ask the purpose of his coming, the gun over his shoulder told her everything.

"Is Father in the field?"

No, he was at home. Shrapnel had crippled his foot and some shot had stayed in his arm as well. Now they had sent him home for his leave, before he should go back to the front again.

"Don't tell the children a thing, Mother!"

For Nikola's mother was still bringing forth children. Six children were asleep in the room, and from the dowelled ceiling over her bed a hollowed log was suspended by chains, and in it an infant was rocking.

"Where does Eržika Dráč go at night to pasture the horses?"

"To the brook," she answered.

His father, wearing the trousers of his soldier's uniform, appeared at the door. They shook hands.

"Did you desert?" he asked, and it occurred to him that assuredly things might have gone worse.

A piece of stale cornbread could still be found, and his mother, sighing, put some of their few remaining potatoes in his knapsack.

Nikola went to a haystack by the woods for his night's rest.

And then for three nights he waited for Eržika; for Eržika, the little bird; Eržika, the little trout; Eržika, who was all pink and black and as fragrant as cherry wood; Eržika, whom he was bound to marry, though he lived beyond seven mountains and seven seas.

From nightfall he lay hidden in the ferns on the fringe of the forest, waiting. Finally his patience was rewarded. He saw her. But she had not come alone. Kalyna Chemčuk, Hafa Subota, and some youth or other, whom he later identified as Ivan Ziatykov, had come along to pasture their horses, too. They built a fire in the middle of the meadow and dragged up two logs, putting one on the fire and sitting down on the other. What was Ivan doing here? The small horses grazed, bending low their necks with the long manes, but when they wandered close to the woods and caught scent of Nikola, they lifted their heads, their nostrils dilated, and they neighed. Their herders turned away from the fire to look at them, afraid perhaps that they might be smelling a bear. But the horses were calm enough.

"Why hasn't that lout been drafted yet?" Nikola wondered, growing angry. "Only a year younger than I, and going on eighteen already." He frowned through the darkness at the fireside ring. "If he touches Eržika, I'll take good aim and kill him at her very feet." At this thought his heart beat wildly. But Ivan was interested in Kalyna and after a time the two went off into the darkness together, deceiving nobody.

Nikola lay on his belly watching the two girls. He felt an impulse to spring up, dash the hundred paces that separated him from them, frighten them out of their wits, seize the one that was his, hold her, and never let go. But instead, he pressed his head into the cool ferns, his chin to his chest. No! He dared not place himself at the mercy of Hafa Subota's tongue. The waiting became painful. Eržika's brightened face, every motion of her body and shifting of her bare feet saddened him. And yet, what would he not have given a few weeks ago for a glimpse of this fire!

Would a bear show up? How lovely that would be. He would kill it when it got just a step away from her, and she could not even guess who had saved her. But a bear did not show up. Would not Eržika go to the forest for firewood? He trembled at this thought, and the fragrance of cherry wood, strangely distinct, came to him. But Eržika did not go to the forest for firewood. The fire was ample, and the log burned slowly and would smolder all the following day.

He spent the night watching the herders, even after they had all wrapped themselves in sacks and lain down to doze in the singed grass, with their bare feet toward the fire.

And he spent yet another night thus. On the third evening, he went far into the village to meet Eržika before she should join the others. He caught sight of her down the road, in the evening twilight. She was riding sidesaddle, with her bare foot way up on the horse's neck. She wore five strings of yellow and red beads, and instead of a saddle she used a brightly colored cloth. She had on a stiff hempen blouse, and her apron had a heavily embroidered sash that was wound around and around her body. She was sixteen years old, she had stuck a few daisies in her black hair, and she was beautiful.

Nikola, in the dusk, blocked her way.

"Ooh! . . . You scared me. Is that you, Nikolka?"

He jumped up on the horse that was following her and pressed the beast firmly with his knees. His whole being thrilled and the blood pounded within him.

Later, holding hands, they stood at the edge of the forest.

"I'll stay here, Eržika."

"Do, Nikolka." Her eyes, black pools always, deepened even more.

But Kalyna, Hafa, and Ivan were approaching with their horses.

"Eržika, Eržika!" they shouted, cupping their hands to their lips.

From that time on, Nikola Šuhaj hid himself in the woods and on the plateau pastures.

If one knew how to avoid the enchanted spots—the crags and the swamps where unclean spirits and malicious nymphs indulged in their capers—the virgin forest was safer than any other place still left in the world. It did not betray. It held dells, ravines, and gorges and the sizable surfaces of uprooted trees, out of whose rotting trunks grew underbrush so dense that even a deer could not penetrate it. Should the authorities want to find Nikola here, it was as though a bird had flown from their hands—just try and catch him! The forests gave forth a fragrance of silence and decay, which all his life he had identified with a feeling of safety and which had never played him false.

He was wont to sleep in abandoned shelters or in haystacks on mountain meadows. These haystacks had a peculiar shape as characteristic of the whole countryside as a smokestack is of an industrial center, a Gothic tower of a medieval town, or a minaret of the Middle East. Each is made of four masts that form a square, with a wooden roof stuck on them; as the pile of hay stored underneath grows or diminishes, the roof may be slid up or down by means of pegs. Enough space is always left between the hay and the roof to provide a good shelter, cozier and safer than a rabbit's lair. Let the authorities, if they would, search ten thousand such haystacks on the mountain meadows of the region!

Here lived Nikola Šuhaj. No cowherd would refuse him milk to prepare corn porridge, no shepherd would deny him cheese made of ewe's milk. His father brought bread to the shelter by the brook and Eržika brought the cornmeal she stole for him from home, the Dráč family being well to do. Whenever he was expecting them in the woods, he would pound a tree trunk with his ax blade so that they might follow the sound to his hiding place of the moment. What did Nikola care that the gendarmes were after him? When the shepherds in their huts told him about it, or when Eržika repeated it to him (how beautiful were her eyes when she was terrified!), he only laughed. Let them chase him! And if they wanted to shoot, they would soon find out who would get hit first.

In Koločava there lived a gendarme sergeant called Lenard Bela, who was out to get Nikola at any cost. He was ambitious to turn this deserter over to the king. The honor of his calling demanded this achievement. Nikola was the first deserter in the region and might set a bad example to others.

Searches of the Šuhajs' cabin were fruitless. The sergeant had given the Šuhaj children a bag of candy for nothing. He had threatened the mother in vain, and it was hopeless to call Petr Šuhaj to the station again. He dared not thrash a soldier from the front and the elder Šuhaj knew it. Perhaps for this very reason the father would admit nothing beyond "I don't know. I haven't seen him, I haven't heard, I really don't know." Lenard had not the remotest suspicion of Eržika, for the charm of her secret had taught her silence. But the herders from the pastures by the brook and various other places let words fall, and he made threats and fair promises simultaneously: if they brought him Nikola, they would get money for brandy; if not, they would get drafted and go to the front right away.

Lenard Bela at that time resembled a hunter tracking down a lynx. He spent entire days in the mountains, examining trails in muddy places, looking into deserted shelters, and, with binoculars focused, sat for hours on end on the hilltops with the best visibility. His vigil always ended in the evening with the hopes of better luck on the morrow, and at night he would dream of Šuhaj. Once he saw him on Krásná (Beautiful) Mountain, walking across the meadow, no more than two or three hundred paces away. Do you know the hunter's state of excitement when he first glimpses within shot the game he has been tracking down for a long time? His feeling is half sudden shock, half joy, mixed with a slight wave of apprehension at the approach of death. It was too late to take a shortcut through the woods to catch up with Nikola; so Lenard, aiming at his feet, sent a shot after him from his carbine. Šuhaj turned, more curious than frightened. He allowed himself to be shot at once more, an easy mark for the pursuer, and then under a furious, senseless fusillade, made quickly for the woods.

What a chase! Such experiences as this make the hunter very unhappy. They give him restless nights and cause him to examine his cartridges and the sight of his gun, and drive him to convince himself of the soundness of his hand and his eye through repeated target practice. They tempt him to believe in witchcraft; he keeps quiet about the incident and torments himself with secret resolutions.

Trying to track down Šuhaj became Lenard's ruling passion. One rainy day, he concluded from the reports of the shepherds that Šuhaj was hiding in an empty shelter by the brook. He disguised himself as a woman, donning a hempen chemise and an apron. He wrapped white linen strips around his feet and fastened his sandals with straps, tied a red kerchief around his head, and put a string of glass beads around his neck. He slung a bag over his shoulder as though he were going into the mountains with salt for sheep or cornmeal for the shepherds. The village policeman followed him.

Nikola watched the supposed woman's approach from afar. When he saw that she was headed for the shelter and only a hundred paces away, he came out with his gun:

"Stay where you are or I'll shoot!"

But the woman kept on coming, waving her hand as though to say, "Don't be a fool, boy, I only want to ask you something." She walked right up to him, took a revolver out of her pocket and struck him in the nose, then grabbed his throat, snatched his gun, and hit him over the head with the butt end. The policeman ran out of the woods and together they beat and kicked Šuhaj until he was limp. Then they took him, dazed and bound, to Koločava. Lenard, who had left his gendarme's uniform in a bundle in the woods, had meanwhile put it on. As he escorted Šuhaj through the village, his smile bespoke a proud self-satisfaction and reflected the hunter's idea of bliss.

The following day, a gendarme took Šuhaj to Chust and thence by rail to Balassagyarmat.

At Balassagyarmat? Just then, the king of Hungary had little appreciation for the heroic deeds of ambitious gendarmes and needed soldiers elsewhere than before courts-martial or in garrison prisons; there would be plenty of time for all that after the War, unless, hoping for mercy, the culprits should meanwhile redeem their misdeeds by death in the field. When Šuhaj's company was on the march, Šuhaj deserted again, with a new gun and fresh ammunition. He did not hesitate: he ran just as a young wolf, breaking away from the leash, trots with his tail and his snout extended where his instinct directs him. To the mountains! To Eržika!

So the old wolf hunt began all over again, in the woods and the ravines and on the plateaus and the slopes of the eastern Carpathian

Mountains. It was waged over a larger terrain, with greater resources and more passion than before.

Sergeant Lenard got reinforcements from Volové. Unfortunately, the main snare in the forest on Suchar, set in a bewitched place that people avoided, did not trap the hunted, but, rather, took one of the hunters.

"Don't fire!" Nikola had shouted when he had seen the plumes of the gendarmes coming toward him. But they had fired, and so had he. A young corporal failed to rise from the swampy black ground. He was cleanly shot through the head.

Nikola's reputation was becoming established. In the whole countryside there was not a hut where shelter or corn porridge would be refused him. For he was the only one of them all, they felt, who had rebelled against poverty. Nikola the hero! He alone was right and the rest were liars, and as long as they would not follow him to the mountains and do away with all the gendarmes, the notaries, the rangers, and the rich Jews, there was no end in sight. Run, Nikolka! Fight, shoot, and kill for yourself and for us! And if you should die, you were born only once and can die only once!

Peace came.

But, good heavens, what kind of peace was this? Was this what they had prayed for so fervently before the icon?

Some demon possessed mankind. Or else somewhere a new comet must have appeared, or possibly the old one was still working, for otherwise God would not have countenanced such great sins among either the powerful or the poor. Now it was time for the men to go down to the plains beyond Tisza for corn to make porridge and for sacks of wheat to make white bread; now they should have gone into the mountains and swiftly floated the rafts down the Terebla. But the men still could not find their senses.

How could the women know what was going on in the world,

when the priest and the mayor, Hersh Wolf, each told different lies about it? But one day at the end of October, when Koločava was already blanketed with snow, the men began to drift back home. Some came with weapons, others without, but to a man they were unshaven, lousy, and irritable. They, too, had pictured peace differently. Certainly they had not expected that their wives' first reaction to their homecoming should be alarm at yet another mouth to feed from the keg of kraut and the handful of potatoes that constituted their garden harvest. The men only now began to notice what they had lazily refused to see during their furloughs: the stables desolate, the haystacks empty, and no supplies at home—nothing, not even a pinch of salt or a handful of flour, only a few potatoes and a little kraut which would hardly last until Christmas. Now this poverty became their particular concern and they began to band together.

And to this excited group somebody brought word that the public notary, Molnár, had sold to an agent from Chust a shoe shipment which was to have been sold to the population at prices fixed by the government. Molnár had become accustomed to such graft and had forgotten that the soldiers were home now but that they still had the frontline habit of united action and were prepared to act.

The news hit the soldiers like a hostile grenade. That evening they gathered in Vasyl Derbák's cabin, filling it. They yelled: "So they would rob us, would they? But we're the ones who went to war, we died in the trenches, and all they did these four years was to steal! Now we're home and now we'll show them!"

They ousted the mayor, Hersh Wolf, and chose a new one, Vasyl Derbák. They elected a military leader, Commander Juraj Lugoš. They would meet the following day, and each one would bring what he could. The notary Molnár was a crook! So was Hersh Wolf! And Abraham Beer another!

Next morning they came with a large number of axes, many army bayonets and revolvers, and some guns and noncommissioned officers' swords: unshaven soldiers in tattered uniforms, assembling with the measured steps of divisions marching to the trenches, anemic striplings, impatient to see what their elders might show them. The women formed anxious groups on the road. Now that the time for action had come, their courage suddenly deserted them. They were like brides, afraid of the joy they had so long awaited. When would something happen? they wondered, fearful, yet impatient. Juraj Lugoš, wearing a commander's sword, ordered, "Forward march! On to Koločava-Horb! Get Molnár the notary!"

But before they could reach the notary's stone dwelling, they first had to pass the gendarme headquarters. They would attend to them first, then! They burst in, not excited and not making too much noise, but matter-of-factly, as befitted soldiers. The station, however, was empty. Sergeant Lenard had heard of the meeting at Vasyl Derbák's; that morning, when told that armed men were assembling at Lazy, he and his whole force had taken to their heels. Only one gun remained in the station, and this the invaders took; then they proceeded to smash up the furnishings. They worked calmly, with the purposive blows of efficient workers. The excitement of the women outside mounted with the noise of the breaking furniture, the sight of the window frames being knocked out from the inside, the crashing of glass, and the soberly professional air of their men, whom they saw thus for the first time. So this was the way it was done? Why didn't you put more passion into your work, boys?

In Molnár's house confusion reigned, as though there were a fire. They had only learned of the riot as the mob was already tearing up the gendarme station. The notary put on narrow white trousers and his coachman's coat, his wife dressed herself in a hempen blouse and a sheepskin coat, while her maid tearfully wound the sandal straps around her feet, already bound, peasant fashion, with linen strips. Wrapping the children in blankets, they ran across the gardens through the snow and crossed the icy waters of the Koločavka. On the opposite shore they made for the woods.

The soldiers found the notary's office deserted. Their eyes fell on the large steel safe. Money! It was bound to be full of money! The notary handled the disbursement of the army pensions for all the three Koločavas. They swung their woodsmen's axes at the safe, but the blades bounced back from the steel walls. They beat it with the blunt ends, but this only cracked the paint and made dents in the metal sides. One man pushed another: "Wait, you don't know how to do it, damn you, give it here!" They all wanted to try their strength, but none succeeded in opening it. They would force it. "Get a strong steel rod, somebody!"

Meanwhile, the notary's apartment was being demolished. This was no longer cold military destruction, for here the women took a hand. With bright red spots burning on their cheeks, with their hearts in their mouths, they had stood stock still at first, stunned by so much splendor, the like of which they had never seen.

"For this?" Jevka Vorobec howled suddenly, and kicked a little table with porcelain vases and figurines on it. The table toppled over and the breaking china tinkled. The women had only needed an example; like mistresses already experienced, they put more passion into their actions than the men who had initiated them. They fell upon the furniture, the upholstered chairs and divans, the cupboards with mirrored panels, the coverlets, the flower stands; they flung themselves on everything that had been bought with their money, really with their tears and their blood. They had starved for four years and their small children had died so that these things might be bought. They smashed the mirrors and the glass doors, and in the kitchen they knocked down a shelf of dishes and wrecked the furniture. They shouted hoarsely without listening to each other; they grew excited over each dress and each piece of silk underwear, tearing at them and throwing them out the window on the heads of

the ones who had not been able to get in. They cut open the featherbeds and shook them out in the October wind, the mob outside
shouting with glee. A piano? So this was the box out of which had
come the tunes they had heard in passing! They knocked the legs
from under it, the thing fell, and they hacked it to pieces.

The work in the apartment was finished while the soldiers in
the office were still struggling with the safe. It lay on the floor with
its paint scratched off and with hundreds of dents made by the
woodsmen's axes. Should they take it to the blacksmith and melt
it in the fire? Not in the fire, it held paper money! Finally they
brought some rods to prop it up, loaded it on a sled, and a few of
the men took it to the cabin of Vasyl Derbák, the new mayor. There
they dropped it in the snow by the side of the road.

It was long past noon when Commander Lugoš led his forces
back to Koločava-Lazy. The eyes of the women glistened as after
an amorous embrace, their nerves vibrated from the work on which
they had lavished their strength. Now the mob turned to the
recently ousted by the people, but still legal, Mayor Wolf, Hersh
Wolf, in front of whose store they had stood in line for days and
when their turn had come had been told that all the corn was gone;
for Wolf had sold the allotments only to those who could bring him
chickens and eggs; for he had sent whole crates of foodstuffs to his
kin, in Volové and Budapest; for he had fed the corn intended for
them to his chickens and had stuffed his geese with it.

Then it was Beer's turn—Beer, who always had some secret
stores but bled the people to whom he sold. They had turned over
to him all their hempen cloth, their wool yarn, their sheep pelts,
their lambs, and their chickens. They had taken in his cows for the
winter in exchange for a sack of cornmeal, and had fed them hay,
which had been in short supply for their own cattle because the
notary had stolen some of it for the army. These reminiscences
made the slackened nerves of the women again grow taut like

violin strings and the blood in their veins course faster. All at once they wanted to fly. They trembled with impatience and kept turning spitefully to the men, who were walking along with the calmness of indifferent bulls.

They plundered the store of the former mayor, Hersh Wolf, and sacked his dwelling. He, too, had fled with his family. They found plenty of corn in the warehouse; in the store a few cans of potato syrup, a little chicory, and some cloth; and in the provision room large quantities of goose fat, flour, and eggs. The supplies were distributed noisily and haphazardly. A crowd of children gathering there tied the provisions in their kerchiefs and scattered them through the village, running back and forth in the snow between their cabins and the store. The men found a cask of wine in the cellar and two demijohns of spirits back of the firewood and in the shed. They drank it up, not in passion or joy, but out of soldiers' thirst.

Then they proceeded to Abraham Beer's store. He also had fled, and his dwelling was wrecked, and his featherbeds scattered to the wind, but hurriedly and without passion, out of necessity, for now they were interested in the stores of flour, beans, hides, and dry goods rather than in destruction. The division of the spoils was accompanied by shouting and quarreling, which Commander Lugoš, accustomed to such scenes from his experience in field kitchens, quelled with blows as well as with authoritative cries. Then they dealt with Mordecai Wolf, Joseph Beer, Kalman Leibovich, and Chaim Beer. The sacking of their small shops proceeded calmly and quietly, for the owners had stood courteously under their signs, waiting for the mob. Their faces had sufficiently expressed their awe of the people's power but had not presented an aspect so unbearably despairing as to provoke fury. Therefore their dwellings, at least, were spared. In any case they had little that might be taken and the mob convinced itself that nothing remained concealed.

God finally heard the entreaties of the eighty-one-year-old Hersh Leib Wolf, distiller and biggest landholder in Koločava. It was not possible that the Almighty, who attends only to the affairs of his Jews, should have missed since morning all the prayers and entreaties spoken in Wolf's time of need. Jehovah had advised him, saying: "Go meet thine enemies and regale those who would do thee evil!" Hersh Leib Wolf obeyed. He commanded the women of his household to roll two barrels of wine from the cellar to the road; hidden in the hayloft back of the house, they would find a barrel of spirits, which they should roll out as well.

It was already evening when the mob neared his inn. He went out to meet them. Addressing the commander and the mayor, he spoke so loud that all could hear: "I am an old man, I understand the ways of the world, and I realize that things have changed. I shall turn over to you all my real estate tomorrow, or the day after, or whenever you may wish it. I shall accompany you to Volové to the district court and have the deeds transferred to you. You know that you won't find any goods in my house. So why pillage? Why hear the wailing of little children? Everything I have is here, and I ask you to enjoy it in health!"

Oh, the foxy old usurer! Was all this that he was telling them true? They knew there were supplies in the house, but, on the other hand, the day's experiences had taught them how small a share would fall to the individual, and they were weary and pillage would cause them no further joy. The barrels tempted them. So did repose.

So they made campfires on the road. The old man brought out all the glasses from the tavern and the women of his household carried out all the dishes that were *treif,* that is, those that the Jew might not use for his own food because they had held things unclean in the Jewish ritualistic sense. The people feasted so that a satisfactory day might end fittingly.

The daughters of Hersh Leib Wolf and the wives of his grand-sons, apprehensive of what would happen when the people should get drunk, watched the activities around the fire through their windows. They trembled with anxiety at what might befall their patriarch, who was out defending the family fortunes. The aged man with his long white beard remained with the crowd and gave no sign of his tenseness: he smiled, he chatted, he was indulgent toward the Jewish boys who had come to have a drink too, if not of wine, at least of spirits, which they mixed with water. At another time he would have driven them away.

The sight of the mob milling around the fires amused the chil-dren of Hersh Leib Wolf's youngest daughters and his great grand-children—large-eyed little girls and small boys with dark or blond or auburn side curls showing beneath their velvet caps. They scram-bled for the windows and, not realizing the gravity of this situation, wanted to sing a Yiddish ditty they had learned from their mothers:

> Oi, oi, oi,
> Tipsy is the goy!
> He is a sot,
> And suffers a lot,
> Oi, oi, oi,
> Because he is a goy!

But their mothers quickly clapped their hands over their mouths and chased them back to bed.

That afternoon, people met Nikola Šuhaj in the village.

"Come along with us, Nikola!"

But Šuhaj merely waved a hand. "I don't want anything. I'm glad I'm home."

He inspected the village and the havoc in front of the house of Hersh Wolf and Abraham Beer and returned again to his father's cabin at the foot of Suchar Mountain, for the gregarious instinct of the front was alien to his temperament. Šuhaj resembled the lynx who stalks his prey alone, who fights alone, and who dies alone, killed by a bullet or hiding powerless in some thicket.

That night a tragedy occurred near the fire in front of Hersh Leib Wolf's tavern. The drunken men were wrangling over the rifle that had been seized at the gendarme headquarters. A shot was fired, and two men were killed instantly. The mob, momentarily stunned, soon grew excited. Hersh Leib Wolf went pale as the question flashed through his mind, "What's going to happen next?" His daughters and the wives of his grandsons sprang away from the windows, pressed their hands to their temples and whispered, "*Shema Yisrael!*"

But when they looked out again, they saw that the old man had made his way through the confused mob to the tipsy mayor, that he was expounding something to him, that he was talking to the commander and ordering the Jewish boys to take away the dead. Ah, what a man grandfather was! What a holy old man! The people crowded after the boys, as they were carrying the corpses, and thus the mob disbanded. After a time there remained only the fires, the practically empty barrels, and, on the snow, trampled almost to the black soil, signs of blood. The name of Jehovah be praised! No fool woman had thought of crying out in the first confusion that the blow had been fired from Wolf's house, nobody had become dead drunk, and therefore nobody could put the idea in people's heads that the liquor and the wine had been poisoned. Hersh Leib Wolf, exhausted and chilled to the bone, could return home. When his womenfolk, full of solicitude, wanted to surround him, he wearily raised his palm, yellowed with age, that they should not annoy him and went to his room. Before he lay down, he talked to the Eternal for a while, reading *Kriat Shma*. And Thursday or on the Sabbath, when the Torah should be exposed in the synagogue, he would read the *Goimel Benchen,* the Prayer of Thanksgiving, with such devoutness as he had not felt in repeating it since the birth of Bondy, his youngest.

Hashem Isborh! The day was ended.

The following morning most of the villagers slept late. In front of the mayor's house stood Israel Rosenthal, the blacksmith, in his leather apron. He was a huge man with a coal black beard and side curls, and he was attacking the safe with blows worthy of a *bar kochba* (Jewish hero).

In vain. The onlookers, at first curious and then amused, all tried their hands as well. But the safe, paintless now, its sides bent and with hundreds of dents, remained there in the snow by the side of the road.

A general assembly of the parish took place outside the church on the day following. The election of the new mayor, Vasyl Derbák, was confirmed, as was that of the commander, Juraj Lugoš. There was little else left to be done. A highway patrol was organized which should prevent goods of any sort from leaving the community and take every new arrival to the commander. But only trouble came of it. The new arrivals were soldiers returning from the fronts, and when Lugoš tried to inspect their knapsacks, they yelled and cursed. Corporal Miša Derbák, the son of the new mayor, making his way home from far out in the Tirol, unshaven, lean, and worn out by the long trip, created a big disturbance at Lugoš's house. He drew out his revolver and tried to shoot the commander, with whom he still had some old unsettled accounts from their days at the front.

Self-government lasted only a day thereafter.

Molnár the notary and Lenard the sergeant had run thirty kilometers to Volové. But Abraham Beer and Hersh Wolf had chosen the better means. They had gone to Chust and looked up the army headquarters at once. There they explained the situation and its dangers. The military authorities at that time had considerable understanding for such incidents. They dispatched a company of infantry and entrusted it to young Lieutenant Mendel Wolf, the son of the only legal mayor of Koločava, Hersh Wolf.

The army invaded Koločava at 5:00 A.M., before daybreak, on the fifth day after the uprising. Fine snow was falling. This time it was Lieutenant Mendel Wolf who said to his men: "Get them! And don't spare any of that rabble!" He would show them that he was no longer a green schoolboy, and he would show them what it meant to pillage the property that should one day be his.

"Get them, boys! Tomorrow the old man will bring wine!"

The soldiers swarmed over the village, but Lieutenant Wolf would not allow himself to miss the chance of visiting his old acquaintances Commander Lugoš and Mayor Derbák. With four other soldiers, Lieutenant Wolf dragged Lugoš out of bed, and the five beat him until he fell at their feet, bloody and unconscious. Then they poured two bucketfuls of water over him, ordered him to dress, and led him away in bonds. Then Wolf went to deal with Vasyl Derbák. The latter was awakened by the rattling of the windowpanes in which the muzzles of guns appeared, and by the pounding on the door. His wife opened the door. He jumped up, still sleepy, and there before him stood Mendel Wolf with two other soldiers.

"Good morning, Mayor. I have taken the liberty of coming to see you." The lieutenant extinguished his burning cigarette against Derbák's nose, drew out his revolver, and aimed at Derbák's forehead as though to shoot him. He stood thus for a moment, enjoying the sight. Then he gave him two blows and ordered the men to bind him.

"Please be so good as to proceed, Mayor!"

Meanwhile the soldiers pillaged the cabins. They beat up whomever they found and arrested all who had weapons. Clothing, dishes, supplies—the villagers' own as well as what they had seized from the merchants—were now thrown outside the doors.

The soldiers poured kerosene in the kegs of sauerkraut, or, if they lacked kerosene, they made water in them.

"Oh you men, you unhappy men, what have you done to us now?" wailed the women to their husbands. "After all, we were better off without you!"

The soldiers stayed in Koločava for two days.

Lieutenant Mendel Wolf established the old order. First of all, he took a little key and opened the safe as it lay in the road in front of Vasyl Derbák's house. He took out and carried away with him all the documents it contained, as well as something over three hundred thousand crowns in cash, before ordering the empty safe to be taken to the notary's demolished office. He commanded that all the articles that had been thrown out of the houses should be taken to his father's shed, and that when his father should return, the merchants might pick out of the piles whatever belonged to them. Then he hired twenty local youths, Jews and Ruthenians, organized them into a national guard, gave them guns, and had the noncommissioned officers of his company drill with them.

Molnár the notary and Sergeant Lenard Bela, with his gendarmes, returned on the third day. Lenard took over the leadership of the national guard.

Revenge is sweet, and Lenard Bela took it. As for the Jews, they took revenge for their past fears and out of fear of future fears. Jewish mothers took revenge for the horrors they had experienced and were willing to have half the village searched for every pot of goose lard that had not yet been accounted for. The national guard, looking for weapons and supplies, robbed and extorted. Nothing was left in the huts except the floors of trodden mud and a few sticks of furniture. Only the patriarch and money lender Hersh Leib Wolf comported himself with as much decorum as ever and sought no revenge against anybody. What could he have gained by it? Or his grandsons and the children of his grandsons?

Things got back to normal. That is, the people again went humbly to Abraham Beer and Hersh Leib Wolf to borrow money: those who still had some assets could sign promissory notes and mortgage their gardens and their cabins. The rich Jews again became mild and benevolent. Everything was as it should be.

When calmness was restored, the national guard had nothing to do. But Sergeant Lenard decided that before he would disband this gang of rogues and ruffians, he would use it for the accomplishment of one other mission. He had only been waiting for such an opportunity. Šuhaj! The old thorn in his side! In fact, he should not be able to sleep peacefully until he should be rid of this vermin that had slipped through his fingers so many times. The month of November promotes the hunter's passion; a fresh snowfall coming down over older snow is a joy to all hunters and incites to adventure.

Lenard learned that Šuhaj was living in his father's shelter, about three hours' walk from the village, on the upper stream of the Koločavka, in a clearing in the Suchar Woods. The place was accessible, as there was not too much snow on the ground and a path ran alongside the river.

"Come on boys," he said to the guard, "we'll make mincemeat out of him!"

They set out, stopping at the foot of Suchar Mountain to get Šuhaj's father; they bound his hands and took him along. In the woods close to their goal, they halted to rest for a time. Lenard, observing from afar the shelter that stood on a small, snow-covered plateau, was making his final preparations and issuing his final orders. He placed his men in a semicircle of which he himself was the center and stationed a gendarme on either wing. The view of the smooth, untrampled snow made the guard catch their breaths. What did Lenard mean? Should they be the targets, at two hundred paces, for Nikola's gun? They dared not run away, they dared not move. "Perhaps Nikola isn't there at all," they comforted themselves. To be sure, a little smoke was issuing from the chimney of the shelter, but that did not necessarily mean anything, because a log in the fireplace might smolder for two days.

"Let him shoot down a few of them," thought Sergeant Lenard, "at least they'll know what they're getting paid for." He bound Petr Šuhaj's hands behind him with a chain and, drawing it so tightly that the cold sweat stood out on the man's forehead, he wound the other end around his own hand.

"Advance!"

The semicircle struck out from the forest and forded the half-frozen stream in a few leaps. They meant to tear across the plateau to the shelter, but this was not as simple as it seemed, for their feet sank in the snow and had to be pulled out again with every step. Lenard protected himself with the elder Šuhaj's body. Drawing the chain, he drove the man ahead and kept him from jumping to the side or falling down to make Lenard an easy mark for his son.

All eyes were fixed on the shelter. Simultaneously they all saw Nikola plunge out the side window and make for the woods with great leaps.

"Halt! Halt! Halt!"

The forest rumbled. A shot was fired. The whole semicircle of them roared. Glee at seeing a creature in flight is man's heritage from his ancestors. The bounding Nikola was pursued by the senseless fusillade of the guard and the well-aimed shots of the gendarmes. They saw him disappear in the woods.

"Forward! Get him!" shouted Lenard, jerking the chain as though it were horse reins. They ran, breathless, stumbling in the snow. But suddenly from the woods ahead they heard a clear and fiercely angry voice calling: "What do you want with me? Why don't you leave me alone?"

"Halt! Halt! Halt!"

They could tell from the direction of his voice that he was at the very edge of the forest, hiding back of one of the old beeches. They fired in that direction. In the general din they could not tell that Nikola, too, was shooting.

Nobody saw just how it happened, but two of the guard fell in the snow. One lay on his back and a stream of blood gushed from his neck. It flowed into the snow and colored it red. For a moment, the members of the guard did not seem to comprehend what had happened. The fusillade diminished until only the gendarmes were firing. Then the distinct, furious voice called out from the forest: "Run, or I'll shoot every last one of you!"

They obeyed this order at once, running back into the woods out of which they had come, stumbling in their own tracks. Sergeant Lenard's shouts were of no avail. Seeing this confusion, Lenard turned Petr Šuhaj by a tug of the chain, pressed Šuhaj's back against his own, and half carrying, half dragging him, retreated too. Petr, beside himself with pain, shouted: "Shoot, Nikola, don't be afraid, shoot!"

Above his father's head a portion of Lenard's head was visible. Twice Nikola aimed at it, but both times he lowered his rifle again.

The gendarmes disappeared in the woods beyond the Koločavka. Once more there was only freezing silence. Two people lay in the small clearing. The one in the crimson snow was already dead. The other, shot in the chest, tried to raise himself on his elbows: "Nikolka! What have you done to me, Nikolka?"

"Why don't any of you leave me alone?" Nikola's voice stormed once more from the forest, as though to excuse him, but still full of wrath.

Meanwhile, Koločava awaited the return of the guard. The community was excited and counted the hours. The impatience of the women mounted when some children who came down to the village from the direction of Suchar Mountain told how a gendarme had hired a sleigh to go up as far as it could to meet the expedition. Whom would it bring? Good God in heaven? Nikola?

But when the sleigh arrived at the gendarme headquarters and the women saw that two corpses were being carried out, they breathed deeply: "Go ahead and kill them, Nikola! Our hawk, Nikola! Our brave lad, Nikola! Why aren't our own menfolk like you? Why do they always start something and never finish it?"

The expedition against Nikola Šuhaj was the last act of the national guard. Shortly thereafter it was disbanded. The leadership of Sergeant Lenard did not last long either, and when people began wondering why they had not seen any gendarmes in the village for quite a time, they found out that he and his men had disappeared to points unknown. Molnár the notary had left with them, and the villagers who walked past his locked office for several days and peered in through the newly glazed windows at the battered safe, now empty, could not guess the reason for these departures. Only the Jews knew that a revolution was brewing in Hungary and that Lenard's guns were more needed down there.

Koločava was without authorities, but life went on. In truth, it was neither better nor worse than before.

And then, one bitter cold winter day, a coachman dressed in a sheepskin coat brought a sleigh to Abraham Beer's door. Two gentlemen, muffled in furs, dismounted. One was recognized as Solomon Perl, a wood merchant from Drahov. The other, a young man, was a stranger. People said that he, too, was a businessman and had come to hire workers. Then, in the dead of winter? And Perl should be bringing him? Somehow those horses were too good for merchants. Abraham Beer put on his fur coat and his felt overshoes and he showed the young man around. He took him along the road first to one end of the village, then to the other. They examined the bridge over the Koločavka, and insofar as they could, they clambered up the hillside over the village and looked down.

The young gentleman was a Romanian officer. The following morning a Romanian army invaded Koločava. The Romanians stayed there. Oh Lord, what new calamity dost thou send down upon the people? The Romanians robbed the haystacks near the village, they stole the cattle, and when the weather made it impossible to go to the winter shelters, they took the only cows that families had kept in their sheds to get a little milk in winter. In exchange, the Romanians gave the people little slips of paper, which, they said, the Czechs would redeem when they got there. They broke into the cabins and assaulted the young girls and on the highways they stopped people with the question, "*Jeste baň?* Have you any money?" and if a man had none, they would knock his teeth out. Lord Jesus, preserve the people from such peace! And if there be no other way out, rather give them war again! In wartimes they at least got financial compensation for the men who were out murdering each other.

Why did Nikola Šuhaj come down to the village? Why did he try to be no better than the rest? Why did he hide his gun in some shelter, just like their husbands, who had left them there instead of using them and were not ashamed to make childish excuses that they would pull them out and get a deer or a boar as soon as the snow went down a bit? Why did Nikola, if he could not save his people, at least not try to get a little revenge?

No, Nikola Šuhaj was no Oleksa Dovbuš after all, for Nikola had come down from his hills. He had come down for a wife. For the handful of ripe cherries which Eržika recalled to him. He lived in his father's house at the foot of Suchar and did not go out except to attend church on Sundays. It seemed as though he could not get his fill of the heat emanating from the bake oven, as though he would never have any desires beyond playing with the children and looking out at the snowdrifts through the clear patches on the windowpane where his hand had rubbed off the moisture.

Again he was one of them, a little worse, if anything, than the rest, since he had cast away the outlaw's stick for which he had been admired so much. A cowardly soldier who had deserted.

One Sunday after Mass, Šuhaj entered the house of old Ivan Dráč. "Neighbor Dráč, give me Eržika!"

This was a little sudden. Eržika, blushing down to the glass beads on her neck, ran out of the overheated room. Old Dráč, who knew nothing about the matter, did not comprehend. What? Why Eržika? What for?

But his son Juraj was there too, Nikola's slightly older contemporary. He had recently returned from the War. Like Nikola, he was still wearing out his soldier's uniform. He loved his sister. Rising from the bench, he faced Šuhaj.

"Give her to you, you bandit? I'd rather throw her in the Terebla."

"I've never robbed a soul!"

No more was said. They paled a bit, standing face-to-face, and sparks shot out from their eyes. Silence. It was evident that only a moment more and nothing but a single shot could ease the tension. Their very uniforms reminded them of killing.

But suddenly the fragrance of cherry wood wafted to Nikola and flooded his whole being so that his taut nerves relaxed. He shrugged his shoulders and turned to go.

"If you Dráčs don't give me Eržika, I'll set fire to your house!"

He walked out, and a great cloud of steam escaped with him.

At the time of the Romanian occupation of Koločava, Nikola Šuhaj was arrested. Armed soldiers came around to get him one morning. It happened after Abraham Beer had drawn the attention of the military authorities to this dangerous man, who had killed, any way you wanted to look at it, at least three people. Abraham Beer was not motivated so much by a desire to please the Romanians and become better acquainted with these new masters (even though to a businessman such ends are not negligible), but because he had some extraordinary and complex plans in regard to Petr Šuhaj. And since after Nikola's arrest he was not sure whether the time was yet ripe for their realization, he did not hesitate to have his sleigh hitched and to travel five hours to Volové to inquire at headquarters about the Šuhaj case.

The military gentlemen listened to him, chatted with him, asked him candidly how much more grain and hay might be levied in Koločava, and then when he was gone they said to each other, "After all, we aren't going to feed a fellow in such a barren section. His case is a war matter, let the Czechs settle with him after they get here."

Nikola Šuhaj was released in two weeks, and Abraham Beer could only furrow his forehead and tug at his beard. The release meant that his plans should have to wait. For how long?

Nikola got Eržika, for Ivan Dráč's fear exceeded his son Juraj's hatred.

Nikola built a broad bed that resembled a manger, a bed with high posts and a low framework. He filled it with straw, which he covered with sheepskins, and placed it in the loft of his father's house. Then he hewed logs at the edge of the forest and with a horse and plow dragged them through the snow down to the valley so that in the spring he might build his own cabin.

The wedding day arrived. Eržika wound a white kerchief over her right wrist and put on a crown with spangles and many small white stars. The church ceremony, performed under the images of fifty saints on the iconostasis, seemed interminable. After the priest's countless repetitions of *pomolin sja* and the deacon's responses of *pomiluj,* the priest finally pressed a wooden Greek cross to their lips with one hand, while with the other he sprinkled them with holy water from the font and joined their hands under his stole. In front of Nikola's native cabin they passed under two loaves of bread that had been tied together, and his mother threw oats on

them, and his younger sister, dipping a bundle of straw in a deco-
rated pail, splashed water on them. The bridal party danced to the
monotonous melodies of a lone little fiddle and feasted on a piece
of wild boar meat which old Petr had brought down (for where
were the foresters of state forests these days?). Only water was drunk.
Late in the evening, in the bedroom, the bridesmaids removed
Eržika's bridal wreath from her head. She kissed it thrice to bid it
farewell; Nikola, too, kissed it three times and then turned it over to
her mother. Thrice he threw over Eržika a kerchief such as was worn
by married women, twice she threw it back to him, and the third time
her bridesmaids wound it around her head and tied it up in back.

Nikola became one of the villagers. Before he should grow old,
or be crushed by a falling tree trunk in the woods or crippled on
a raft in the sharp bends of the Terebla, he had every expectation
of having many children and not enough corn porridge, much want
and a few transitory joys.

The snow in the mountains south of Koločava had not yet melted,
but on the northern slopes the coltsfoot was already in bloom.

Nikola heard that the Romanians were felling timber, way out
somewhere near Vučkov, and paying the workers cash instead of
scrip. In the cabin, the last of the corn had been used up.

Nikola put on his sheepskin coat, furry side out. He swung his
ax over his shoulder and went out to see if he could get a job.

He crossed the ridge to the south, traversed the watersheds of
two rivers, and was descending to Vučkov along a stream through
the woods on the warm side of the mountains. The soil was swelling
with springtime and the exuberant stream bounded in great waves,
hiding the rocks that caused the rapids. Nikola approached a sun-
lit pasture where a sulfur spring issued from the ground. The
Jewesses of Vučkov were wont to come up here, bringing their
own tubs, in which they would heat the water over a hot rock and

bathe their limbs to treat the rheumatism acquired down below in their shops.

At the moment, five boys were grazing their horses here. They had built a fire to burn some juniper that interfered with the growth of the grass. The season of the year had warmed their blood and made them as spirited as the colt that one of them was riding. Another boy, small and stocky, was chasing the rest, cracking his short-handled whip. He climbed up on a boulder and, artfully swinging the whip over his head, snapped it again and again, with short sharp cracks that resounded over the valley. He was shouting, "I am Šuhaj! I'm Nikola Šuhaj!"

Šuhaj stopped in his tracks and smiled, but more in surprise than in merriment. So great then was his fame? And it reached way out here?

He left the path and walked up to the boy, avoiding the skillful circlings of the long whip. Frowning, he boomed, "Hoo! *I* am Šuhaj and I'll eat you up!"

The boy faltered, but seeing the twinkle in Nikola's eyes, he grinned. The others had flocked around him and he called out, pointing at Nikola, "He says that he's Šuhaj!"

The herders burst into roguish laughter and, retreating a little to be on the safe side, shouted, "Šuhaj! Šuhaj! Šuhaj!"

"The real Šuhaj!" smiled Nikola.

"Well, if you're Šuhaj, give us a million dollars," said the one on horseback.

"And where is your bough?" asked another.

"What bough?"

"You don't even know that Šuhaj has a bough?"

"No."

"Then you don't know very much," and the boys again burst into laughter.

The smiling Nikola turned and walked away.

"Šuhaj wasn't a shrimp like you," yelled the one on horseback, ready to press the beast between his knees and ride away, should Nikola turn. And the short stocky one called: "And he had longer whiskers!"

But Nikola did not turn again.

"Where's your bough?" one of them clamored, and the others took up the cry, cupping their hands to their lips, "Lend us your bough, Šuhaj, lend us your little green bough!"

Nikola crossed the pasture and continued through the woods.

Was his fame really so great?

The rhythm of his gait woke up old memories, which fell in line with his steps.

Did he really have a green bough? The children were right. How many times had people shot at him? At the front and at home? Was there any kind of firearm that had not been used against him? At Kraśnik, only three men of his platoon had remained and he had been one of them and had not even been wounded. He had come out all alone from the bridgehead at Stokhod. And Kraśnik! The Black Swamp! Suchar! Was there another man alive who could have evaded such a shower of bullets? No, in his case it could not have been Chance. It was not Chance. But what was even more remarkable than his escapes was the fact that every time he had been certain that nothing would happen to him. Even at Kraśnik and at Stokhod, when every hope had seemed madness, and in a hundred other situations, at Krásná, at Black Swamp, on Suchar! He had known that nothing could happen to him, that no missile could touch him, whether shot from a pistol, or a cannon, or a machine gun. Was this a gift? Yes, it was a remarkable gift, and it was his.

At the thought, a chill ran down Nikola's spine. The shouts of the children had died down long since.

Perhaps he could really have become an Oleksa Dovbuš. Perhaps he had really abandoned his fame for a woman. Had he thrown away his great gift uselessly and in vain, without getting any more out of it than his bare life?

Nikola Šuhaj's pace grew slower. The soil was muddy and his steps soundless. To the left of him the brook murmured and rushed, rolling in turbid waves where there should have been waterfalls.

How was it possible to live so miserably, so wretchedly, when one held an enchanted bough in his hand? Or did it only work in wartimes and had it now lost its potency?

2

Nikola Šuhaj

Abraham Beer came out of his room, where he had been conversing with Jehovah, his master and friend. With one phylactery over his forehead and the straps of the other wound around his left wrist (to which the blood flows direct from the heart), his shoulders wrapped in a black and white striped prayer shawl, tallith, he had recited the *Shachris,* the morning prayer: "*Ma toivi oihulechu Jankoif!* How good it is to dwell in thy tents, O Jacob!"

Now he stood in front of his shop, in which the customer could spend three hundred crowns and still carry his purchases off in a basket on his back. He was thinking about his own affairs. These were complex and tangled, and much reflection, ingenuity, and labor were needed to unravel and arrange them and tangle them up all over again. The left corner of his partly open mouth was drawn up, as was his left nostril; his left eye was half shut, his forehead wrinkled. He was plucking at his blond beard as though it were a harp. All the Jews of Koločava stood thus in front of their shops after *Shachris,* and each one's business was as complicated and as full of problems as was his, and might be dealt with in any of a dozen different ways, or not at all. For business is not only making money, it is a philosophy, a political science; it has all the complexity of life; it is an outlook on life and is a passion no lesser than love. Articles of trade are the creation of the Almighty and were made to give joy to his children. And truly, there is no joy greater than playing with them and making them change hands.

Things looked bad, thought Abraham Beer. New masters again. The Czechs. Law and order? It would seem that there might be order, but there wasn't. The Czechs were here, and nobody knew what they would be like. Their president was a professor, he wrote books, but, I ask you, what could a professor know about business? They said he had written some book or other about a ritual murder, about that Anežka Hrůza, and that unfortunate Hilsner, who got out of jail only recently. That looked pretty good, but you couldn't ever tell. To be sure, the Jews would have to get on with the Czechs. What else could they do if they wanted to live? And even so, it was better than in Poland or Romania. And Hungary. Oi, oioioioi! Bela Kun. God Almighty deliver us! Such a Jew who renounced his God was worse than ten thousand Christians. A Jewish head, and the soul of a Gentile! The Eternal would send some terrible punishment down on him. Tsk, tsk, one preferred even the Czechs.

But how would they line up? With the Gentiles or with the Jewish people? Would they realize that this country could not be run without Jews? It was possible that they would not see that. Or maybe it would be two, three, or even ten years before they did. Even a Christian brain would have to take it in sometime. But what would happen in the meanwhile? Painful thought! Business was bad; no cattle; grain was no good for starting anything; there was only liquor, the Wolfs were able to laugh at the world. Oi, oioioi! Would there at least be something doing in real estate? Ah, such worries! When would they get rid of that Nikola Šuhaj? A rotten lout, an outlaw! Let him cool his heels in jail for a year, the rogue!

Abraham Beer opened the left corner of his mouth a little wider and raised his left nostril a little higher. For the matter of the Šuhajs was the most important of all.

The whole business was very involved and had developed somewhat as follows:

The people who had been born in these mountains no longer lived in one empire, but belonged to Poland, or Hungary, or Czechoslovakia. It was unwise to set up tariff walls right in front of people's noses, but a good businessman had to know how to make the most of even such a circumstance as that. Another matter: the narrow strips of cultivable land and pasture were constantly being divided and subdivided into strips still narrower. When a girl was married, her father would give her a few square fathoms of land to raise hemp; when he died, his sons would divide up his holdings between them. Such strips would be scattered over the whole valley, one here, another there, and the peasants, to have at least part of their possessions together, would trade the strips among themselves, making up the difference in value by a payment in kind—a cow, or three sheep, or ten meters of hempen cloth, or the like.

It goes without saying that such bargains would be carried out in an informal, neighborly manner, without lawyers or courts, for which there was neither time nor money. Thus the land register did not record the actual holder of the land, but some forgotten past owner. Of these very ones, many now lived in Hungary or Galicia. Abraham Beer made it his business to go to Volové, take a look at the records, ascertain such cases, and write to a Jewish friend in Poland or to one in Hungary. Then either of these Jews would go around to see a Ruthenian living in his respective town, and would say to him, "Hey, you, don't you own some real estate in Koločava in Czechoslovakia?"

"Eh!" the Ruthenian would answer. "Where would I get it? You know well enough that I'm a woodcutter. My father did leave me something there, now that you mention it, but we fixed it up somehow with my sister and her husband. But they don't have it anymore, either. They sold a part of it and exchanged the rest. You'll have to find out about that in Koločava."

"Wait," the Jew would say, "I know all that. But nowadays, what with all these new governments, there is so much red tape that I need to have you sign a paper that you're selling that land to me."

"And what'll you give me for it?"

"What'll I give you? I'll give you three guldens."

The Ruthenian would consider. He would not understand a thing about it. Why should he not sell something that did not belong to him? And if a Jew wanted to get taken in, why should he stop him?

"Give me five."

"What for, in heaven's name?" the Jew would shout. "For your mark, when it'll cost me some more money to have it certified? If you don't want to sign, never mind, I'll get what I need somewhere else."

So the Jew would buy the land for three Polish guldens and twenty groshes, or for fifty Hungarian crowns, and would sell it to Abraham Beer in Koločava for two hundred Czech crowns. And Abraham Beer would take all the documents pertaining to the transfer to the district court at Volové and would have the papers made out in his own name. This was the way it had been done with the meadow (among other places) where old Petr Šuhaj was still making hay.

Abraham Beer's expression grew more and more worried.

The Lord knew, two hundred crowns was a lot of money to pay out when there was no telling when one could take over the property. By the Jewish Peter and Paul Day? Oi, oioioi! Of course he could sell to somebody in the city—it was always better for an outsider to wrangle with a peasant—but that was just the point: he could not afford to sell. The meadow in question bordered on one that he owned already, which had been flooded by the Koločavka for three days the preceding spring, and when the river had receded to its regular banks, his beautiful plot, for which he had been offered sixty thousand crowns, was an expanse of drift, where not even a willow could take root. He just had to have Šuhaj's meadow, such an opportunity would never present itself again. He was not afraid to tell old man Šuhaj that his, Šuhaj's, meadow was really his, Beer's, but how could he get rid of the young Šuhaj? Seven daggers seemed ready to leap out of each of his eyes, and it would be child's play for those bandit's hands of his to strangle a man. Ah, such troubles! One had to wait till one saw what the Czechs would be like.

But look there! Where was Isaac Hershkovich running so hard with little Teivi Menchl? There was another fine rogue for you, that Isaac Hershkovich! Such a pig head. How many sheepskins the fellow had sold to make into coats for the dragoons! Tsk, tsk! How much money he had made! Ah, might he be struck dead!— But where were they hurrying so, just as though they were going to a fire?

"Well?" wondered Abraham Beer as they passed him. His wide-toothed grin and outstretched palms were interrogative. But Isaac Hershkovich obviously had no time to waste. He merely waved his hand as though to say "What's the use of talking?" and ran on.

"Well?" Abraham Beer said to himself, gazing after them. "What's happened to that pig head?"

Something had really happened to Isaac Hershkovich. He and Teivi were bound for the gendarme headquarters, where Hershkovich excitedly told the sergeant all about it.

This day, the sixteenth of July, Isaac Hershkovich was to go up to the mountain pasture at Douhé Gruny (which was the common pasture for the small cattle of the neighborhood) to get the average annual proceeds from his six sheep, namely six gelets of milk, that is to say, sixty liters, or the cheese that had been made from it. Since he wanted his cheese to be kosher and was afraid that the shepherds might make it without washing their hands right after they had handled a piece of bacon or that they might muddle things up in some other way, he wanted to oversee personally the making of the cheese and to take along for rennet a piece of the stomach of a calf that had been killed in the proper ritual manner. So, on the previous day, he had measured out some cornmeal into a sack, in the amount that was required of him, for feeding the shepherds and their dogs, and had placed in another sack the wooden buckets to hold the cheese; he had requested his sister's son, Teivi, to go along and help him carry the load. After they had prayed for the success of their undertaking, they had set out. Since to get to Douhé Gruny one had to go by way of Suchar Mountain, take the path alongside the brook, cross the horse pasture, and then proceed down the side of Tisová Mountain, a good five hours' journey in all, they had left early in the afternoon, planning to spend the night up there.

The shelter at Douhé Gruny was very plain. It had a slanting roof made of twigs for protection against the dew and a little fence to keep the cattle from licking the sleepers' noses at night. On the fence hung a few milking pails. In the evening, they had sat with the shepherds before the fire in front of the shelter and had supped on the wheat bread, cheese, and onions they had brought up with them. Then they had just lolled around, watching the flames and the stars. Suddenly the dogs had begun to sniff and bark wildly, and had all started running in the same direction. A shot had been heard, and then another, and Isaac Hershkovich had seen one of the dogs topple. "*Riboinoi shel oilom!* Lord of the earth!" Isaac had cried and had fallen on his face. Then the shots had come thick and fast through the darkness, and from near at hand. The echoes had made them multiply. Isaac Hershkovich, pressing his body into the grass and his nose into the cold earth, had whispered a long chain of "*Shema Yisrael*—Hear me, O King, thy Jew is calling!"

Then a voice had been heard behind him: "Get up!" The command had to be repeated several times and accompanied by a kick before Isaac Hershkovich had obeyed. Teivi, pale as a sheet, had stood beside him, facing two men. The shepherds had scattered in all directions. The men had worn old military uniforms, with cloths tied over their noses and mouths. The bareheaded one, with his black hair tumbling over his forehead, had held a gun. The other had on an old army cap with the rim turned down and fastened under his chin, as during the War the soldiers had worn them in winter to keep their ears from freezing. In the glow of the fire, Isaac Hershkovich had been able to see three more men lying in wait about two hundred paces away, aiming their guns at him. The one in the cap had kicked the fire with his boot to dim the blaze and scatter the embers.

"Hands up!" he had commanded. No, Isaac Hershkovich could raise his hands no higher. "What's in the shelter?"

"Cheese," Isaac had gasped, his teeth chattering.

"We need it. Go on home!" But the other one had noticed his good boots.

"Wait, take your boots off!" he had ordered, and when Isaac had complied, he had seized them. Then they had gone into the shelter and had carried off a keg of cheese and another of curds from goat's milk. As they had been rolling the kegs past the fire, the mask of the one in the cap had slid down from his mouth and Isaac Hershkovich had recognized Nikola Šuhaj.

"Nikola Šuhaj?" the sergeant thought to himself.

The excited Hershkovich told about his terror, about how the fellows had taken eight hundred crowns that belonged to him, and repeated the episode of the stolen boots.

"Nikola Šuhaj?" mused the sergeant. He knew of the young man: Abraham Beer had told about him and had requested his arrest. But since Šuhaj behaved with propriety, it was not altogether clear to the sergeant whether Nikola's past exploits should be considered as heroism on the field of battle against the Magyars or as threefold murder; he had made a report to national headquarters. To be sure, this was a different matter entirely. Official orders dealing with Carpathian Ruthenia were very strict. In Slovakia, there was still fighting. In Hungary, the communists were at the helm. The formation of holdup gangs could not be tolerated here. The sergeant would intervene with a mailed fist.

But things had not happened just exactly as Isaac Hershkovich had described them. No dog had been shot, no men had lain in wait at two hundred paces, aiming their guns at him. There had been only Nikola Šuhaj and one companion, as the latter confessed afterward at Chust. If, however, it were possible to credit Isaac Hershkovich with good faith in these two errors (for he may have thought he actually saw these things), it is utterly impossible to do so in the matter of the eight hundred crowns, even though it may be claimed that he did not intend to hurt anybody by his statement. His business, too, was a bit complicated. On the morrow he was to pay Mendel Blutreich of Horb something over seven hundred crowns, the balance due after a very involved and turbulent accounting of mutual debts. But he could not pay it, because he needed the money to buy hides. Mendel would be furious and would not believe Isaac's story even after Isaac should have sworn to it in court at Šuhaj's trial, for he would know, as knew all Jews, that the dear Lord did not understand the Gentile language and had no intention of giving even a moment's notice to some Czechoslovak court or other at Chust. But could a businessman miss such an opportunity?

"Did Šuhaj see that you recognized him?" asked the gendarme.

"Merciful God, no, he would have killed me!"

"And have you told anybody about it?"

"No, I came running straight down here. I only stopped to borrow some shoes at the butcher's but he wasn't home and I didn't tell the children anything."

The sergeant decided to keep Šuhaj under observation for a few days. It would be necessary to destroy the whole gang.

"Good," he said. "Don't tell a soul. And you," he thundered at Teivi Menchl, "if you blab, I'll lock you up!"

Teivi could not understand why he should be shouted at in this way.

During the following days the sergeant could not find anything suspicious. On the third day, Nikola Šuhaj was arrested up on a hilltop where he and Eržika were haying. There was a haystack there, and they were sleeping between the roof and the hay, Eržika's head reclining on his shoulder and his face nestled against her hair, when the gendarme woke them up. The sun had already risen.

Before noon, they had him at the gendarme headquarters, in bonds, with a scowl on his face. They let him wait for a while.

"Who was with you at Douhé Gruny?" asked the sergeant when he came in.

"We had nothing to eat. Nobody has. Not a grain of corn, nor a piece of cheese, nor a head of cabbage. We couldn't starve to death."

"Nobody is asking you about that. Who were the four men with you?"

Šuhaj eyed the gendarme in surprise. "Only one was along. But I won't tell who."

"Oho," said the sergeant mildly, "a peasant cavalier! Tie him up again!"

When Šuhaj's hands had been bound again, he struck him in the face. "Well, who were they?"

Šuhaj drew his head down between his shoulders and wanted to butt the gendarme like a ram. But one of the men grabbed him from behind.

"Well, so who were the four?"

Nikola, gritting his teeth, fought with his elbows and kicked with his feet. They threw him to the floor three times, and each time he got up again. They finally had to give him a few lashes with a cowhide to tame him.

They bound his feet and tied him to the sewing machine which belonged to the sergeant's wife and had been placed in the office. They knew who Nikola Šuhaj was, and did not dare put him in the jail; it had been wrecked by storms the previous autumn, and the Romanians had gone to no special trouble to repair it.

The news spread over the six hundred cottages scattered along the Koločavka valley and over the fourteen square kilometers of inhabited mountain slopes.

Šuhaj? Nikola Šuhaj? So Eržika Dráč had not succeeded in bridling him, in keeping him bound to the marriage bed, and they had misjudged him! So the gendarmes had caught him! May the devil strike them! Nikolka would get away from the Czechs, the same as he had escaped from the Hungarians and the Romanians. He would run to the mountains and strike back.

The news went direct to Abraham Beer's heart. How? What? When? Where? The name of the Eternal be praised! At last! Tomorrow, or the next day, he would go to tell Petr Šuhaj that his, Šuhaj's, meadow actually belonged to him, Abraham Beer.

What voice was that in the night? Whose was it?

None of the gendarmes had so far had time to escort Šuhaj to Volové, and so for the second night Nikola was sitting on the floor next to the sewing machine. The pain from the cowhide lashes had passed, as had the unbearable numbness in his foot and his first wild fury. His limbs when he was quiet felt as inert as though they belonged to a stranger. The petroleum lamp on the braced table was lit, and outside the windows shone the stars. Three gendarmes snored on their army cots. Nikola had already abandoned his occupation of the first night, to which he had looked forward with such high hopes all day, namely, the effort to loosen the bonds on his hands or reach the knots with his teeth. It had led nowhere and had only made his limbs the more painful. His eyes roamed over the gendarmes' guns on the wall, and their bolts, shining in the lamplight, were putting him to sleep.

"Shall I get out of this all right?" was the only thought—and this day the last thought—to occupy his mind.

"I am going to get out of it!" he answered himself for the hundredth time, and his weary heart for the hundredth time beat a little faster.

Then, leaning his head against the iron base of the sewing machine, he fell into a leaden sleep in which every muscle ached with the least motion, yet the strength to wake up was lacking. The strange music of the Koločava night came in from the river, the dull thuds made by the turning of the wheel at the mill where wool was being beaten. Nikola heard these sounds as though from a distance, an incalculable distance, from one so great that nobody could ever succeed in overcoming it.

He slept. Later he knew quite positively that he had been asleep. And suddenly that voice spoke into the quiet, saying, "Nothing can happen to you!"

It rang into the night with a strange metallic clearness. Nikola sprang up, but the shackles dug into his flesh and hurt him unbearably. He woke up. What was this? The three gendarmes continued to sleep on their cots, not one of them having moved. And then, the words came once more, softly now, from that insurmountable distance where the mill wheel had sounded before: "You're going to get out of this."

Nikola stared wildly into the yellow lamplight. Whose voice had spoken to him? Whose miraculous voice?

The sounds from the mill seemed to come into the room, the dull thuds of wood against wood with wool in between seemed to grow louder. He did not go back to sleep again that night. He tried to, but could not. Whose voice had it been? Then the windows lit up with the approach of morning. The alarm clock went off; the gendarmes arose, dressed, and breakfasted, acting as though they did not see him. Then for a time they untied him from the sewing machine and led him out; then they bound him again and went away, one by one, until finally only the provisional gendarme, Vlásek, remained with him.

It was just before noon. Vlásek sat at the table, writing something in a thick ledger and smoking a cigarette. His back was turned to Nikola and they were alone. Nikola's eyes wandered restlessly over the doorknob and the three window latches, passing back and forth over their metal sheen. Nikola's mind was working again. The nocturnal voice still filled his being. He could certainly get out of this. He had extricated himself from worse situations. He had a green bough. No missile could touch him, whether shot from a pistol or a revolver or a cannon or a machine gun.

But how? By force? Not for the time being. By entreaties? Ridiculous thought. Through the aid of friends? Possibly, but only while being transferred to Volové or Chust. Or should he wait until he arrived there, where his position would be considerably more difficult? No! There was still another way to be tried.

He had chosen for its execution the provisional gendarme, Vlásek, the very one who was sitting here with him. He did not know why he had chosen this one particularly, but the idea had come to him suddenly on the preceding day as he had watched the man laughing. Perhaps it had been his expression or the sound of his laughter; Nikola had not analyzed it.

"I'm not a beggar," Nikola said suddenly. "I have cattle. Maybe if I sold them I'd get sixteen thousand for them."

The provisional gendarme did not consider Nikola worth a turn of his head.

"The Czechs won't stay here," went on Nikola after a pause.

The gendarme continued smoking his cigarette and writing in his ledger. Only the scratching of his pen on the paper could be heard. His back was broad, the green cloth of his uniform was stretched tightly across it.

"The Germans were here and they left, the Russians were here and they're gone, the Romanians have disappeared, and so have the Magyars."

Vlásek did not turn, but tore a piece of paper off the page. The sound was startling in its suddenness. The gendarme had torn it off to make a note of Šuhaj's remarks.

"In a few weeks you'll be leaving too, and then nobody's going to ask you what happened to Nikola Šuhaj."

Silence again. One could hear one's own pulse beats. One could smell the aroma of the gendarme's cigarette.

The most fateful hour of Nikola's life had arrived. But Nikola could not realize its full importance; he only knew it as the hour that should decide whether he would stay tied to a sewing machine or whether he would get out in the sunshine and fresh air.

At noon, Eržika brought him his lunch. The gendarme turned his chair to face them and stuck a bayonet on the rifle that he laid across his knee.

Šuhaj did not want any corn porridge, he refused it as he had done on the two previous days, but he took the pitcher of milk in his manacled hands and drank, staring straight in Eržika's eyes as he did so. His stare had a piercing intentness.

"Sell both the cows you brought me," he whispered between gulps, ". . . to Abraham Beer. . . . Have Father sell the horse . . . to Hersh Wolf. . . . Right away. At once. . . . Borrow what you can. . . . Bring it to the gendarme . . . now. . . . Right away!"

Eržika left and the gendarme turned back to his ledger.

Had he not heard? Nikola wondered, his heart pounding. And would Eržika manage to get back while Vlásek was alone?

Eržika managed it. She came with thirty thousand crowns and laid the bills down on the table near the gendarme. But Vlásek was too absorbed in his work to have time to look at the roll of banknotes or at Eržika's departing form.

The silence was insufferable. The July afternoon cast broad beams of sunlight through the windows. The gendarme lazily lit a fresh cigarette and in the bluish haze its smoke formed wavy lines.

"How much might we have here?" thought Vlásek, surveying the bankroll out of the corner of his eye. Twenty-five? Thirty? There wasn't a great deal. It took that much nowadays to get a cow. Well, maybe two cows. He stooped down, as though looking for something in the bottom drawer of the desk, covering the money with his body, and shoved it in his pocket. Who could pin anything on him? Anyhow, he was fed up with this service in the sticks, it could go to the devil!

He got up and looked down at Šuhaj with indifferent eyes.

"Your hands are all swollen. Wait a minute, I'll loosen the rope a bit and you can rub your joints!"

He took the shackles off Nikola's wrists and walked out. Nikola removed the rest of the bonds, stretched himself painfully, his head swimming, and then jumped through the window into the garden.

When the gendarme returned, now knowing exactly how much money there was, he surveyed the room with its open window and also noticed the desk where he had left the memorandum of Šuhaj's treasonable utterances. He struck a match, burned the paper, and rubbed the cinders in his fingers until nothing was left of it.

Then he waited for the return of the sergeant, for the breaking of the storm. It would be nasty. But what of it? He needed that money. How had it happened? Well, he had had to leave the room, the house was empty, Šuhaj had escaped in the meanwhile. Would a disciplinary investigation ensue? Would he get kicked out? What of it!

So well did they keep the official secret at the gendarme headquarters that not until two hours after the alarm over Nikola had been raised did Abraham Beer set out for Petr Šuhaj's place at the foot of Suchar Mountain to tell him that this time he, Abraham Beer, would make the hay on the meadow by the Koločavka. Before this dangerous undertaking he repeated his prayers, the *Tefilah* and the *Derech,* and even on his way he still spoke to his God somewhat as follows: "Isn't it thy sacred duty to help me? When I pile up a fortune for myself, don't I do it for one of thine own people and for thy greater glory? Therefore, really for thee! Help me, O Lord! Thou canst not do otherwise!"

Nevertheless, when he drew near to the Šuhaj house, his heart was pounding fast. But the children told him that their father was not at home, that he had gone to the pasture on Suchar. It was not very far away. Abraham Beer decided to follow him there.

At the crossroads in the woods, past the bend where a pine log served as a bridge across the Koločavka, he learned how Lot's wife must have felt when she turned back and saw the brimstone and fire of the Lord raining down upon Sodom and Gomorrah. For, standing at the crossroads with a gun over his shoulder, was Nikola Šuhaj.

"*Shema Yisrael,*" whispered Abraham Beer, and he, too, felt the blood freezing in his veins and his body turning into a pillar of salt.

Šuhaj looked down at him and started walking toward him rapidly. Abraham Beer trembled.

"Tell them that they won't get me anymore now! Not alive, they won't," he uttered vehemently.

Then he turned on his heel and made for the woods with long steps. His movements were always eager and his gait quick.

Abraham Beer remained a pillar of salt for yet a time. He gave up the idea of going to the pasture to see Petr Šuhaj, for the Lord Jehovah had given him a sign.

He reached inside his shirt under the armpit and then smelled of his fingers. It was well to do that in times of sudden fright, perhaps because it made one conscious again of one's own existence. He started back, but it took a long time before his knees lost their shakiness and his steps became firm once more.

By the time he got home, it was already dusk. The heavily shaded lamp that hung from the ceiling of the shop was already lit. It flooded the center of the room with a yellow glow while the corners remained in obscurity. In the store there were customers again and wares to be sold, even though it was hard to squeeze a penny out of the people. The store was also a meeting place for the Jewish younger set. Several boys and two girls were lolling around on crates, leaning against barrels and the counter, chatting, meddling in everything, and getting underfoot. Abraham Beer's wife waited on the customers, and his seventeen-year-old Hanele (she was the only child still left at home, the name of the Lord be praised!) stood talking to an old peasant wearing a broad belt; supported by her young friends, she was trying to convince him that she could not knock fifty pennies off the price of the scythe that he was constantly testing with his knuckles. Abraham Beer did not like these gatherings in his store. This time he just walked through, paying no attention to anything, except to give a nasty look to a fresh young Jew who had seated himself back of the counter. The youth got up at once.

Abraham Beer went into the room back of the shop. Three stars had risen in the sky, and therefore it was time to read the *Ma'ariv*. He set his hat down more firmly on his head and, turning to a corner of the room, he prayed: "Praised be Jehovah, our Lord, the king of the earth, whose word makes darkness descend; in his wisdom he opens the gates of heaven and in his sagacity causes night and day to alternate and the seasons to change and the stars to follow on their courses in the vault of heaven according to his own will."

This day he spoke the words of the *Ma'ariv* with particular warmth and emphasis, for he had never sensed the proximity of his God more clearly. He knew that Jehovah had stood by him. Glory to the Eternal who watched over his people, glory to the King of Kings who since the beginning of time had kept in mind only his people's well-being! Glory to Jehovah, who cared for every Jew, knowing that his celestial throne rested on the steps of Israel and that the prayer of each individual was more powerful than the angels, and magnified his power and glory. How wise was Jehovah, who had sent Petr Šuhaj to the pasture at the right hour and had placed Nikola Šuhaj at the crossroads at the very moment when his servant Abraham Beer was to pass there, and thus had saved his servant's life! Turned to the bare wall near the sofa, where nothing could bother or distract him, Abraham Beer, swaying his body to and fro, spinning around, snapping his fingers, muttering, chanting, gave his mind wholly to prayer and to his Lord.

It was impossible all evening to speak of the miracle on Suchar, for to have done so would have meant speaking before the whole Jewish community. For even during supper the whole house was full of those forward boys—was Mama looking after that child with the proper caution?—and those perpetually hungry girls of the blacksmith, who were in any case coming over to see Hanele only for what leftovers from supper Mama would give them in the kitchen.

Not till night, after they were in bed, did Abraham Beer say to his wife, "Today the Lord delivered me from a great danger!"

"May his name be praised," Esther Beer responded fervently.

And when she had heard the whole account, her eyes growing rounder and rounder, she lifted her plump arms from under the featherbed as though in benediction, turned her gaze upward, and praised the Lord once more: "*Hoshem Isborh!*"

He repeated *Kriat Shma,* a bedtime prayer: "In the name of Jehovah, the God of Israel, with Michael on my right hand, Gabriel on my left, Oriel before me, and Raphael behind me, and over me the majesty of God!"

And then another idea struck him, and he poked his wife with his finger just as she was dropping off to sleep: "Don't say a word to that child, she'd only get frightened. She will find out all too soon that Šuhaj has escaped. . . . Let us only hope no evil comes of it!"

Had Dovbuš's rifle come up out of the ground at Brázy, where just before his death this celebrated outlaw had buried it deep in the mountainside? It was said to move through the underground darkness a shade closer to the surface each year, and when it shall have gleamed entire in the sunlight, like the bennet or the anemone blossoms in the mountain pastures in the springtime, the world shall have been given a new Oleksa Dovbuš, who, like the old one, shall take from the rich, and give to the poor, and fight the ruling classes, and never kill anybody, except out of just revenge or in self-defense.

Assuredly at Brázy the rifle must have moved to the surface.

Nikola Šuhaj was at large in the woods. He roamed, swift as a deer, over the countryside. He ate at the shelters and in mountain cabins, where he paid royally for each bowlful of corn porridge; he slept in the haystacks and under trees, laughing if his chest was bedewed in the morning.

In the place where a wooden cross with two transverse bars marked the highest point of the steep highway, he was holding up the mail from Volové. Wearing Alpine boots with army puttees and an old army uniform, unarmed, and with his face uncovered, he would be seen standing in the middle of the road, with the palm of his hand upraised: "Halt, I'm Nikola Šuhaj!"

Four men with kerchiefs over their noses would be standing behind him, two of them aiming at the vehicle with army repeaters, and if one of the travelers should, perchance, have the courage to look out, he could see that the muzzles of both rifles would be aimed directly between his eyes.

"All out and hands up! Everybody give everything he has, unless he be poor and we know it!"

In the narrow valley of the Terebla he was holding up the vans on their way to the fair at Chust. A crowded wagon would be going along the road, its Jewish owner walking alongside with a whip. If a stranger on foot should ask him, "Tell me, how many people will your wagon hold, anyhow?" he would not realize the maliciousness of the question, but would answer cordially, "As many as can get in, sir. Just go ahead and climb in."

The chassis would resemble a beehive, the axle would squeak, the horses would be proceeding at a snail's pace. At the bridge across the creek an empty farm wagon, unhitched, would be blocking the road. Four or five men would be standing in front of it, two of them armed. The one without a mask would put his finger before his lips in warning, and with long and menacing steps would advance toward the wagon. It would all be very mystifying. The horses would stop. "Everybody out!" Nikola Šuhaj would beckon with his hand, without a sound, but his easy motion would have the force of a command at once mysterious and inexorable. Not a soul would refuse to obey. Then Šuhaj, still silent, would slowly raise his hands over his head, and they would gradually follow suit, bewildered, and as though in a daze. He would point at one of them with his finger, and the man would approach compliantly. And then things would happen fast: a sounding slap, a few light passes at his pockets, then the order, "Get in the ditch! Lie down, facedown! Next!"

Again: a slap, a turn at the pockets, the ditch, next! Jews, well-to-do peasants, *kerons* (employment agents), Americans who after the War had brought their dollars from America to the land of their birth and whom Nikola particularly delighted in robbing.

After a time, there would be a long row of motionless people lined up in the ditch, while the driver, clutching his whip, would still be out in the road, his eyes popping out of his head. Šuhaj's companions would pull the farm wagon out of the way and get behind the prisoners.

"Everybody back in the wagon," Šuhaj would shout at the top of his lungs, his thundering tones even fiercer than the silence that had preceded them. They would jump up and run to the wagon. "Get going! Hurry!"

The Jew would lash the horses and they, with craned necks and raised heads, would even try to trot, while two of the bandits would aim their army repeaters at the wagon from behind. Not until they were far away, out of the range of gunshot or at the other side of a bend in the road, would the robbed ones begin to scream and get excited, the Americans firing their revolvers straight up in the air to raise an alarm that of course nobody would answer or even hear, pretending to want to go back and make the bandits give up all the things they had seized from them. Meanwhile, Nikola would be waiting for another vehicle. And as the second wagonload was sent on its way, Nikola, followed by his pals, would be making for the woods with his long calm strides.

People would meet him in the woods on Suchar, looking just as they had known him to look in the old days when he had lived in his father's cabin: dark eyed, dark haired, with a mustache, with the small chin and prominent forehead characteristic of reckless horsemen and crack shots. He always wore a broad belt trimmed in multicolored leather, such as would protect his ribs if he fell or if a log hit him. He wore narrow trousers, sandals with straps wound around and around his legs above the ankles, a hempen shirt with bright glass buttons. He carried one gun over his shoulder and another suspended from his neck in back, like a cavalryman. On the stock of each gun a large cross had been carved with a knife. Sometimes he would ask people from the village about the gendarmes; at other times he would laugh and joke with them; other times, for no apparent reason, he would hand out money to children and old women. When he met some respected citizen of Koločava at the ford or on the highway, the priest or the schoolteacher perhaps, he would chat with him, inquire after the health of his family, and would say at parting, "Father, will you do me a favor?"

"Well, what is it, Nikolka?"

"Please tell the gendarmes that you saw me up here. I'd like to give them a little exercise."

But on other occasions he would hurry along, frowning, and pay no heed to anyone.

One time under Tisová Mountain three Jews were laboriously ascending to the pasture, their heavy load of sacks of salt for the cattle and cornmeal for the shepherds slung over their shoulders. Suddenly Šuhaj stood before them, as though he had dropped from the skies. He stood there silently, looking them over, while they prayed and grew pale.

"Hey, you *sloim nachamkes,* stop leaning against that tree and look up! Tomorrow the bailiff will be selling Eržika's cow; here is some money, buy it; someday I'll be down to get it!" And truly no cow in the whole district would be better tended and fed, or more carefully watched, than that particular one.

Sometimes Nikola would rob, at other times not.

"If only I were at the other side of the ford already," thought Bernard Hahn of Horb. "Once I get that far, I won't be afraid of running into Nikola anymore this trip." He cracked his whip at his little horse. But Nikola did not keep him in suspense all the way to the ford; he appeared just a hundred paces ahead, with the palm of his hand upraised. Hahn jumped down from the wagon, the blood rushing to his face and his heart filling with a desperate determination.

"You won't get this money, Nikola. I'm going to Chust to buy the children some shoes," he said emphatically, in a voice that sought to be steady.

"Let's see how much you have there!" Nikola ordered.

Hahn drew out a grimy notebook, opened it on the page where he kept his banknotes, but drew back, clutching it to his breast, and was determined not to give it up.

"Hand it over," Šuhaj cried crossly, tore the book out of his hands, and turned the pages. "You have five children?"

"Seven."

"Well, Bernard, your money wouldn't go very far on shoes for that big a number; here, take this, and get them good ones!" And he added several green hundred-crown bills to the collection in the notebook.

"What do you call your youngest?"

"*Faigele,* Birdie."

"Give her my regards."

He even appeared way down in Chust, dressed in store clothes and a raincoat, walked into an inn, sat down directly under the electric light, was served like any stranger, and listened for an hour while people talked of his exploits. For to go unrecognized was great fun. After he had gone, under the beer tray at the table where he had sat, the waiter found a card bearing the only words that Šuhaj had learned to write while he had been with the Hungarian regiment: *Šuhaj Miklos.* The guests jumped up and ran to the empty chair that he had occupied, as though something were still to be seen there; they read the card, pulling it out of each other's hands, and grew excited.

One night, Šuhaj slept in the big shed on Stiňák Mountain; he brought some sweet brandy to the German milkmaids there and danced with them to the singing of a local tune. In the morning he robbed a Czech engineer of his money and his horses in a nearby valley; an hour later he held up the notary from a neighboring town, and in the afternoon he was already far away by the shallow stream of the Rika, where at the moment the wife of the prefect of the Volové police was taking a dip and giving her dog a bath.

Šuhaj stood there watching her; he smiled and twirled his black mustache. "You're a pretty enough woman, but my Eržika is even prettier. I'm Nikola Šuhaj!"

And while the woman stood there, dressed in her blue bathing suit and knee-deep in water, not knowing what to do or what attitude to take, Šuhaj laughed, "Remember me to your husband, Madam," and strode away.

The gendarmes were helpless. They were frantic. They thrashed Eržika, they thrashed old Petr Šuhaj, they thrashed Ivan Dráč, they thrashed Nikola's brothers and sisters. They arrested his friends and all those who might possibly have been his friends. Koločava, which was obviously abetting the bandit, was assessed to pay thirty thousand crowns in taxes.

The Czech gendarmes did not leave as Šuhaj had predicted to Vlásek. On the contrary, their power was strengthened. And Šuhaj himself was to be its touchstone. There could be no order, and the authority of the new state could not be established as long as this bandit was at large, as long as legends should be woven around his person, as long as questioning eyes should follow with secret joy the gendarmes' unsuccessful contest with him, as long as Nikola Šuhaj's name should be on everybody's lips, a synonym for heroism. The provincial government at Uzhgorod was as aware of the situation as the Koločava post itself, and central headquarters sent out strict orders, instructions, and explanations that only served to excite the gendarmes at Koločava. Their number was increased to thirty. They occupied the school, they settled themselves in Kalman Leibovich's hayloft, and all day long they filled his tavern with cigarette smoke, beer-bottle corks, and the stench of their boots. A captain was named head of these concentrated forces, and almost the only duty left to the old sergeant was acquainting the new men with the countryside and local conditions. The sergeant, therefore, hated Vlásek like the plague (no matter what the truth of Šuhaj's escape may have been) and he made a report to the disciplinary commission in which he expressed the gravest suspicions. The other gendarmes also looked down on Vlásek, gay comrade and good fellow though he was, because, anyway one considered the matter, it was his fault that they had to live in this bandit's nest of a village and go clambering up these mountain slopes.

"Arrest everybody the least bit suspicious!" the captain ordered.

They did so. Only the Šuhajs went free, for the captain believed that if Nikola could not be caught in any other way, Eržika would make good bait.

They only kept searching the Šuhaj premises three times a night, four times a night. Then they would quit for a few days, to lull the family into the false hope that the gendarmes had given up their endeavors, and then they would start searching all over again. Three times a night they would get them out of bed, examine the whole cabin, hold hearings, and make threats; three times a night they would place their bayonets against the Šuhajs' chests. For, until people were brought to the verge of despair, and until their nerves were shaken, they would not talk. The gendarmes arrested many suspects, and, if need be, they would arrest half the village without injustice to a soul.

But these men who were held were peasants, whose every step to the landlords' forests for wood, for game, for berries, or for fodder was a misdemeanor of one sort or another, or at least a trespass (or if, perchance, it was neither, they did not even know that it was not). Such people knew how to hold their tongues. In Chust they lied frightfully, scorning their judges, and did not even make an effort to conceal the fact that they were lying.

How did it happen that in these wholesale arrests Vasyl Derbák Derbačok and his son Adam Chrepta were passed up?

Vasyl Derbák Derbačok was unsuspected, for he had a good cabin, was an able farmer, and nobody knew anything against him. In a region where people went to the pastures for days on end, it was not possible to suspect everyone who spent a night away from home.

One day, however, a shepherd boy brought the gendarmes an old army rifle that he had found under the moss in the woods. The metal was not tarnished, for the firearm had been recently cleaned. Therefore, they reburied it in its place and kept watch there for five days. On the sixth day, they caught Adam Chrepta. They had intended to shadow the weapon's owner, but since the boy was unknown to them, and since he had merely looked at the rifle and walked off again without it, they arrested him.

"To frighten the bears? Ho-ho, Sonny, such fairy tales are for little children!"

They searched him and found three hundred crowns in his possession.

"You earned them? And you wouldn't like to tell us how?"

The cabin of Adam's father, Vasyl Derbák Derbačok, who that day was not at home, was thoroughly searched. Nothing, however, was found. So they took Adam and locked him up.

Adam Chrepta was the illegitimate son of Derbák Derbačok, but he lived with his father's family, and Derbák Derbačok loved the handsome blond lad better than his other children, perhaps because the boy recalled to him the time of his youth, the only joyous period of his life.

When Derbák Derbačok returned from the pasture and heard what had happened, he faltered. He said to himself, "Run to the gendarme headquarters and entreat them to give up your son!" But what a foolish idea! Who had ever heard of a case where the Koločava gendarmes had allowed themselves to be moved by persuasion? Who had ever even tried to move them?

But Derbák Derbačok succeeded. He talked. It was possible to say a great deal in two and a half hours, even when a person tried to keep most of it to himself and was forced to rack his brains to answer the torrent of questions in a manner that would at least appear plausible. He did not tell everything. He particularly avoided revealing anything about Ihnat Sopko and Danilo Jasinko, who knew every bit as much on him as he did on them. But, in any case, he talked enough, and the captain of the gendarmes, in accordance with the bargain that the man was tacitly offering him, became convinced that there would be time enough later to arrest both father and son, and that meanwhile it would be well to use them both for his own purposes. This Šuhaj affair was becoming too serious. So much depended on it, even for him personally. All right. Adam Chrepta was freed. They released him.

Derbák Derbačok and Adam left the schoolhouse, now turned into the gendarme headquarters—Adam, happy and smiling, Derbák Derbačok, with a perspiring brow and a confused mind.

The captain's views were confirmed. The pursuit of Šuhaj was no unique case in which mysterious alliances and secret contacts played a part, but a perfectly banal matter, centering around his home and his love affair, around the cabin at the foot of Suchar Mountain and Eržika. These baits would have to bring results. These baits should bring results. Šuhaj was spending most of his time in the valleys around Suchar, and both his father and his wife were meeting him there. Very well!

"Leave them alone for a few days," the captain told the sergeant in reference to the nocturnal inspections at the Šuhaj homestead, "and watch the house from the outside."

Out on the pasture between Šuhaj's cabin and the Suchar Woods, there were two haystacks about three hundred meters apart, and with a like distance between the cabin and the nearer of them. Three gendarmes hid in a haystack to carry out the orders. But since they came late in the evening, they did not suspect that Eržika and Nikola's younger sister Anča had already been asleep for an hour in the other one. Both girls preferred the autumn mist to the gendarmes' nightly interference with their slumbers. And so it happened that in the morning fog, as the women were jumping down from the hay, the valley and mountain slope above began to resound with cries of "Halt! . . . Halt! . . . Halt!"

Both the women started running for their lives. Shots were fired, for the gendarmes thought that the one in back was Šuhaj in disguise. Eržika and Anča tore across the pasture and flew into the woods. There they slowed down, gasping for breath.

But Eržika could not go on. She sank, more dead than alive, under a pine. Her head bowed lower and lower, until it touched a jutting root.

"What's the matter, Eržika?"

Anča looked. Eržika was as pale as death, and her hempen clothes were soaking with blood. Great quantities of blood.

"Jesus! Mary! They've shot Eržika!"

But the girl was mistaken. Eržika had miscarried. Anča darted deeper into the woods. She made for the valleys and pastures where Nikola was apt to have spent the night. As she ran, she kept shouting, "Nikola! . . . Nikola! . . . Nikola!"

In the fog, her voice sounded desperate and terrible.

The gendarmes in the surprise of the moment had dashed into the woods and had advanced a short distance. But soon it became apparent to them that this was foolish. Three people in a virgin forest? Whom would they find? They returned, cross and irritated.

From the edge of the woods they could see Petr Šuhaj, his wife, and their three older children examining the premises, trying to see what had occurred. They watched Petr go back to the haystack. Then they attacked the family, dragging the parents to the cabin. The two younger boys followed, shrieking. Only the fourteen-year-old Juraj resisted. Twice they threw him to the ground, but each time he got up, and, with teeth gnashing and eyes glowing like a young wolf's, he struck back. Finally, they twisted his arm and dragged him along.

They stood Petr against the wall of the cabin, and while one of them put a bayonet against his chest, the other thrashed him. As for Juraj, he lay howling, facedown, in the grass, after a few blows.

"Where is Nikola? Where is Eržika? Where did they go? We'll kill you!"

At that moment, a dreadful shriek was heard from the forest—a cry whose words could not be distinguished. It was uttered by Nikola. There he stood. The gendarmes, turning, were making ready to aim their rifles at him when they heard a shot and one of them fell to the ground. The two remaining ones leaped back of the cabin and sent a volley of shots toward the woods.

That evening, the Šuhajs' cabin burned down. It blazed like a pile of dry tinder. The ailing Eržika had to be carried out.

That was the way it had been done in the villages in Siberia when one of their number had been murdered. Use terror! Get them down through terror! Had the gendarmes escaped the bullets of the Russians, the Serbians, the Italians, the Austrians, the Germans, and the Bolsheviks only to let a bandit do them in? And had they fought on Siberian plains and among the Dolomite rocks only to perish in this robbers' village?

The funeral of the murdered gendarme was held on the third day. No, it was not like a funeral, but more like a review of armed forces in the face of the enemy, like a military demonstration in a silently hostile Siberian village.

A fully equipped company of soldiers had arrived from Chust to honor the fallen legionnaire as befitted him. Their heavy tread between the picket and board fences of Koločava was reminiscent of war, and the very atmosphere had the semblance and flavor of war, as though a heavy, ashen-colored cloud were floating over the valley and making it difficult to breathe freely.

The soldiers carried the wreath-covered coffin out of the schoolhouse. The signals given, the infantry and the gendarmes rendered the last homage to their dead comrade. The drumbeats resounded in the stillness like a distant and menacing cannon. The inhabitants of Koločava, hiding back of the fences in their yards or behind the windows of their houses, watched the black and gold robes of the Catholic clergy and the surplices of the altar boys, the officials in full dress uniform, and all that multitude of gentlemen who could destroy Koločava and avenge one of their own number with a single stroke of the pen. The somber procession of gendarmes, marching in columns of four; the beats of the cymbals, echoing loudly between the house walls; the slow, warlike advance under which the pebbles and rubble of the road were made to crunch— all these impressions were evil and somehow aroused a foreboding of starvation. The single bell that was left in the Greek Catholic church was tolling, and its double peals fell on the village as threateningly as though there were a flood by night. Koločava kept silent.

Only the old Jews who came out to stand in front of the signs on their stores and artisans' workshops comprehended the purpose of this powerful demonstration. Even though they were mindful of it, they did not allow themselves to be carried away by emotion. Puckering the corners of their mouths, they thought, "Eh, a bad business! They should lock up Eržika and let Nikola's pals go free, because people cannot be caught by what is good in them, they must be caught on what is wicked in them."

This article of faith had been discovered by the white-bearded Hasid Hersh Leib Wolf, perhaps in the Mosaic canon, or possibly in the very holy, mystic *Zohar*. The Jews accepted it as their own, for they did not approve of the gendarmes' tactics.

»»» 3 «««

Oleksa Dovbuš

Outlaws! Black Lads!

In propitious times, when the luck of heroes was on their side, they founded ruling dynasties; much more often, however, their bodies hung from the gallows and most frequently of all they were shot in the back and ended on the moss in the woods in a pool of blood. But the fate of these last was glory greater than that of kings for the very reason that they had failed to found dynasties, that they had remained local, familiar. They had taken upon themselves the suffering and the burdens of the people and had achieved what the mountaineers had not dared try, yet had always wanted passionately: they had avenged injustice, killed members of the ruling classes, deprived them of their unfairly accumulated fortunes, destroyed by fire and the sword, for pleasure, for revenge, as a warning against the future, and out of fear of what the future might hold. These outlaws were the children of the people's dreams, for in cold reality the people had never ventured to rebel and had never achieved the happiness of mass revenge.

See, that flat boulder yonder used to be the banquet table of Oleksa Dovbuš. He used to meet his Black Lads at this spring over here. There, beneath the ancient pine, they used to split their spoils; over there they danced the wild *arkan,* standing in a row with their arms around each other's shoulders, tapping the ground with their heels and squatting down. He went out that way to set fire to the lord's castle after having lured away the garrison. Over there used to be a tavern, where he joined a Jewish wedding party and departed with leather bags full of money and jewels. In this direction lies the thrice-accursed village of Kosmače, where lived Dzvinka, his treacherous sweetheart, and over there is Black Mountain, where he lies buried amidst his treasures.

They are false, the stories that the ruling classes have invented about him, and false also are the books that have been written only to dim his glory.

Oleksa Dovbuš did not live in the middle of the eighteenth century at the time of the struggle between Augustus and Stanislaus Leszinsky in Poland, or following the stormy revolt of Rakoczy in Hungary; nor did he flourish during the severe civil strife in Romania that led to the war with Russia; he did not loot the countryside during the seven years when it was filled with deserters from the armies of Rakoczy, Gienieawski, and Golc, in mountains crowded with peasants who had fled from the manors of Sir Josef Potocký and were willing to face the gallows in preference to bearing the injustices of a heterogeneous soldiery and the oppression of the lord's henchmen and agents. Above all, it is not true that he was shot in the village of Kosmače by Štefan Dzvinka when he came to demand a dowry due to one of his fellows. And the year 1745 is a bookish figure, desolate and meaningless. Oleksa Dovbuš did not live in any particular period. He lived thousands of years ago or centuries ago, he lives today, he will survive tomorrow. For Oleksa Dovbuš is not one man, he is a nation, he represents the flare of its revenge and its passionate longing for justice.

Well then, what is the real story of Oleksa Dovbuš?

Here is the way things really happened:

Once upon a time, there lived a weak shepherd, poor, infirm, and simpleminded, by the name of Oleksa Dovbuš. For (to use the idiom of the preachers and the interpreters of the Holy Writ) it was to be demonstrated through him that each one of us, no matter how timid, humble, and poor, can perform great deeds, if it be God's will that he should do so. Dovbuš used all the money he earned tending sheep to buy a pocket pistol and wandered, limping, over the village, much to the amusement of the children, who used to run after him. And if any of the shepherds had to take a thrashing, it would be he. Nobody held a high opinion of him.

But the Lord gave him great strength as a reward for a service he once performed for him. Beyond Tisová, on Black Mountain, on the side of one of the peaks, there was a deep chasm, overhung by a cliff. Therein dwelt the devil, who would sit on that cliff, mocking God and blaspheming. God would send a flash of lightning down on him, but the devil would jump into the abyss, and the thunder would only serve to break off a piece of rock. Then the devil would crawl out and begin deriding God again. God would send down another flash, but the Unclean One would disappear once more in the pit. It went on this way for a long time. Once Dovbuš happened to be there and see this game, so he turned his back on the lightning bolts, aimed his pocket pistol at the devil, and shot him down. The devil fell into the chasm and sank head-first deep into the earth. Only a cloud of smoke was left of him. Then the Archangel Gabriel appeared to Dovbuš and said, "Thou hast done God a good turn by ridding the world of the devil. What wishest thou for thy reward?"

Dovbuš meditated for a long time, and finally he answered, "People consider me of little account, but I should like to prove to them that I can do great deeds and be useful to them. May God make me the strongest man in the world that I might defeat my enemies and punish wrongs! May God grant that nobody conquer me and no missile hit me!"

And when he came back among the other shepherds and they began poking fun at him again and wanted to thrash him, he threw them to the ground like so many pebbles.

From thenceforth, Oleksa Dovbuš became a leader. He stood for Truth and punished human injustice. He was cruel to the rulers, merciful and kind to the people. He took from the rich and gave to the poor. With the fifty Black Lads whom he gathered about him, he set fire to the castles of the wicked lords and the houses of their officials. He held up Jewish shops, took brandy for himself and his band, and poured out the rest. He threw pawned articles out into the street so that everybody might pick out his own belongings. Once he attacked a nobleman's estate and carried away whole sacks full of pure gold ducats. He loaded these sacks on his lads' backs and made holes in them with his hatchet-handled cane. Wherever his lads went, they scattered gold pieces, and the poor thronged around them and picked them up. The lords and the Jews alike mended their ways for fear of him.

He lived on one of the mountains, where his lads hewed him a throne in the rock; there he would sit and issue orders to the people. He conducted expeditions as far as Romania and Turkey to rob the infidels. Bringing the spoils home, he gave aid to the needy who asked for it. He ordered his lads to bury his treasure in the cliff in such a manner that nobody could ever steal it, and they obeyed. Nowadays men could build railroads and dynamite whole mountainsides, but they would never succeed in opening or breaking up that cliff, which holds his gold and silver and precious stones and well-oiled weapons. If the cliff should expose its treasures, they would glisten so mightily that the entire world would be dazzled. But this wealth is awaiting the appearance of a new Dovbuš, who is due to come someday. For before he died, Oleksa buried his dagger in the earth on Brázy. Each year the dagger moves the breadth of a poppy seed closer to the surface, and when it shall be fully exposed to the sun, a new Oleksa Dovbuš shall be born who shall be the darling of the people and a terror to the rulers, a defender of Truth, and an avenger of Injustice.

Dovbuš scattered all the armies sent out against him as though they were flocks of birds. When the Emperor heard of this invincible man, he sent word for Dovbuš to come to Vienna, that he wanted to come to terms with him. But actually he intended to trick him, and when Dovbuš was drawing near to the palace, the Emperor sent his troops out to kill him and stood looking out of the window to see what would happen. And all the missiles that were fired bounced back from Dovbuš and killed the ones who had fired them. The Emperor, seeing this, ordered the firing to cease immediately and made an agreement with Dovbuš. He allowed him to fight freely over the length and breadth of the land as long as he would spare the imperial soldiers, and he gave him heavy sealed documents setting forth this privilege. Dovbuš remained the guest of the Emperor and his court for three days. For seven years thereafter he pillaged the countryside, and as long as he lived the poor were well off.

He was destroyed by a woman, that everlasting enemy of man, that shameful root of all evil. He fell in love with a woman, forgot his mission, and perished. Ah, the devil's own treacherous breed! Her name was Dzvinka, she lived in Kosmače and was married. In an unguarded moment she wormed his secret out of him, swearing a tenfold oath not to tell a living soul: the invulnerable Dovbuš could be killed only by a silver bullet that had been hidden in a bowl of spring wheat that had been handed to the priest to be blessed on each of the twelve holiest days of the year. The bullet was to have twelve masses said over it by twelve priests.

But Dzvinka told Štefan, her husband.

One day, Dovbuš and his Black Lads set out to capture a castle. "Tomorrow we shall have to get early under way, my lads," Dovbuš said to them, "so we shall go to bed early tonight. We shall stop at Kosmače and see Dzvinka."

"Oleksík, little father, do not go to Kosmače, for we had an evil dream!"

"My lads, my dear gallants, how foolish you are! Charge each rifle with two bullets and wait for me here at the foot of the hill while I go up and ask whether Dzvinka will give us some supper!"

He came to her window, upon which the setting sun was casting its reflection. "Little friend," he called, "are you asleep or are you awake? And will you give us some supper?"

Dzvinka did not answer him, but she thought to herself, "I'm not asleep, I'm listening, I'm getting supper, and it will be a notable one! How people will marvel!"

"Are you asleep or awake, my heart, and will you give Dovbuš lodging for the night?"

This time she answered. "I'm not asleep and I hear you well, but I have no lodging for bandits. Štefan is away and supper is not ready!"

"Open the door, bitch, or do you want me to break it down?"

"I do not want you to break it down, but I'm not going to open it."

Dovbuš grew angry and pressed his body against the door. Štefan, watching from the loft, loaded his pistol with a single bullet. The door creaked, the locks were yielding. Dzvinka, terrified, whispered through the keyhole, "Oleksík, my soul, do not come in. I'm not resisting of my own free will, but Štefan is watching from the loft."

The door bent inward. From above, Štefan shot the silver bullet. He aimed at the heart and hit the right lung. But the blood gushed from the left side also.

Dovbuš lay before the cabin door in a pool of blood. He was all alone. "Ah, Štefan," he cried, "so you have killed me for a bitch!"

Štefan answered from the loft, "You should not have loved her or confided in her. Good faith in a bitch is like the foam on running water."

Where were his gallant lads now? If he should call, they were too far away to hear him; if he should whistle, they were too far away to come to him. Nevertheless, when he called, they did hear him, and when he whistled, they came, like a flock of sheep. "Oleksík, little father, why didn't you heed us? Dovbušík, why didn't you kill her?"

"How could I kill her, when I love her so very, very much? Go and ask her if she too loves me!"

Dzvinka was weeping. "If I did not love him, I would not be wearing white and adorning myself with gold and silver!"

"Oh, my gallant lads, I feel so ill! Take me away from this place! Lay me under a beech, where I may bid you farewell and die as befits an outlaw!"

They laid him under a silver beech. "Oleksík, little father, shall we thrash the bitch to death or shall we shoot her?"

"Neither beat nor shoot her. Burn the cabin, but let her go in peace."

The lads mourned: "Oleksík, little father, what will become of us without you? How shall we spend our youth? How shall we win castles? Advise us! Shall we go to Hungary or to Romania?"

"Do not go out to pillage, lads! Go home and farm! You have three lumps of gold. Bury one with me, give the second to the bitch, and divide the third among yourselves. Abandon your war clubs and stop shedding human blood. Human blood is not water and should be spared. You must not roam over the world, pillaging; you cannot succeed alone, and your leader is gone. Make a stretcher of your war clubs, my gallant lads, and carry me to Black Mountain. I have loved the place and wish to die there. On the cliff there are two pines, they are my little sisters, and two maples, my brothers. Bury me beneath them."

They bore him to Black Mountain on their clubs. There he died and was buried in the shadow of wild crags in an unknown spot amidst his treasures, which, if exposed, would dazzle the world.

God loved Dovbuš and glorified him even after death; for on the very first day in the year—no sooner, no later—that the sun casts its first gleams on his grave and touches his heart, the world greets Easter Sunday, the greatest holiday of all Christian souls.

The rest of the region did not know how stifling the atmosphere had been in Koločava on the day of the gendarme's funeral.

It only knew that Nikola Šuhaj was alive and that he was living in the woods. A man in the woods was like a fish in the lake: everybody knew he was there but nobody knew just where. The murky depths of both water and forest held in them something mysterious that intrigued the fisherman, the ranger, and the passerby.

The women sitting before their doors in the warm sunlight of autumn afternoons would work and talk as they had done from time immemorial. Each one of them would have a distaff held over her left side by her apron string, with a tuft of sheep's wool wound around its end, and, working the spindle with her right hand, moistening her left thumb with her lower lip, would spin heavy thread. But they were no longer discussing their old favorite subject, reminiscent of ancient legends and the Bible, and one in which, heaven knew why, they had always found such delight: namely, snakes. They were no longer talking about the human snake-kings, who by whistling could summon their snakes at any time and could drop them from both sleeves of their fur coats; nor about the conjuring of snakes on the feast of the Annunciation, when all the underground vermin crawled out in the sun; nor about the prosperity that snakes brought to the cabins in which they were allowed to reside; nor about their revenge in causing children to be born with snakelike features and scaly bodies. No, they would talk instead of Oleksa Dovbuš, of Dovža, or of Pinta; of the one whose body the pandours (brutal Croatian soldiers) had branded with glowing twenty-heller pieces. And they would call out the witchlike crones, who knew how it had happened. Sucking on their short pipes with the pointed lids, they would climb down from their perch back of the oven, come out in front of the house, and recall the past.

The women would also talk about Nikola—Nikola the Invulnerable, Nikola the hero and the brave lover. He was in the mountains now. The gendarmes were organizing expeditions against him, were surrounding him with cordons of crack shots who were firing countless bullets at him, but he would stand on a mossy boulder and wave a green bough, repulsing the bullets. Then he would disappear at will: perhaps to his treasure hoard in a Suchar ravine, a cave more splendid than all the cathedrals in the world, but one whose exact location was unknown even to his truest friends, for he would not approach it otherwise than with deer hooves fastened underneath his sandals, so as to leave no human tracks. Or then again, he would wander over the countryside, appearing suddenly, to stop the mails, the rich Jews, the *kerons,* and the gentlemen with these words: "I am Šuhaj!"

The three words would suffice to make people's knees grow weak, would cause their palms to sweat and their pocketbooks to open up. Then they would allow themselves to be thrashed and laid in a row in the ditch like the rungs of a ladder. Ho! Ho! Ho! Had anybody ever heard of anything as funny? Ha! Ha! Ha!

Have you heard the incident of the baron? Somewhere out in Bohemia there lived a nobleman who rented the local game preserve and was paying two foresters to watch his deer. And all of a sudden the rumor spread that a bear was in the hunting preserve. It was said he had killed a peasant's horse; he had just knocked him over with his paw and eaten out his brains. The foresters had begun to set out raspberry juice for him to drink. To get him out of the habit of finding his food for himself, they trained him to come to the clearing for meat. They knew how things would go: the bear would grow fat and lazy so that even beating him with sticks would only make him growl and show his teeth, but would not induce him to leave his food. They even dug the baron a hunting trench and covered it with boards so that not even an artillery could shoot its way through to him. Then they telegraphed: "Will your lordship please come, the game is quite certain."

Three cars arrived with the gentlemen, who brought supplies, wine, cooking utensils. It looked like a military expedition. They hired horses and about eight local men and went out after the bear: to the mountains, where his lordship had a hunting lodge. But when they drew near the lodge and saw it through the trees, they wondered, "What have we here?" Something big and red could be discerned over the door. They quickened their pace: good heavens, what was it? The place looked like a butcher shop. The baron and his foresters ran ahead and then stopped dead in their tracks with horror: the bear! He hung from the door of the lodge, but he had been dressed, or rather undressed. Nikolka had skinned him to save them the pains. Ha! Ha!

Did you know Marijka Ivanyš of Točka? The Ivanyš' cabin was located high up the mountainside. One day toward nightfall Marijka looked out the window and saw somebody coming toward the house. "Where might he be going?" she wondered, as it was too late in the day to get anywhere. Holy Virgin, the man had a rifle over his shoulder! She called her husband and he grew alarmed: "Marijka, it's Nikola!"

The stranger walked up and greeted them: "Glory to Jesus Christ!"

"Glory forever, amen," Marijka answered, frightened to death as might be expected; and then they just stood there, looking at each other and not saying a word. Nikola was grinning. Finally, Ivanyš gathered the courage to ask, "And who might you be, brother?"

Nikola burst out laughing and his white teeth gleamed: "Brother, you know very well who I am. I shot a deer out yonder, so give me a hand! Let's bring it in here. You can salt it down and maybe smoke a piece, and someday I'll be back to help you eat it."

Sure enough, he came two or three times after that. Then he stopped coming. At Hafa Hurdzan's, where he saw that there was nothing to eat in the cabin, he gave the children money. And he would take brandy to the German milkmaids on one mountain and candy to the shepherds on another. What did Nikola care for a hundred-crown note? Or what did a thousand crowns matter? He would go to his cave and get some more.

One could talk about Nikola all day long. And from one end of the mountains to the other there was not a place where somebody had not clearly identified him, disguised as a peasant, a gentleman, a forester, a priest, a soldier, a woman. And if there were people who had no imagination and had never glimpsed him, at least they must have heard the sound of a reed resounding from the fringe of the forest at twilight. That was Nikola playing, for nobody could play the shepherd's pipe as beautifully as he; for even he would sometimes get lonely in the woods and pour out his longing for Eržika in sweet music.

In darkened rooms at night, as the beech logs burned low in the ovens and the old crones finished their pipefuls of tobacco mixed with walnut leaves, people would still be talking about Nikola. And mothers would say to their children: "Don't you bother me, I have no more corn porridge, and Nikola will hear your whining!" The children warming themselves on the top of the oven would then stare into the darkness and Nikola would become for them a personage from the world of fairy tales. They would shiver with terror and delight. Perhaps he really was crouching out there under the window, listening to what was being said about him! Someday they might meet him face-to-face and he would give them candy and a handful of gold.

Who were Nikola's pals? On Sundays, the men from the mountain cabins went down to the village. Wearing their sheepskin coats furry side out, with sleeves reaching far below their fingertips, they formed white interweaving groups; they greeted each other in the name of Jesus, and then they proceeded to talk about Šuhaj. What a joy it was to hear new details of how he had humiliated the upper classes, who were tormenting them with summonses to Volové and Chust and were unwilling to pay them anything for the notes issued by the Romanians! What pleasure to hear about rich Jews whose money had brought them no blessing! Let Nikola shoot the gendarmes, the devil take them, who led them to jail in chains and stole their army pistols and muzzleloaders out of their cabins and tried them for every piece of wood out of the forest and every trout out of the brook and spied like fiends for tobacco plants in their potato patches!

Had you seen that big-mouthed fellow yonder, the one in the town clothes and green hunting hat, who was strutting around in front of the church and not associating with anybody? That was a *keron,* an agent who got them jobs for shares of their pay, a beast and an accursed swindler who juggled the figures in the wage agreements with the entrepreneurs and overcharged the workers for their fares and their joint purchases of foodstuffs. He was an illiterate man from a mountain cabin the same as the rest of them, but now he was putting on airs, swaggering with a cigar in his mouth (that mouth which had many times felt the force of woodcutters' fists!). Not a head of the shaggy sheepskin-clad group turned to look after him; they followed him only with their eyes. Ha, ha, he looked glum, for all he tried to appear unconcerned! Nikola had taken his money as he had been bringing it home from Chust.

But which of these men were Nikola's accomplices?

They were here among the rest, blessing themselves before the iconostand with the Greek sign of the cross, just like anybody else, and singing "*Hospodi, pomiluj!* Lord, have mercy!" the same as everyone. Probably everybody was meeting and greeting them daily. But still, they were meeting Nikola as well, and were covering their faces with blue cloths. Who were they? Which ones of the crowd? This secret was as exciting as the murky depths of the water and the woods or the idea of snake-kings.

The Jewish younger set of Koločava was also very much interested in the question of Šuhaj's partners in crime. (They no longer called them merely his companions.) These Jewish youths, changing from handsome children into unattractive adolescents with unclean skin, long earlocks, and a premature, fuzzy growth of beard, had never done much work. Now that their fathers' businesses—trucking, selling, or the crafts, as the case might be—had come to a standstill, they did nothing at all. They would spend their days visiting each other. They sat around on the stoops of the shops, swung on the carriage shafts in the courtyards, lolled on the turner's bench and the lumber in Pinkas Glaser's carpenter shop. In their boredom, they helped Srul Rosenthal blow the bellows. They peeked into kitchens and wondered where they might get a cigarette or something to eat. They argued, poked fun at each other, and discussed Šuhaj.

They would ask one another, "Where does Šuhaj exchange his money, hey? And what has he done with the box of felt hats that he took from the post from Volové, eh? And what has he done with all the sugar? And where has he put the two bundles of cloth from Hersh Wolf?"

"Is it possible that Abraham Beer . . . ?"

"Who was talking about Abraham Beer? Nobody said a thing, one way or the other. One was only asking what has Šuhaj done with the banknotes, the cloth, the sugar, and the felt hats?! Maybe he has eaten them all, eh, what do you think, you dummy?"

Abraham Beer? They all wondered, idly toying with the sawdust on the lumber in Glaser's workshop. Abraham Beer? They wondered, thinking of Hanele, a mangy Polish Jew, whose father had come from Poland, a half-naked beggar! Might the flesh fall off him like this sawdust, the cur, who wanted to devour everything for himself! The devil always helped the rich, and the poor always had to go without.

Well, and how could Petr Šuhaj be building a new cabin for his family when he had not borrowed the money for it anywhere? Neither at Hersh Wolf's nor at Abraham Beer's nor at Hersh Leib Wolf's! And where had Fedor Burkalo acquired the money to buy a cow? And Adam Chrepta the money for cigarettes, when not a single one of them was working? Listen: there was little eight-year-old Icho Kahan from Majdan, who lived at Hersh Leib Wolf's house and got his meals with various Jewish families because Majdan had no Jewish teachers and the boy had to learn Hebrew. A child like that knew everything because everybody talked in his presence. Ask him! Ask him whether by any chance old Isaac Fuchs hasn't been transporting lumber from Koločava by night? And whether by any chance there hasn't been something hidden under this lumber?

Truly, one was surrounded by robbers. Robbers and murderers! And after all, the worst of them was Abraham Beer! The situation was as bad as in the woods: here it was man eat man. Except that in the end Abraham Beer would gobble up everybody else.

The old Jews recited all the prayers prescribed by their Law: in the morning, and before the stars had risen and after they had risen, before going to sleep, before meals and after meals, and before and after each drink of water. When they were not praying or thinking of their complicated affairs, they were wondering about Šuhaj. And they would say, "Eh, a bad business!"

When the major of the gendarmes arrived in Koločava to inspect the assembled detachment, a Jewish delegation gave him their opinion outright: "You're not going to catch Šuhaj with Eržika as the bait, you'll catch him on his comrades. For people cannot be caught on what is good in them, but on what is evil. Lock up Eržika and let his friends go free!"

The major of the gendarmes had no comprehension for such talmudic wisdom and did not answer. His time was short and he asked that one of the Jewish gentlemen, perhaps Mr. Abraham Beer, come to see him on the morrow.

But during the night he had Vasyl Derbák Derbačok brought in by the back door of the schoolhouse and he said to him, "You've been tricking us, you rascal! You lead us around on Šuhaj's trail, but always manage to get us there after he has already gone. You never take us where he is at the moment."

"Can I fly from the mountains to Koločava like a bird? And can you fly back there like birds?"

The point was well taken, but the major was right nevertheless. While Vasyl Derbák Derbačok tried to keep the gendarmes in a good humor (which was not easy) and kept them hot on Šuhaj's trail, he took care that they should not catch Nikola napping, for he was especially afraid lest Šuhaj be arrested and talk. He hoped and continued to believe that Nikola would save himself and he wanted nothing more fervently. Perhaps Šuhaj would escape, maybe he would hide himself for good, or maybe . . . no, Derbák Derbačok knew no other alternative.

What more did Nikola want, anyway? He had enough, and so had his friends. The gendarmes were getting urgent: where had Šuhaj been yesterday? Where had he slept? Who had been with him? Where was he today? Derbák Derbačok would lead them to him! This double dealing and double danger made Derbák Derbačok suffer considerably, the more so as he did not wish to report innocent people and could not report Ihnat Sopko and Danilo Jasinko. His one-track mind could not bear such duplicity. He was sleeping poorly, had lost weight, and looked ill. What did Nikola expect, and why did he not save them all from such an untenable situation? If it was God's will, in spite of Derbačok's wishes, that Nikola should fall into the hands of the gendarmes, then . . . then . . . yes, then let God give him to them in a condition beyond speech!

"Listen," said the major of the gendarmes to Derbák Derbačok, "I'll give you six weeks. That's more than long enough. Within that time you will help us get Šuhaj. If not, we shall arrest you and your boy. He's twenty years old already, so you know how it will turn out for him. Until that time, you may have dealings with Šuhaj. But you alone, not your boy! And you shall tell us whom else he sees. Everybody he sees! Is that clear?"

He fixed his stern gaze on Derbačok's eyes as they struggled for calmness. Then he turned to the captain of the gendarmes. "Captain," he said, "please note the date. Six weeks from today you will arrest them both and turn them over to the courts. . . . And you, Derbák Derbačok, may go now."

Derbák Derbačok left the gendarme headquarters with his heart heavier than when he had come.

While Derbák Derbačok was wavering between the desire that Šuhaj might escape and the hope that he might die, Abraham Beer had already solved the problem: yes, let the gendarmes get Šuhaj, but let them get him dead! Otherwise, Abraham Beer was in accord with the views of the Jewish community and for the officer's benefit he translated Hersh Leib Wolf's theological precept into practical terms:

"Arrest Eržika, Major, and let his pals go! You'll never trap him with Eržika, believe me, Major, as there is a God above me! Eržika is his chief spy in the community. To be sure, they have other messengers, because every child is aware that whatever move Eržika may make she is certain to be followed by gendarmes in disguise, and she, naturally, knows this too. As long as she stays in Koločava, all your efforts are useless. And the captain won't take him alive either! Fie, Major, just try to find one particular grain in a pile of wheat! The captain would need half of the whole Czechoslovak army for that! Let Šuhaj's comrades go, promise them to drop the charges against them, and set a price on his head, Major! The Jewish community will offer a reward, too, and within two weeks the whole affair will be settled. Somebody will shoot him, or will do him in with an ax, or will bring him in bonds, or . . . some other way. If I'm wrong, Major, may the pestilence strike me!"

With the first signs of spring, as the sun beat down upon the softening snowdrifts and the first cracks began to form in the ice that stretched over the swift streams, Nikola seemed to go on a rampage. He who had preserved the age-old tradition of outlaws, to kill only in self-defense, now began to murder right and left. He, the hero, who had always appeared with his face exposed and had been one against many, now did not shrink from working after dark when it was necessary to use an ax and spatter the cabin beams with blood.

The evening after the fair of Volové three Jewish merchants from the city were shot. They were riding in a peasant wagon, not over five hundred paces distant from the last houses of Volové. And how they had been shot! Nikola, the wonder shooter, who had formerly missed neither a deer nor a bear nor a human being, was suddenly missing at thirty paces. The merchants had been shot in the stomach, and, since they had remained alive, he had run the wheels of the wagon over their throats as they lay in the melting snow. But they still lived for a few hours and thus were able to answer the official who conducted the investigation.

The whole family of a Ruthenian peasant who had just returned from America was put to death in their cabin near the village. In the mountains, a Jew was shot and robbed. Murders, assassinations! Not a week passed but what a killing took place. What was Nikola Šuhaj about?

Terror descended upon the countryside.

The division of gendarmes was increased to number sixty men. But it seemed as though no investigation could get past the stubborn heads of the people in this bandit's den of a village. It ended with them, and nothing came out.

They had seen nothing; they had heard nothing; they knew nothing; they had not caught sight of Nikola for months; nobody had met him in the woods or on the pasture; he had not come in to drink in their winter shelters. Two road workers who at the time of the holdup at Volové had not yet left their gravel piles three hundred paces away, and whose bellies were still wet from the way they had crawled in the ditch and crouched there in the thawing snow as the shots were being fired, had not even heard any shots and knew nothing whatever about it. The girl who was the eyewitness to the holdup on the highway denied everything. And the Jew who had been robbed in his own house and had escaped alive by a miracle was still trembling as he told the judge at Chust: "I don't know anything, Your Honor, I lost the money, I don't want to lose my life as well!"

Terror gripped the countryside, and the woman who described one of the murderers of the American's family had her house burned by incendiaries.

"Lock up Eržika! Let Šuhaj's friends go free! Offer a reward for his capture!" repeated the Jews, and since they made an article of faith out of every formulated opinion, they repeated it with all their might, furiously, consistently, and with passion. They screamed it in the ears of the gendarme officers, they bombarded the district government at Volové with it, they stormed in their Yiddish newspapers in Ruthenian towns, they sent complaints about it to Prague. The gendarmes, raging over their own failure, made nervous by the Jews and the press, by the reprimands they were getting from central headquarters, and by the stubbornness of the Ruthenians, were becoming subject to bursts of anti-Semitism.

They called Derbák Derbačok and multiplied their threats.

But Derbák Derbačok was like a ram: "I don't know. I couldn't say where he is, I haven't seen him for two months."

"You're lying."

"I'm not."

Then, when it seemed that the captain of the gendarmes would pounce on him, that he would call the sergeant to arrest him immediately, Derbák Derbačok called out the words that staggered them so completely: "Nikola isn't guilty of all that at all!"

The captain was momentarily dumbfounded, for the fellow had voiced the captain's most secret suspicion.

"You're a liar, you cur!" He clutched at the man's throat. "Liar! Liar! Liar!"

The captain's stamping changed into a rapid pacing up and down the classroom.

"How do you know that?" he called out, stopping before the peasant. Without waiting for an answer, he commenced to pace again.

It sounded improbable, impossible, and yet, Derbák Derbačok had uttered the captain's own secret thought. For really, had Šuhaj sprouted wings, that he should have been able to rob here in the morning and seventy kilometers away by evening? Such speed was suspicious. But if Derbačok was right, then somebody else must have been committing murder at Šuhaj's expense! How horrible! Had they more than one bandit to deal with? In that case, they would have not one gang of criminals to face, but a whole region of thieves and assassins! It was horrible. Horrible!

The cross-examination of Derbačok started all over again.

The captain resumed his seat at the desk. "How do you know that?"

"Nikola never killed anybody. Excepting gendarmes," he corrected himself at once, and the officer rewarded him with a piercing glance.

"I asked you: how do you know that Šuhaj isn't committing all those crimes? Who told you?"

"Nobody told me. But I know. Nikola never missed beast or man. . . . He doesn't go around shooting people in the belly. And he doesn't kill with an ax. And he doesn't break into people's houses at night."

"Where is Šuhaj?"

"I haven't heard for two months."

"Is he still alive?"

"I don't know."

"Then who is doing it all?"

"I couldn't say."

He really did not know. After the gendarme (himself near collapse) had tormented him for two hours and was beginning to threaten him anew, Derbák Derbačok burst out screaming: "Arrest me then! And Adam too! Lock me up! And lock up Adam too! Do you think I'm less afraid of Nikola's bullet than of your jail? When the whole village knows that you bring me down here nights! The devil should have broken my legs under me the first time I came here! I know nothing, nothing, nothing!"

"To arrest him or to let him go?" wondered the captain. His own limbs were trembling with fatigue and excitement. Horrible! Horrible! Regiments of robbers and cutthroats! He nervously passed the back of his hand over his forehead. Derbák Derbačok was ready for everything; he no longer feared anything, for at one of the questions of this day's cross-examination a happy thought had passed through his mind, a thought which was now gaining shape and magnitude. Yes, perhaps Nikola was no longer alive. Certainly he was around no longer. Maybe he had run away. Maybe he had hidden forever. Maybe he had saved himself. "Lord Jesus Christ, grant that it should be so, and that he should come back no more!"

But Derbák Derbačok's hopes were false, for Šuhaj was alive. He had not run away, but was hiding in Zvorec.

Zvorec was a community on a mountainside, made up of four cabins that were about half a kilometer apart from each other in a valley so narrow that four soldiers marching abreast with their arms stretched out from their sides would only reach across it, and so deep that in summer the sun shone up there for only seven hours a day. The grass from the sides had to be brought down on sleds gliding down in the dew or after a summer rain, for in winter neither a horse nor a human being had yet succeeded in scaling the steep slope.

He had come there in a strange manner.

Old Olena Derbák, Derbák Derbačok's mother, had given him something to drink. It had happened in winter, when he had been spending the night at the Derbák cabin and Eržika had come over to see him. At the time, he had not paid any attention to the peculiar flavor of the milk, and had only recalled it afterward, when the snakes' eggs that it had contained were already hatching within him and it was already too late. Yet both Eržika and his brother Juraj had warned him against the Derbáks! Derbák Derbačok had denied everything. So he was communicating with the gendarmes, was he? Well, he'd like to know who in the whole village was not being questioned at the gendarme headquarters these days? Nikola had believed him. But Derbačok's mother was a witch. She had the evil eye, she knew how to prepare enchanted brews, she had power over snakes and at twilight could turn herself into a toad or a black cat. People had been aware of these things for a long time. Nikola had not believed them, and now his unbelief was costing him dearly.

One night, when he was staying in the shelter on Suchar, he was seized with sudden stomach cramps. He burned with fever and hundreds of brooks seemed to be murmuring in his brain. In the morning, after he had staggered out into the cold and taken a few hundred steps through the valley, he wanted to lie down somewhere in the snow under a tree and stay there, come what may. With all his might he had to keep reminding his aching head that this was the very thing he must not do, for it was the very thing desired by the unclean powers which had fallen upon him.

He walked on, seeing whiteness all around him and rings before his eyes. He knew that he must go on.

How did he manage to get through the snow-clad valley as far as Majdan? He did not know. The witch of Majdan, the most renowned witch of the whole region, was at home.

"Glory to Jesus Christ!" he greeted her, entering the room. His head swam.

"Glory forever, amen," the witch responded. "You are Nikola Šuhaj."

He was not even much surprised that she should know him.

"I knew that you were coming. You should have come sooner. I've been expecting you for three days and three nights."

He was conscious only of her lustrous eyes.

"Some witch has given you something to drink. She has set snakes' eggs to hatch within you."

There flashed through his mind the image of old Olena with the ugly gray pigtails showing under her kerchief. He recalled the night when Eržika had come over to see him.

"The snakes will leave you."

His sight became strangely clearer, but he had eyes only for the witch, as though she were alone in the world. He saw her fill a pan with red-hot charcoal from the oven and put it in the middle of the room.

"They'll leave you right now, this minute. The fire will consume them."

She gave him something to drink and told him to pray. Nikola repeated the Lord's Prayer in his mind, and she, mumbling some sort of incantation, circled around him, faster and faster, until she was bobbing about like a whirligig. The words of her exorcism became more and more unintelligible. Šuhaj could see nothing but her eyes. Then he had a violent attack of vomiting. It seemed to him that all his entrails would come up, that he would bring up his very soul. And suddenly he saw that his vomit was swarming with snakes, small and large, that snakes were slinking out of his mouth, that all of them crawled in the direction of the pan and disappeared in its consuming flames.

He felt weak. He could barely stand.

"Now you are well again. Go up in the loft and get a good night's sleep! In the morning you will be strong."

And sure enough, in the morning he felt well. The witch of Majdan was a powerful witch.

"Thank you!" he said to her in parting and gave her a reward.

"I thank you, too, Nikola Šuhaj."

He went out into the woods, to the deserted shelter. That day he shot and killed the biggest bear of his career. "Heigh ho!" he shouted to it when he saw it on a woody path at three hundred paces. The bear stood up on its hind legs and he shot it in the breast. He saw it fall on an old beech tree and claw at the bark and send splinters of wood flying. That day everything was gay and clear and Nikola felt joy in his heart.

But Olena Derbák's spell had been too powerful. The cramps and the fevers returned, stronger than before; then the scorching fevers gave way to chills which could not be driven out, no matter how many logs he fed to the open hearth fire with such great effort. He could sleep for only a few minutes at a time and would wake up with a start, for he would see flames all around him and it would seem to him that the shelter was on fire. The morning! If only he could live until morning!

He knew not whether it was morning or afternoon. He only knew that he had to go. And this "Go! Go! Go!" he repeated to himself a hundred times, kneeling and groping for his sheepskin coat and putting it on. "Go! Go!" As he got out in the cold, he violently forced his poor brain to keep repeating the command, as though he were mortally afraid lest he forget this most important of words. He came to a cabin in Zvorec. He entered.

"I'm Nikola Šuhaj. Get somebody who can write!"

Suddenly he was sitting alone on a bench in a room with a floor of trampled-down mud. He faced a big baking oven from the top of which some children were staring down at him. They seemed to belong up there, back of the chimney. The room held another large misshapen thing that almost filled it, barely leaving space for the bed and the table. He had to blink his eyes several times (heavens, what was the creature?) before he could identify it as a hand loom.

Soon a man stood before him, holding a pencil and a piece of brown paper such as is used for wrapping tobacco. Evidently the one who could write! The master of the house, the wife, and some other people were out in the hall, peering in through the open door.

"Write!" Nikola ordered, and dictated a letter: "*'Come to treat me. If anybody learns my whereabouts, both your children will perish. Nikola Šuhaj.'* Take that to the doctor in Volové!"

Swaying, he looked through the mist at the people: "This is Zvorec?"

"Zvorec," nodded the man who could write.

"It will burn up if anybody finds out where I am."

Only one more thought passed through his brain before he lost consciousness: "Nothing is going to happen to me. I have that gift from God."

The district health officer was ashamed. He was dreadfully ashamed. Driving his buggy up the steepest highway in the republic, he considered the whole miserable business. How many times had he followed this dreadful road up the mountain and then down the valley of the Terebla, a four-hour trip by buggy and an hour's walk besides—to treat a bandit! A comical situation! A plot for a farce! For the most stupid farce on earth! But what could he do about it? Granted, the fulfillment of the threat was not imminent, for friends were unreliable (at this point he stopped to muse on some particular incident of his own experience to prove it); they would not dream of being true beyond the grave, nor risk danger to carry out the orders of a dead comrade. But still! The responsibility of looking out for his children and the nagging and hysterics when he should have been forced to tell his wife! To be sure, he had succumbed to the general fear of Šuhaj's omnipotence and omnipresence. Not until now that he knew Šuhaj so well had he been wise enough to realize that nothing at all would have happened. But how could he have mentioned Šuhaj's name to his wife at first? Šuhaj! Should he report him now? Ha, ha! "Doctor, in Christ's name! You're telling us that now after two months' time! Do you know how much the persecution of Šuhaj has cost the State during that period? And you, the public health officer, have failed to report a case of typhus?". . . Fie!

The horse climbed up the mountainside laboriously, in part through what remained of the snow, in part over rocks. Somewhere below a lark was singing in the sun. The doctor held the reins lightly, and as he smoked his cigar he had enough time to think about his position.

What could he do about the typhus? Some antipyretics, some camphor injections to stimulate the heart. And, to be sure, the diet was important. But that could not be observed at Zvorec, unless he (ha, ha!) should go so far as even to bring up supplies from Volové. But that magnificent chap (what a fine stock were these Šuhajs!), with his bearlike chest and a heart like a dog's, who had run around in the snow with a temperature of one hundred four degrees Fahrenheit, would pull through by himself. If only he would know enough not to stuff himself full of corn porridge! Why was he going up to see him, anyhow? Had he fallen in love with the lad? Or did he want to give him some fatherly advice: "Stop it, Nikola, and give yourself up voluntarily!" What nonsense! Or: "Nikola, repent!" That was like telling a beast of the forest, a wolf or a bear, to repent! Of what, good heavens?

Why, then, was he going up there? Brrr! Mainly, it seemed, in order that he might at some future time testify before the provincial court at Chust as a witness of evidence to Šuhaj's alibi in certain crimes. How unpleasantly the buggy was jogging along and jolting! A one-year-old child, creeping on all fours, could have passed it! Giddyap! Get a move on there, nag! And who would pay for these trips? His boy was to go to Bohemia to high school next fall, and the girl could not stay forever in this Jewish hole, either. He needed the money badly. At the next-to-last call Šuhaj had again offered him a handful of hundred-crown notes, with some thousand-crown bills thrown in; it appeared that Šuhaj was gradually raising his remuneration. And again he had told Šuhaj crossly, "Let that go for the present, there will be time enough for that later." Hmm. . . . For the present! How he needed the money! Should he take it? Money, drawn out of some traveler's pocket? One day that might get him into a pretty mess!

This damned country! Here one couldn't scrape together a hundred crowns in the whole village, including the parson, and the people did not call the doctor except to rouse him at night in the hour of death, and then it was in vain and of course without pay. Well, this was the famous mountain country, Verchovina! Here from the summit it lay before one as on a platter: hills, black forests, and in the valleys a ribbon of bright green. It was beautiful only in pictures. Rye did poorly here; a little oats, with the straw a scant nine inches long, grew on some of the hillsides. Nothing could come out of the rocks except more rocks. Hmm. . . . Money taken from some traveler. Fie! No! If Šuhaj should be taken alive, a nasty scandal (if not worse) would come out of this anyhow; but he would not take the money from him. . . . He could only console himself with the hope that they would not get him alive.

The district health officer continued to go to Zvorec, to give Nikola antipyretics and injections of camphor to stimulate the heart. Once, indeed, he brought a bottle of cognac from Volové that Šuhaj might mix it with his milk. And he said nothing.

Zvorec, too, kept silent. These people lived in an isolated region, surrounded by woods belonging to absentee landlords, and although a goodly half of their actions violated the property laws, their violations went unpunished. Such people learned early in life that silence was a necessary means of augmenting their livelihood. Moreover, the threat of arson was frightening. And why should they make a single move to give anything away when for years they had not been as well off as now that Nikola lived in their midst? Did one of them need any money? Nikola was staying in the village!

Danilo Jasinko, a dark, angular peasant, had come up from Koločava several times. Nikola was ready to have a little beef broth. But where was it to come from, when the Jewish butcher in Koločava was not selling any beef and it would have been necessary to go thirty kilometers to Volové to fetch it? So Danilo Jasinko would come, leading a whole live cow for Nikola. Not purchased, to be sure. One man does not eat a cow unaided.

"You're not going to die, are you Nikolka?" Danilo would ask Šuhaj, with a compassionate look at the waxen face out of which gleamed a pair of deep-set dark eyes.

"No," Nikola would answer in a weak voice. And then Nikola, still lying in his high, crude, wooden, mangerlike bed, would ask, "What's the news?"

"What should it be? Nothing!" Danilo Jasinko would lie.

"You're not doing any more robbing?"

"Unh-uh!" For Danilo could hold things back even from those he loved.

"Don't do it, boys," and the dark eyes would look softly in those of his friend. "And what's Eržika doing?"

"What should she be doing? She's staying with Ivan Dráč, with her father."

"Nobody making up to her?"

"Not that I've heard."

Again long days would elapse when he spoke to no one and was alone with his thoughts. The wounded wolf that has crawled in the thicket wants nothing, but only waits to see whether the spirit of the woods that is in him will revive again or whether it will leave him to lose itself somewhere up in the crowns of the beeches.

The windows of these old cabins were small, barely eighteen inches square, so that only the head but not the shoulders could pass through them: protection against thieves. Looking out, one could see the opposite slope, two squares of green forest reflecting the March sun. There was nobody to talk to. The man of the house had hitched up and was to be gone for two days and nights to the springs in another part of the mountains to fetch two barrels of salt water (for they had run out of salt over the winter). The children, dressed in shirts, were dozing on top of the baking oven back of the chimney. The housewife sat at the loom, weaving woolen yarn into cloth, the loom squeaking and pounding as wood hit against wood. From time to time, a two-year-old child toddled up to her and demanded the breast.

Nikola had a power from God. But its safety had to be guarded jealously and not discussed with anybody, not even with himself in his own mind, lest the mysterious and intangible suffer through handling. It lay buried deep under all the layers of his soul: a gleaming white point that shone through his subconscious to his consciousness.

No, nothing could happen to him, not even in this dim room with the large oven, with the little squares of bright green and the squeaks and thuds of the loom. Olena's spell was strong, but his own strength was stronger.

What would happen next? He did not know; he only knew that all would be well, that he would leave here for the green brightness out there on the opposite slope, that people would love him and fear him again, that he would see Eržika again, and that he would never be caught, for no missile could touch him, whether fired from a rifle, a pistol, a cannon, or a machine gun.

The man of the house came back with his load of salt water.

First he grumbled about the tax collectors who were stationed at the springs and were collecting fifteen hellers for a bucketful. Nowadays one had to pay for even a bit of salt! Then he proceeded to tell the news from out in the world. He told about the crimes in the region, about the murder after the fair at Volové, the wiping out of the American's family, the bloody holdup on the mountain pasture. Just recently a Hungarian dealer had been killed on the road to a shelter, two Jews had been shot to death, a farmer had been seriously wounded and robbed. The whole countryside was talking about it. All the papers, they said, were writing about it, even abroad, and the force of gendarmes was constantly being strengthened.

Nikola was listening breathlessly.

"They're looking for you. They believe that you're doing it all."

Nikola's sick heart beat faster. "How's that?" he asked. "Do people believe that?"

"Well, there it is. You know how people are. Fools! Sure they believe it!"

Somebody was committing murder in his name? Some coward was hiding himself behind him? The blood rushed to Nikola's head, pounding in his temples. Oh, to jump up, to grab his gun, then, right away, to go, to run and thrash the cowards and murderers! But the arms on which he tried to raise himself bent under his weight, and he sank back in the hay. He wanted to howl like a wolf.

A few days later, when the faithful Danilo Jasinko came around, dragging a calf behind him, Nikola fixed his dark eyes on him and gave him a long and reproving look: "You're not robbing?"

"Unh-uh," answered Jasinko, looking Nikola full in the face.

"One hears that there's much murder going on in the country."

"There are a few rumors. They say some Jew was killed."

"I understand they're blaming me."

"Well, they haven't caught anybody."

Nikola's eyes glowed wildly in the dim room. For the first time they glowed again with the old, deep-green fire, resembling the eyes of lynxes and wolves peering from dark thickets. For within Nikola the spirit of the woods was coming to life again.

"I'll kill them. As there is a God above me, I'll kill them! Tell everybody!"

Danilo continued to look Nikola in the eye. But his heart fluttered as when a flock of flying birds flap their wings: he knew that Nikola had spoken the truth.

Inside the cabin the days passed gray and sad, and on the opposite slope the sun shone and a breeze such as would cool one's head swayed the verdure. The nights were close and beyond the two little windows the stars gleamed austerely.

Nikola Šuhaj was getting well. He tried to drag himself around the room, against the doctor's orders, he ate what the doctor had forbidden, and he slept a great deal.

One Sunday in spring, as the last traces of snow were disappearing from the northern slopes, when the hillsides had blossomed with anemones and the paths were quickly drying, Nikola's hosts dressed themselves all in white, the wife hung all her red and yellow beads around her neck and wrapped her youngest in a white shawl, and for the first time that year they went down to Koločava to church.

Nikola crept outside the cabin and sat down on the doorstep. He raised his face to the sun and inhaled the healing fragrance that could make men, beasts, and trees whole. He looked in the verdant forest and listened to the bubbling of the brook and longed for his people, whom he could not touch. He thought of Eržika, for this sunny Sunday morning reminded him of her.

Suddenly he started. A man had emerged from the woods and was coming up the path to the cabin with rapid strides. Who could it be and what did he want? Nikola wished to hide. But before he was able to rise to his enfeebled feet, he recognized the arriver. In a short time they were gazing into each other's eyes: Nikola, on the doorstep, and a few paces away, his brother Juraj, a lad of fifteen, thin, tall for his age, with eyes as glistening, a forehead as arched, and a chin as small as Nikola's own. They surveyed each other in silence, without surprise, and full of joy at the meeting.

"You're not going to die, Nikolka?"

"No, I'm not going to die, Juraj."

The boy joined his brother on the stoop and together they looked out over the countryside. The valley was flooded with light, and the brook was murmuring in the ravine. It tempted one to put his hands in it and feel the force of the swift chill current. When would he be able to crawl out of his den and again become a part of all that was around him? Nikola wondered.

All would be well, felt Juraj. Everything was fragrant from the sun, the earth, and the waters.

"Who told you I was here?"

"Nobody, Nikolka."

"Then how did you find me?"

"I've been looking for you for a long time, but last night all at once I knew you were here."

It was too hot for the time of year, and the sun's rays were burning too hard. Clouds arose over the ravine, mounted in the sky, and turned ashen. There would be a storm.

For a long time the brothers did not speak. People of this region were often silent. Neither the deep mountain valleys through which they had to go for hours without hearing any sound other than the humming of the water, nor the primeval forests whose silence was unbroken even by small game, nor the birds, nor the mountain pastures where the stock munched the blades of grass so patiently had taught people to converse. Words were only for everyday necessities; emotions had to be expressed by a glance, a pressure of the hand, a tune played on a reed pipe, a prayer.

Yes, Juraj had come to be with Nikola and would stay. When Nikola was well again, they would go out in the woods together. He would not go back home. The region was overrun with gendarmes, who were invading their unfinished cabin day and night, even several times a night, dragging them out of their beds, scattering their belongings, thrashing the family. The father was going to run away too. He would take the cattle to the pasture and leave the mother up there somewhere with the smaller children and then would go to Poland or Romania. He, Juraj, would stay with Nikola.

Nikola gazed up the ravine. Its sides were parted by a huge gray-blue curtain—the sky, suspended straight from above. Over this curtain little clouds were floating, dazzlingly white and absurd in their smallness and restlessness. The cabin at Zvorec already lay in the deep shadow, but the sun was still flooding the valley.

"You believed that I was doing all that killing?"

Juraj turned to his brother in astonishment. Why should he have believed otherwise? He, a fifteen-year-old, had also come to kill.

Who, then, was doing it?

Ihnat Sopko perhaps, or Danilo Jasinko, or maybe Vasyl Derbák Derbačok with his natural son, Adam Chrepta, or perhaps all of them together, or, then again, maybe none of them. Juraj did not know. He only knew that Derbák Derbačok was a traitor and his mother a witch, that Derbák Derbačok was in touch with the gendarmes, and that it was he who was constantly sending them to the Šuhajs'.

"Do you know that I'll kill the person who murders in my name?"

"I know."

How could Juraj help knowing? Nikola could accomplish anything he desired.

"Derbačok will have to be killed, too," Juraj remarked.

"Possibly," answered Nikola.

The gray-blue curtain that was the sky had spread overhead to where they sat, and it filled the whole valley before them. Only small hillocks remained in front of it, nothing showed in back of it, and on it a few small snowy-white clouds flew wildly. The air grew cooler, almost cold. A great silence hung about them. The trees became rigid, straining to capture the first raindrops when these should fall.

The first gust of wind blew sharply. The trees that stood alone bent their sides. All at once the valley disappeared, and they could see only a bit of roof overhead and a very green lawn before their eyes. The first large raindrops fell on the roof, and lightning that reached over the whole surface of the sky illuminated the darkness that had come over the world. A clap of thunder pealed, rolling broadly over the clouds. Then lightning started whizzing above and around them. Here! There! The skies opened in a downpour of rain which pelted the small plot of grass in front of them.

Both boys stayed on the stoop. Juraj laid his hand on his brother's knee and Nikola covered it with his palm. They watched the storm with joyous eyes.

In storms like this the Jews down in the valley would be praying, "Let us rejoice, our Jehovah, that thou art so strong!" But Nikola and Juraj knew how things really were: when there was lightning like this, God was pursuing the devil. "You'll never get me," the devil would say to God. "Oh yes, I will," God would answer. "I'll hide in a calf." "I'll kill the calf and give people another in his place." "I'll hide inside a man." "I'll kill the man and create another." "I'll hide in a sliver of wood cut on a Sunday." And then God would not answer. For a sliver of wood cut on a Sunday was one place where God could not enter.

The skies were all aflame with lightning and the world a continuous peal of thunder. The ends of the lightning flashes lashed the lawn. Here! There! Here again! The devil was bound to be hidden right around here somewhere. But they were not afraid. Nothing that came out of the mountains and the woods in the daytime needed to be feared, only that which came from the people down below. This storm did not concern them; it was a matter between God and the devil. The two boys, hand in hand, looked the god of the earth full in the face. It was one of those moments when the god of the earth spoke, within man and without him. It was one of those moments that decided about life and death.

"Well, and what now, Šuhaj?" the district health officer, raising his eyebrows, asked Nikola, as he announced that he would not come back to Zvorec anymore. "What are you relying on? Your friends? Friends are trash, they will betray you!"

Nikola's heart contracted a little.

"No, I won't take your money." He refused Nikola's handful of notes. "I consider that I came in the first place, and have continued to come, under irresistible compulsion. I hope that you won't repay me by telling anybody that I've been treating you here." Content to have found the proper legal formula, he departed as an "unsatisfied creditor."

Nikola remained standing in the center of the room, alone. He had a lump in his throat. His friends would betray him. The doctor was right. . . . Would Eržika betray him, too? . . . Oh, how he longed for her now, as the eager new blood coursed through his body! How he wanted her!

So she, too, would betray him, and he would stand alone against the whole human world? Well, what of it! He shook off the unpleasant feeling and squared his shoulders. Standing with feet wide apart and firmly planted on the floor, he felt the strength of the solid earth beneath him flowing into his body. He had within him a power from heaven, and this power would never betray him. He could stand alone, if need be, against the whole human world.

He crossed the threshold, and, putting two fingers in his mouth, he whistled. For Juraj was out in the woods. It had been necessary to hide him from the doctor. He came.

"Tomorrow we shall move on from here, Juraj."

From thenceforth, the brothers never left each other again.

And from thenceforth people again met Nikola Šuhaj in the woods and on the highways. But they saw him less and less often in the company of his masked friends. Now there were only these two: Nikola in his Alpine boots with the puttees and the lanky fifteen-year-old lad in the traditional costume of the locality, in sandals, narrow trousers, a coarse woolen coat, and a belt that protected his ribs from injury. They kept circling the country, first here, then there: not treacherous assassins, but honorable outlaws who met both friend and foe face-to-face.

Again they held up the post and various vehicles. Their two figures would step out of the ditch onto the highway: a boy with a pistol to his hip, ready to shoot, and with a wicked glimmer in his eye, and the calm Nikola with his gun slung over his shoulder, leading the way and pronouncing his magic formula, "I'm Nikola Šuhaj!" It was no longer necessary to intimidate with blows; the dreadful name sufficed. Nobody dared to offer any resistance; people knew him, as did the drivers of the post coaches, who, having hidden their money packets in their boots or under their seats, smiled through their fears as they confided, "Today, Nikola, I don't believe you will find much on us!"

What joy for Juraj to be a bandit! What a delight for one who hitherto had himself been full of fear to cause others to cringe!

What a proud feeling to stand on the road with a pistol on his hip, to gaze at people who had gone pale and were holding their hands up over their heads, and to be able to think, "If the fancy strikes me I shall shoot you, Mr. Official, and if this fancy does not strike me I shall not shoot you, but instead, I shall shoot you, you moldy Jew with the popping eyes and the red chin!" What a satisfaction it was to sit in the woods with Nikola, hidden by a beech tree, and to see two gendarmes pass down the path ten paces away, and to realize that the difference between their life and death depended on a small pressure applied by the forefinger to the trigger! Pray, you dogs, to Juraj Šuhaj, not to exert that pressure, and guard against any move that might cause the fire in his smoldering eyes to mount by even a fraction of a degree!

One time they came down from the woods to the highway, where the valley was so narrow as to leave room only for the road and the river Terebla. They sat on the rocky shore, watching the rafts glide past and gain on the swift current. "May you arrive in safety!" they called to the raftsmen, in keeping with traditional custom, and waved. Recognizing Nikola, the raftsmen answered "Thank you," but their words could not be heard. They stood at the wooden blocks to which the sweeps were fastened, they steered the rafts as they flew downstream at a fiendish speed, zigzagging lightly over the places where a few weeks hence huge boulders would protrude from the water and piles of drift would protect the shores.

"Someone is coming," said Juraj, who was sitting higher up the bank, and motioned with his head in the direction of the curve in the road.

A cart drawn by two nags came rolling over the gravel. A bearded man wearing a torn rusty coat stood in it in a typically Jewish pose. The puckered corner of his mouth signified both that his attention was fixed on a manual task and that his mind was occupied with a painful train of thought. The horses were approaching at a brisk trot as he held the reins.

"Oh, that's only Pinkas Meisler," said Nikola. There was nothing to be had from Pinkas Meisler.

"Well, anyhow, I'll take a look to see what he's delivering," Juraj answered.

But Meisler was not delivering anything to anybody. He had only a hen for his own consumption, one that the *schecter* (Jewish butcher) had killed according to the proper ritual. That was the very reason he was hurrying his horses over the uneven gravel road: it was Friday and he wanted to get home early in the afternoon, since the hen was intended for the Sabbath eve supper and his wife would have to be through with all her work in the kitchen before the first three stars should rise in the sky.

Juraj jumped on the road. "Stop! Šuhaj!" and he held the gun on his hip, ready to shoot.

"*Shema Yisrael!*" The Jew cracked his whip at the horses and shut his eyes; his face suddenly drew up in mortal terror, and the image of the hen cooking on the stove flashed through his mind.

The cart whizzed past Juraj. Ping! Juraj sent a bullet after it. Pinkas Meisler dropped the reins and fell over backward, and the frightened horses galloped wildly on, the gravel crunching under their hoofs. Ho, ho! How funny it was!

Nikola ran up on the highway. Astounded, he stared for a second after the runaway horses and the reins they were dragging after them in the road, as though he could not believe his eyes. Then a furious anger possessed him. Had he been able to do so, he should have knocked his brother to the ground with a single blow. He roared at him, "What are you doing, damn you?"

Juraj looked at him in surprise. What was the trouble? Why was he angry? Did it make any difference to Nikola whether he killed one man or ten? Or did the Jew matter? He could not understand.

Nikola quickly set out in the direction in which the cart had gone, as though he wished to overtake the runaway horses that would get tangled up somewhere in their harness before they would stop or else would break their legs. Juraj followed him. And only after a long while, when they had left the highway for the woods, walking as wordlessly as a stern father and his reproved son, did Nikola say, "Don't you ever do anything like that again!"

He spoke crossly, but nevertheless he spoke like a father who was already getting over his anger. After all, he could not stay vexed with Juraj over a Pinkas Meisler! That very night, when he returned from an expedition to Koločava-Negrovec (whither he had gone to slip four one-thousand-crown notes under the bereaved Mrs. Meisler's window) and found Juraj asleep in the shelter, he covered the boy with his coat and gazed on him tenderly in the moonlight. What joy that the lad had come to him! Perhaps he loved nobody else as well as he did this child. Without a doubt, he trusted nobody else as fully.

Yes, there was Eržika! Whenever he would look at the two peaks of one of the mountains, so like a woman's breasts, he would think of her, and when, chin in hand, he would sit on a boulder, watching the current of the river and the soft line between two waves, he would disturb himself with thoughts of her body. At night, he would go to sleep in the shelter with her in his mind, his being full of her fragrance, and when he would play his reed pipe in the evening, he would have the sweet impression that she stood behind him, listening, and that she would embrace him from the back as soon as his song should cease. On sunny days, he would spend hours lying hidden behind the rocky ledge on the bluff that overhung Koločava, fixedly watching old Dráč's cabin through a looted field glass. He would pass through the same reactions he had experienced upon his return from the War, when he had lurked by night in the forest near the pasture by the brook and, trembling with longing and jealousy, had gazed toward the fire where she had sat with Hafa, Kalyna, and Ivan Ziatykov. Would she come out of her father's cabin? Would he behold her as she went in her bloused chemise, which she wore tucked under her apron strings, to fetch a pail of water? Who was it that had already passed the house three times? Nikola's eyes would shine again with a wildfire. If the man went in to see her, he would shoot him as he was leaving her! He would take good aim and get him even at this distance.

Ah yes, he loved Eržika! But for all that, she was different from Juraj. The boy belonged to the woods and was part of Nikola's days. Eržika was something removed from every day, she resembled, rather, a Sunday in the springtime, or lightning in the mountains, or even more, a melody played on his reed pipe.

Why did Juraj dislike Eržika so much?

In addition, there were his friends! But already they belonged to his past, and their contacts, insofar as they had been preserved, were only a habit that would soon cease. They still came to see him, they shaved him, they brought him cornmeal and cheese made of ewe's milk, and sometimes they still took part in his expeditions: Ihnat Sopko, Danilo Jasinko, Vasyl Derbák Derbačok, and his natural son, Adam Chrepta—the ones who were not in prison. But what a wall of ice now stood between them! They gazed in each other's eyes, but still, it was as though they were looking through a frosted window that separated the room from the out-of-doors. Juraj was right to frown his dislike in their presence and always to keep his hand on his gun, ready to shoot.

Consider Derbák Derbačok of the uncertain, shifty eyes, who came to him so seldom these days and went to the gendarmes so often, and whose mother, the witch, had given him a snaky brew to drink! And was it not Adam Chrepta, to judge from the gait, who had circled around father-in-law Dráč's cabin? And among these four who sat here, not knowing what to say, was there not at least one who had helped wipe out the American's family and had wounded the three Jews at the Volové fair and then had run over their throats with the wagon? And all in his name! All in his name! Nikola's blood boiled, his eyes traveled from one to another of them, stopping for a moment on each. They felt these glances, and for all they returned his gaze firmly, the chills ran down their spines.

"Adam," Nikola once said suddenly to Adam Chrepta as they sat under the hazel trees on Suchar Mountain (and he calmly continued to eat his bread and cheese), "tell your father that his horse is lying over there on the pasture. Tell him that Juraj pierced it with his bayonet without my knowledge. Your father is a traitor, that's why he doesn't come among us anymore! This is a warning . . . to you, too, Adam!" At these words Nikola gave him a sharp look.

Adam Chrepta turned pale.

Juraj was sitting apart from them on a rotted stump; his black eyes shone like the eyes of a lynx, and he held his gun over his knee, in readiness. The others noticed only now that he sat four paces away from the rest and that with a single movement of his finger he could kill whomsoever of them he might wish.

»»» **4** «««

Eržika

Why did Juraj dislike Eržika so much?

It was the age-old fear all creatures feel toward what is strange to them and toward what stays too close to them, toward anything, therefore, that may bring them death. It is fear such as this that makes the fox slink away with his bushy tail outstretched when danger has touched his snout and causes the deer to leap for the nearest thicket. Eržika was strange to him, she lived too near him, and she might cause death.

At this time she was living with her father, Ivan Dráč, and her brother, Juraj, in the middle of Koločava. It was far more difficult to see her than when she had still lived in the Šuhajs' cabin, which stood on the outskirts of the woods, far beyond the village. But only a few half-burned beams remained of that, and the new house going up on the meadow was still roofless, for Petr Šuhaj had taken his cattle, his wife, and his younger children high up to the pastures in the mountains, while he himself had made his way to Hungary.

Nikola was seeing her nevertheless. For how could he have lived without Eržika? She would run away from her father and her brother at night; although the cabin was surrounded by gendarmes, she would make her way in the darkness, as crafty as a weasel, to meet her husband. And when, twice a week, she went up to the pasture to fetch home the milk from her father's cows, even though she was well watched by gendarme sentries posted in ditches and behind trees along the way, she could tell exactly when a moment of safety arrived. The two could always find places where she might slip past the guards and where he might be waiting for her for a smile and a hurried embrace.

When Eržika failed to come to an appointed meeting, Nikola would leave his brother's side in their haystack hiding place and venture down into the village. He would creep among the sunflowers and between the bean stakes near the garden fences; he would lie in hiding in the hemp for long minutes at a time to determine the location of the sentries; he would swing over the stiles; he would come to her room and, pressing his face against hers, wake her with tender whispers. For how could he have lived without this warmth, this cherry wood fragrance, without these limbs that were as smooth as the flow of water between two ripples?

Had Juraj Dráč not loved his sister, he would have hated her for this behavior. He lectured her, he shouted, he swore that he would kill Nikola, but she remained unruffled, industrious, and apathetic to his jealousy; she walked past him, keeping her thoughts to herself. Why should she get angry when things would never be any different? Her brother loved her, he would not beat her, and if, in his anger, he shook her by the shoulders a bit, it did not hurt much.

While Juraj Dráč was watching Eržika, Juraj Šuhaj watched Nikola. In the evenings when he could read in his brother's face the signs of approaching danger, he followed each of Nikola's restless movements with eyes full of suspicion. And at night, when Nikola left him without telling where he was bound, Juraj would half raise himself on the straw and his gaze would be sad and reproachful.

Nikola had spent the whole previous afternoon on the rocky waste above Koločava, hiding behind a boulder and watching the yard and the windows of the Dráč cabin through his binoculars. He had not seen Eržika for ten days. But that night, when he descended to the network of the village gardens, it happened that he could not get to his wife. Perhaps the door creaked as he stole into the hallway, maybe it happened by chance that Juraj Dráč flew out of the living room just then, and furiously screaming "Who's there?" summoned the gendarmes. Nikola barely managed to run out into the darkness. Cross and unhappy, he did not get back in the mountains until daybreak.

Juraj Šuhaj was no longer asleep, but awaited his brother like a jealous wife her husband. He sat at the foot of the haystack, eating cornbread, and as Nikola approached, he examined him searchingly. Nikola did not go up to sleep under the roof of the haystack. He, too, sat down, leaning his back against a bundle of hay; he set his gun down by his side and looked out into the morning that was being born.

Juraj spoke: "You've been with Eržika!"

Nikola did not answer.

"Yes, you have!"

The sun had not yet risen over the mountains; only the cold light that precedes it was present. A kite perched motionless on a haystack pole on the opposite slope and waited expectantly for the first ray to warm it.

"Because you are so pale. You're always so pale in the mornings after you've been with her."

Nikola heard his brother's voice, he understood the drift of his words, but he was not interested. They did not reach him, but stopped two steps away from him just as though a stranger were addressing someone else.

"You, Nikola, listen!" Juraj was saying, and his voice sounded as worried as that of an older brother reproving a younger. "Oleksa Dovbuš was invulnerable, too, and nobody knew how to kill him. And then his mistress, Dzvinka, wormed his secret out of him."

The sun was rising over the mountain. Its first stabbing gleam pained their eyes. Rapidly the landscape became tinted with gold. Opposite, the summits of the mountains shone already, and the glow was descending in the valley. Nobody had a right to deny him the wife that God had given him! Would it be necessary to kill Juraj Dráč? Why should Juraj Dráč hate him when he had never done him any harm? The kite sat motionless on the haystack pole, as though it had been killed, mounted, and placed there.

And then Juraj uttered the dreadful words that had been tormenting him for some time. "Eržika is a sorceress," he said quietly, with his eyes on the ground. He feared those words.

A little white cloud was rising from the black-wooded mountain pass before them. Alone in a clear, glowing atmosphere, it seemed as solid as a loaf of bread; it was pushing its way up, unbroken, over the pine tops. What would Eržika say if someday her brother should be found in the pasture, dead?

"I know what Eržika does with you at night, and why you are always so pale in the morning."

If a stream of words continues to roll long enough, even though they are mumbled in a boyishly timid and low manner, their force eventually reaches one's consciousness.

"She changes you into a horse at night and rides you till morning."

What was the boy babbling about?

"You, Nikola, listen. Couldn't you try to deal with her like the Verecký farmer?"

The Verecký farmer? Nikola knew that story, of course. The farmer's wife had been a sorceress and had turned him into a horse at night. But once, on a witch's advice, he had only pretended to be asleep, and when she had bent over him to work her magic, he had seized her by the hair and refused to let go, and behold! Her hair had turned into a mane, the woman had become a mare, and that night until dawn it had been he who had done the riding. In the morning, he had had the mare shod at the blacksmith's, had taken her to the stable, and had gone about his work. At noon, when he had come home to dinner, he found his wife in bed, in mortal pain; her hands and feet had been pierced with nails. All right. But what had the Verecký farmer to do with Nikola?

"Or better still, Nikola, kill her!"

Nikola's eyes roamed over the mountain peaks and the luminous sky. What was the lad saying?

"Or no, you don't have to, Nikola, I'll kill her myself."

Only then did Nikola look at his brother. He gazed at him long and in much the same way as he might have looked down at a puppy by his side, a puppy that, fearing for his master's welfare, has shown its gums as though to bite. He said, "Eržika isn't to blame for anything."

The whole world was sparklingly clear. The kite's head ducked in the feathers on its neck; it stretched its body, spread its wings, and took off in rapid flight. He had not seen Eržika for eleven days! Was Eržika flying away from him? Yes, something was happening. He could feel it. He had felt it in a slight difference in her embrace the last time, in her momentary tremble—a tremble so slight that only a lover could have perceived it, and even he could not have been positive abut it.

But Juraj, for whom feelings and knowledge were not yet divorced from each other, was aware of a change and scented the approach of death.

"What are you fellows good for?" the captain of the gendarmes was saying. "Not to be able to win a nineteen-year-old girl! And you standing guard over her bed at night at that!" The captain clung tenaciously to his plan of catching Šuhaj with Eržika as the bait.

One evening, when the cow was in from the pasture and Eržika was milking it in the twilight, it happened that a shadow darkened the whitewashed door of the cowshed at her back. Turning, she got such a fright that she nearly dropped the milking pail she held between her knees, for from the silhouetted outline of the cap, she recognized a gendarme. She had had a rest from them for some time.

"How are you, Eržika?" a man's voice asked gaily.

No, there was no need to be frightened, he had not come in any official capacity. He had heard that she had received some bear-skins from her husband, and he should like to get one to send to his brother-in-law in Bohemia. For a time they bargained in front of the shed. He was pleasant; he said that there was no sense in tormenting Nikola's family, and, as they were parting, he tried to pat her on the hair. That was the way it started. Perhaps Nikola was right: perhaps Eržika was not to blame for anything. Maybe the one to blame was Juraj Dráč, who these days was seeing her to the pasture, and who had been keeping her and Nikola apart so long. Maybe the captain of the gendarmes was most to blame. But possibly it was nobody's fault. Perhaps Eržika yielded to the gendarme sergeant's force because he held too important a position to permit open resistance; maybe she only wished to make easier her own and her husband's lots; chances are that she even admired the gendarme's tall figure, his curly hair, and his white hand with the ring on its finger. Certain it is that as her knees grew weak, she pushed him away with her hands and became flushed and tac-iturn. Had she known how to cry, she would have cried.

Koločava was a damnable place, not unlike the villages in Siberia. People lived as though it were in an occupied zone. The expres-sions on their faces were at once mocking and malicious, and since the time when a tax of thirty thousand crowns had been levied against the village as punishment for its having abetted a bandit, there came to be not one, but a hundred Nikola Šuhajs, all with the urge to kill. The peasant women were timid and reserved, and went out of their way to avoid the gendarmes. The Jewish girls back of the counters and on the steps of their fathers' shops were pleasantly talkative and laughed delightfully, but their stern-faced mothers watched them constantly, and there was always a brother in evidence, standing around with his hands in his pockets, whistling idly and looking unconcerned, but making it impossible to so much as see the girls across the street, let alone touch them. And therefore, if a man did not feel like lolling back of the gendarme barracks to watch the clouds roll from one mountain to another, and if he found no pleasure in playing cards from morning till night, there was nothing else left for him to do but get drunk at Kalman Leibovich's or Hersh Wolf's.

"She is wonderfully sweet," thought Sergeant Svozil, and was pleased with his thought. Creeping stealthily through the garden between the river and the Dráč cabin at twilight (before the sentries were stationed), he repeated this sentiment to himself, for his own enjoyment and as an excuse. Then he, in his turn, tiptoed over the path and waited long minutes between the sunflowers and the climbing beanstalks to watch what was going on in the cabin and to hope that Eržika would come out to him soon.

Professional zeal had given way to erotic need. He had wanted to show off before his pals, but now he said nothing; he had wanted to come to the captain with definite information regarding Šuhaj's whereabouts, but now he had stopped bothering about Šuhaj. She was so wonderfully sweet. Did she love him? He could not tell. The question tormented him, even as he tried to persuade himself that this was only a temporary affair. He did not know. She did not talk (ah, how terribly silent these mountaineers could be about everything!); she did not say anything when he kissed her and crushed her shoulders. She kept still when he was gentle with her, and, if he forced her to answer him, she would say calmly, "Yes, I'm fond of you." But her tone of voice would be the same as though she were saying, "I'm fond of red beads." No, not even that, for assuredly she would have said, "I'm *very* fond of red beads." She was a cat, a cat that never spoke and always gazed, and a man never knew what was going on back of those wide-open eyes of hers; a cat whose thoughts were her own, who came calmly and calmly went away wherever it pleased her.

But when Eržika's shadow appeared in the yard at twilight, and her bare feet flashed over the stile, and her beads twinkled for a moment, the tall, curly haired boy's face would light up: "Ah, my darling!" And at once he would think, "Yes, I have some beads for you, or would you prefer a piece of the moon? I'd get that for you, too." He would run to meet her. He would kiss her.

One evening, after it had grown completely dark and she said, "I'm going now, my brother will be looking for me," Sergeant Svozil thought of something else. "How does the witch of Majdan know that we're going together?" he asked, laughing and tickling her ribs with his thumb.

The witch of Majdan certainly could not know anything about it. Nobody knew of it.

"When I was there on official duty the day before yesterday, I had her tell my fortune, and she said I would die soon. She wouldn't say when, but I could tell from her eyes that it would be within a month and a day. Well, and that could happen only because of you!" He laughed as though it were a joke.

She disengaged herself from his embrace and regarded him dispassionately with those great dark eyes beyond which he could not see. He was a dear, this big boy. It was a pity that he should die! He was not one of them, but he was good to her and brought her presents. A pity! If the witch of Majdan said he would die, it was so.

"What do you think of it?" Svozil asked her gaily.

"Nothing. I have to go now."

She ran away and left him standing there, still filled with desire and with her sweetness.

That night, as he lay in the schoolroom occupied by the gendarmes, his dreams of her were rudely interrupted. It was after one o'clock. Vasyl Derbák Derbačok had come running to the gendarme headquarters to report that Nikola Šuhaj and Juraj Šuhaj were spending the night in a certain lone haystack that stood between the pasture and the copse on one of the nearby mountains. In daylight, it was possible to walk the distance in three hours. The pasture was small and could be surrounded easily.

The gendarme on duty awakened the captain and the old sergeant at once. Those two took a quick glance at the map as they were getting dressed. They gave an immediate alarm for the whole force to get ready. The men were to advance as fast as possible before dawn. Further commands were to follow. Derbák Derbačok would come along. The captain was all excited.

In the school, the gendarmes, so suddenly roused from their slumbers and with an unpleasant sensation along their spines, were throwing on their clothes, lacing their boots, and tightening their belts. The ones who were quartered in Hersh Wolf's and Kalman Leibovich's haylofts crawled half dressed down the ladders and into the thick night mist. The lights of their lanterns, blurred by the fog, flickered to and fro in the yard. The assembled unit started off into the white darkness, leaving behind it an unconscious, sleeping village.

It happened that at half past three, just as Eržika was leaving her yard to take the geese to the brook, she saw Sergeant Svozil running up the road fully armed. He had been detained on duty in the village and now was trying to catch up with the others. When he glimpsed Eržika, he smiled rather excitedly, slowed up, then stopped. Should he tell her or not? He told her.

"We're going to fetch Nikola for you. By noon he'll come walking down; that is, if we don't have to carry him!"

He smiled again, this time in an embarrassed manner, as though he did not know whether he had caused her joy or pain, and as though he himself were uncertain which he wished to have caused her with his announcement. Then he trotted on into the darkness.

By noon? The words struck her. That would give them just time enough to accomplish their purpose! For she, too, knew where Nikola was sleeping these nights. The day before yesterday she had been up there with him.

She left the geese out in the road and dashed back in the cabin to put on her sandals. "If we don't have to carry him!" But simultaneously another idea flashed through her mind: the witch of Majdan. A pity the sergeant had to die. Swiftly she wound her sandal straps over the linen strips on her feet. Her father and her brother were still asleep.

She ran for the mountains. The fog lay over the valley like a milky flood. Cabins were swallowed up in it, and one could see only two paces ahead. She did not think, did not ask herself anything, not even whether she had time, whether she could get there before they did. She only ran through meadows and over paths.

By five o'clock she had arrived at the woods. Breathing fast, she passed the palm of her hand over her forehead and eyes. Maybe she had arrived here first. Then she took a wood path up. Somewhere to the side of her, a few rocks clattered a little as, breaking under the foot of a human or a wild animal, they rolled down. She took a few swift steps. Lord Jesus Christ! Ahead of her in the fog were the gendarmes! To the right of her and to the left, deploying as they climbed the mountain with their guns in their hands.

There was neither need nor time for reflection. She ran to the right, wishing to circle around them. She sprang over rocks and roots, waded knee-deep in mud on the shores of streams, fell again and again, and bruised her knees. All in vain. They were ahead of her everywhere in the fog, silent, proceeding calmly and as though mechanically, ever up and ahead.

Dear God in heaven, what should she do? Go back to the left? They were there as well. Her strength was failing, and soon it would be too late. Their destination could no longer be very far ahead—perhaps one kilometer, or possibly one and a half. For a time she followed the gendarmes at thirty paces, barely within sight of individual helmets, which emerged alone from the whiteness of the fog, as though they belonged to disembodied heads. In her silent sandals she stepped as softly as a cat stalking its prey. She got her breath and for the first time since she had left home she began to reflect. They were not chasing her, she realized. It was Nikola they wanted, and since they must already be near to him, they would avoid shooting, for that would put him on his guard. She quickened her gait, hiding behind trees and boulders, until she caught up with the line. She picked a space through which she might pass between two of the men.

Blessing herself with the triple sign of the cross (according to Greek Orthodox usage), she started off. She flew through the line and raced forward. She was aware of some commotion behind her, of rocks rolling and branches crackling, and then, silence. As though of their own volition, her sandals bore her over boulders and avoided steep rocks, dashed over ferns and rushed through the underbrush, which seemed to part at her approach. The god of the earth was with her. Something within her kept calling "Nikola! Nikola!" She wished the underbrush was more sparse, and in a flash it became so, and she saw before her the shadow of the haystack, rising out of a lake of mist.

"Nikolaaaaaaa, run!"

She herself grew frightened as her own resounding shriek pierced the quiet air. She was still able to distinguish two human forms part from the shadow of the haystack as they leaped down from it; she saw the taller one disappear in the shining whiteness of the fog and the shorter, stouter one raise his gun and take aim. Then, simultaneously with the shot that rang out, something seemed to hit her at the nape of the neck; blows struck her down and her head was pushed to the ground, crushing the fine gravel into her forehead and up her nose. She heard more shots, a large number of them. The gravel in her face was very painful.

The first ones to reach the village that morning were four frowning gendarmes. Two of them carried a stretcher, on which lay a man, ghastly pale, but still alive. It was not Nikola, but a gendarme.

Koločava had been informed of the night expedition by Hersh Wolf and Kalman Leibovich. People stood quietly outside their cabin doors, behind their garden fences. The summer morning brightened the red bean blossoms on their green stalks and opened the first sunflowers. But Koločava felt something of the same horror as had gripped it on that autumn day when the murdered gendarme had been buried. The ominous procession passed, but the people continued to stand motionless. What had happened? For this was only the beginning, and they wanted to know all.

Only after a considerable time was their patience rewarded. A party of the gendarmes came, leading Eržika, and Koločava trembled in excitement. Eržika was pale and her face was scratched from the rocks and swollen from gendarmes' blows. But she walked erect, looked people straight in the face out of eyes that reflected naught but calmness. Her gaze held no traces either of suffering or of triumphant joy.

Toward noon, the remainder of the unit arrived. Marching in ranks of four, separated from the people by the fences, the gendarmes gave the impression of being on parade on a racetrack. The pebbles and the rubble crunched beneath their feet. Their countenances were sullen and evil. And in this unit marched two men, in step, with their heads bowed only a little lower than the rest, but belonging here only in external appearance; their minds were wandering far afield. "If only I could get away from here!" one of them, Sergeant Vlásek, was thinking. "No matter how badly the disciplinary investigation turns out, just so it is over!" Was the wounded man still alive? The second colleague to go! And as Vlásek thought of the thirty thousand crowns which he had accepted as a bribe, the number thirty recalled to him a memory of his schoolboy days: a class in biblical history and the dark picture of Judas Iscariot on the Mount of Olives in his textbook. As boys, they had despised the traitor and had pierced his eyes in the picture with pins.

A few ranks ahead of Vlásek marched a young giant with curly hair. His childlike soul was weeping within him, "Why? My God, why? Have I hurt her in any way? Is it possible that she still loves a murderer and a bandit?"

In its turn the unit passed. Would Koločava see anything more? And so Nikola had not been caught? No, people would see nothing further. Silence. The parched noon hung over the valley. In two or three hours they would go and inquire in the Jewish shops, where, meanwhile, something more would be learned. The farmers, the women in their red kerchiefs, and the small boys with hats like men and in hempen shirts that reached down to their ankles all went back into the cabins.

But the Jewish community buzzed like a beehive. In front of the stores they were whispering mysteriously, talking, shouting, shrugging their shoulders, gesticulating. Some of the Jews with black earlocks, others with auburn or blond or gray ones, some with long beards and others without, some wearing caftans, others in store clothes they had purchased in Chust, all were using what information they had to put two and two together. Their conclusions were fairly accurate. Striking the backs of their right hands against the palms of their left, they fretted, "Pig heads! Here we've been telling them for months, 'Lock up Eržika! Let his pals go!' No use! A Gentile is a horse! *Meise beheime!* A fool's story!"

Abraham Beer was standing among them. He neither shouted nor grew visibly excited. Only his restless fingers were plucking his beard, and his head, covered with a skullcap, kept swaying from side to side. Through it ran a refrain in decrescendo, "Oi, oioioioi!" The throbbing of his pulse was barely perceptible, and the palms of his hands were damp with sweat. What torture he had undergone since morning, when he had learned that this time the gendarmes had a sure thing! The whole morning had seemed unreal, a terrible game with strange actors, yet with his own life as the stake. The game was the more horrible as he could not take part in it and was doomed to do nothing but wait. He was aghast at the thought that tonight he might be lost forever to Hanele, to his wife, to everything for which he had lived. At the same time, he could not give up the hope that this night he might be as happy as the angels in heaven.

It all ended differently, in a gray, withered, disappointing manner. He did not win, for Nikola had not been brought in dead. On the other hand, he did not lose, and, for the time being, he was safe (for which the name of Jehovah be praised!), for Nikola had not been brought in alive either. For the time being! But that meant that his terrible uncertainty was beginning all over again!

Oioioioi, why had he ever become involved with Nikola? He did not know how it had all come about; he had not been very well able to refuse, for he had been afraid. He had made money out of the association. Certainly, he had made money. Quite a good deal, a fortune, on goods and money changing! But the business could not last forever. Somebody would find out sometime that old Isaac Fuchs, who was leaving Koločava nights with a load of lumber, was stopping twenty kilometers away at a deserted hut and loading the crates that had been piled there to be delivered in the city. Or Abraham Beer himself would be discovered on his way to appraise the goods. Or those sniveling Jewish bumpkins would get wind of something. They were the worst of all. They lolled about all day, they did no work, they banded together in everybody's yards like dogs; they reeked of Zionism and hated him, Abraham Beer, because God had given more to him than to the rest. . . . Or else, one of Nikola's pals would get caught and would drop a hint, and the gendarmes would ferret out the rest. Or . . . ah, how could he tell what might happen? He did not want to work with Nikola anymore, the Lord knew, he was ready to quit. But what could he do? Could he give somebody ten thousand crowns and say to him, "Go and kill Nikolka!"? Ah . . . ah . . . ah, perish the very thought, with the Lord Jehovah's aid!

Already he had tried various alternatives. "I'm not going to deal with you after today, Nikola, it does not suit me anymore," he had said as one night they had met by appointment on the slope above the village.

"All right," Nikola had answered. "But I'll write a letter about it to Chust and I'll set fire to your house."

How many times he had asked him directly and had sent word to him to leave, to run away to America! He himself would have helped Nikola make his way to a Jewish friend's in Galicia, who would have sent him to an acquaintance in Kracków, who would have guided him to a business associate in Vratislaw, and this last one would have helped him to get to America somehow. Nikola was crazy. He thought that he could overcome the whole world. Or, possibly, he did not believe this, and was merely crazy. Oi, oioioioi! Life was dreadfully complicated and frightfully difficult. Abraham Beer had taken a long trip to seek counsel from a miracle-working rabbi, to whom he had given all of a thousand crowns as a gift. "Should I move away from Koločava, Rabbi?" The holy man's wise eyes had gazed at him long and thoughtfully: "A poor man is like a dead man. If you leave, Šuhaj will burn your house and destroy all that is yours. Do not leave Koločava! The Eternal will not allow you to be killed."

True, these words bolstered Abraham Beer's morale considerably. And yet . . . and yet . . . and yet . . . what if the Eternal should permit it? Oi, oioioioi! Life was dreadfully difficult.

On the steps to the shop the Jews were yelling, expostulating, and wrangling. Abraham Beer stood among them silent, with nervous fingers plucking his beard like a harp. He was not listening to them. Nikola had not been brought in dead. What was the use of arguing about anything else?

A few hundred paces away, Vasyl Derbák Derbačok and his son, Adam Chrepta, roamed aimlessly through cabin, barn, and garden. They did not know what to talk about or what to do with their hands, and their sluggish blood coursed no faster than did that of Abraham Beer. They, too, awaited the return of the expedition with tremulous hearts, which stood still when the gendarmes, bearing stretchers, appeared in the street. Father and son leaned over their fence and craned their necks to be a few inches closer to the dead or the wounded, and to ascertain a split second sooner whether the one lying there was the one they expected it to be. Their disappointment showed in their faces. They waited. Then came Eržika, in bonds. They continued to wait, the blood pounding in their temples; time seemed to stop. Then the procession of wrathful gendarmes filed past, and after that, nothing more, nothing, nothing at all; they saw their hopes flow down the river and disappear in the distance.

And then they walked to and fro together, in the potato patch between the cabin and the river. They did not speak, and behind their moist foreheads persisted the question: What next, now that this great opportunity had been lost?

Meanwhile, Nikola and Juraj were sitting in the grass on the mountain summit. Their danger had long since passed, and their blood had cooled. Overhead, the white noonday sun glowed from a cloudless, unbrokenly blue sky. Down in the valley it would probably be very hot, but up here a breeze was blowing; it rippled the low grass and puffed out their homespun shirts. Juraj plucked some bennets, geraniums, and buttercups, and trimmed his hat with them.

Nikola was filled with a feeling of blessed security. Their rifles lay cast aside, no longer necessary, for here, above the treetops, they were as safe as in a castle tower from which they could see everything but where nobody could reach them. He was permeated with a deep joy; he drew it in with his breath and it spread over his whole body. He was like a soaring bird.

Deep down in the valley, in barely visible cabins, people were living. They feared those in power, they lied to them, they worried and worked, and their brows grew wrinkled and their hands calloused. A man hired out to work was a dog on a chain to whom the masters threw a bone. Work was not joy, except possibly when one was building one's own house or bringing in a good harvest; not otherwise. It was joy, rather, to sit on the hot rocks on the shore of the Terebla, to gaze into the blueness and the verdure and to listen to the song of birds. It was joy to experience the feeling of safety on top of the mountain, with the shadowless world below and the white sun above and the wind all around. It was happiness to love Eržika. It was delight to have a band of men as sunburned as oneself, with hands as resolute as one's own, and of friendly and merry minds. It was pleasure to give to others, to rejoice in the joy of others. It was joy not to pass through life unnoticed, but to be loved and hated. It was good to have Juraj only three feet away, for his eyes were devoted and he had flowers on his hat. It was a joy to be Nikola Šuhaj.

In a semicircle around them were the mountains, wooded with silvery forests, the river Koločavka with its green valley, the human dwellings down below, the huge arch of the sky above, and the burning sun. All formed one harmonious whole. He loved these hills and forests, which always offered a safe refuge. They had never betrayed him and would never allow him to perish—they and their

God—for he, Nikola, was the flesh of their flesh and the blood of their blood. Gladness flowed to him out of the earth, was borne to him by the wind, and warmed him through the rays of the sun.

Juraj, brother Juraj! The boy lay here quietly at Nikola's side, a big, thin, human puppy, true and devoted; his head was in the grass and his eyes were fixed on his master, not daring to interrupt his thoughts.

"Juraj, Eržika isn't to blame for anything. Eržika is a brave woman." There could be no joy of which this name was not a part. Nikola smiled. He was glad that he could say this on such a happy day and could remind him of their old conversation. He wanted to talk about Eržika, brave, self-sacrificing, longing, and most dear to him—Eržika, who this day had risked her life for their sakes. He wished that his brother, too, might love her.

But Juraj did not move and only gazed wide eyed, like a puppy.

Suddenly he said, "Come, let's burn Derbačok's cabin!"

For Juraj did not allow himself to yield to a feeling of security. He thought of the morning, of the escape from the shelter; the whistling sound of the gendarmes' bullets overhead was still in his ears. Nikola was to have been murdered, only because there existed a Vasyl Derbák Derbačok and an Adam Chrepta who wanted him out of the way. Nikola had always been good to them. Yet, if he let them live, he would be murdered.

Derbák Derbačok? Nikola considered. All right, Juraj was right. But why talk about Derbačok? Why not about Eržika?

"Derbačok and Adam are traitors. They must be killed," Juraj continued.

Nikola looked at his brother. The boy had flowers on his hat and his eyes were fixed on Nikola's lips. The two had already discussed the subject on their way up. Adam had come to them on the previous day, bringing cheese and a sack of cornmeal, and had shaved Nikola. He had demanded money for his share of the returns from the sale of some cloth. Now it was clear to Nikola why Adam had been in such haste. True, they had observed the law of the wilderness: they had not been so trusting as to go to sleep in front of him or to show him where they slept; they had parted from him before sundown, two kilometers away, and in order to confuse him had gone in another direction. But instead, he had fooled them. He, in his turn, had pretended to head toward the village, but apparently he had followed them and had seen where they slept. The night had been clear. He had been able to risk the trip and be down in the valley before the fog had fallen.

Again Nikola looked out over the countryside. Koločava lay below, a long row of crumbs that could be brushed into a little heap and gathered up in the palm of his hand. What would happen when he would blow them out of his hand? Nothing would be changed, and nobody could tell that there had ever been a Koločava. And down below, hidden in it somewhere, small, invisible, lived Derbák Derbačok and his son, and the gendarmes lolled about in the lofts. What could they do to him, when all these enormous wonders roundabout him—mountains and forests, clouds and the sun—were all united with him, when he was the flesh of their flesh and the blood of their blood?

He glanced at his brother and smiled, "They cannot hurt us, Juraj!"

"And what have you ever done to harm Derbačok and Adam?" frowned Juraj.

Nikola continued to smile. He would blow them away, not that he feared them, but because nobody could betray him and go unpunished.

"Eržika is a wonderful woman, Juraj!"

"I'm terribly hungry, Nikola!"

To be sure! The boy had not eaten since the previous day. Nikola rose. He slung a gun over his shoulder. He surveyed the countryside again and once more filled his lungs with the air and the strength of the mountains.

"Come then, let us go to Suchar!"

They descended to the region of trees. The sun beat down on them and the wind made the homespun of their shirts flutter.

"Tonight we'll go down to Koločava, Juraj. We'll take a lot of ammunition along."

Juraj only half understood. But it would be all right. Everything that Nikola did was all right.

That night, Derbák Derbačok's cabin burned. At eleven o'clock it flared up like a heap of fagots and the dry smokeless flames licked the starry sky.

Marijka, Derbačok's wife, was awakened by the glare in the yard and the crackling of the fire. She shrieked in fright and rushed to her children. They all jumped out of bed and ran for the door. But horrors! The door was fastened from the outside. They beat their bodies against it furiously, but without avail. "Nikola!" The thought flashed simultaneously through Derbačok's and Adam's minds, and the bright light and the howling and bellowing of the cattle in the barn gave this name a fearful significance. The mother shouted desperately. Axes! Axes! Axes! The windows were too small to allow anyone to crawl through them. The flames crackled. Finally an ax was found somewhere in the storeroom.

They escaped from the cabin in the nick of time. The dwelling and the barn were a mass of flames. Ready to venture freeing the cattle, they ran to the barn. But there, too, the gate was barred with young birch trunks thrust crosswise between the doorposts. Shots began to resound, bullets to riddle the yard. Somebody was shouting. The shots could be heard coming from somewhere in the distance. The Derbačoks fled in terror. The mother carried an infant in her arms and dragged another behind her.

The bell in the church steeple started to peal with measured sounds that filled the inhabitants of wooden cabins with fear. Women in long homespun chemises appeared on the thresholds and the drowsy men hastily began to draw on their trousers. A few gendarmes walked swiftly toward the fire.

What was going on? Somebody was shooting from the slope above the village: dozens of shots from a magazine. All heads turned in that direction.

Where was the fire? At Vasyl Derbák Derbačok's! There was only one man who could be responsible.

An elliptical zone of light surrounded the burning buildings: it was four hundred paces long, three hundred broad, and enclosed a cross section of a street with shining pebbles, sharply green garden beds, and two neighboring cabins that cast shadows somehow too long for this bright, noonlike light. A row of human shapes stood on the boundary line between broad daylight and night. All were turned toward the strange, unnatural fire, where nobody was battling the flames, nobody was trying to carry things out, nobody was lamenting or calling to God and the holy saints, where there was an amazing silence, and where dry flames pointed straight up to the stars.

Out of the darkness, shots struck the daylight zone and riddled the ground and prevented everyone from entering it. The long, drawn-out peals of the church bell gave to the horrible occasion a supernatural quality, while above the flames, in the darkness as well as in the light, floated the fearful name of the outlaw Nikola Šuhaj. This name towered overhead like a bird of prey with motionless wings.

Derbák Derbačok had betrayed. Nobody could betray Nikola and evade punishment. Toward morning, only two charred beams remained of Derbák Derbačok's cabin. And in the cinders of the barn lay the charred bodies of two cows with protruding bellies, hissing with white steam. The bell had long since stopped pealing.

The shooting had ceased. Only the dull thuds of the mill wheel sounded in the dawning day.

The frenzied laughter of the Jews expressed their fury and unbounded scorn: "The hogs! The idiots! The pig heads! They've let Eržika go!" For Eržika's stay in the regional court at Chust did not last long. She ate the cornbread her father brought her, she scrubbed the cell three times, she lent a willing ear to the life histories of some of the women who were jailed with her and enjoyed their respect without reciprocating their confidences. Several times the warden took her before the investigating judge. This gentleman, clean shaven and wearing a pince-nez, worked in a beautiful bright room where a young lady wrote on the typewriter. Eržika sat down, her hands folded in her lap, and looking the gentleman with the pince-nez calmly in the eyes, she lied and lied, without even trying to sound credible.

At the third or fourth interview, he told her, "See here, Mrs. Šuhaj, your cry, 'Nikola, run!' was heard distinctly by at least ten men, and many more heard you call out without distinguishing your words. And yet, you claim that you did not cry out at all and that you ran only because you were afraid of the gendarmes. We have ascertained that nobody ever goes to the spot where you broke through the gendarmes' ranks, and that far and wide there is no pasture. You claim, however, that you were bound for a pasture at that early hour. Your own brother, Juraj, has testified that he has had to protect you from your husband, that Nikola Šuhaj has annoyed you in your very house, and that he himself frightened him away one night. Still you assert that you have not seen Šuhaj for nearly a year. How are you going to explain all these discrepancies? I mean to do well by you, Mrs. Šuhaj! Tell the truth! It will help your case!"

But Eržika kept silent, and even though the investigating judge cross-examined her over and over, her statement remained unchanged:

she had been bound for the pasture; she had not cried out; she had not seen Nikola since the previous summer. Yes, the gendarmes had invented the whole story; yes, her brother was angry at her; yes, there was a pasture up there.

"Well, as you like, Mrs. Šuhaj. I'll write it down. But if you think that such lies will do you any good, you're very much mistaken." He dictated Eržika's statement to the stenographer; she pounded her keys, the typewriter clicked, and finally Eržika signed her mark to the document.

The captain from Koločava secured her dismissal from Chust.

His nerves were shattered. When Eržika ruined his great expedition, he was in despair. When the division that he had sent out on the dark hillside to get the Šuhajs, the night of the fire, came back without them, he raged. (Ah, the cowards! Apparently they did not want to find them! Apparently it suited them very well to have the outlaws keep on the move and be able to set more fires! His own gendarmes would soon be beginning to believe the twaddle about Šuhaj's invulnerability!) But he clung tenaciously to his original plan. Eržika! She was his first and now his last, his only hope. Upon her depended the success or the failure of his mission, his honor, and his career.

He called on the president of the regional court. "Believe me, sir, she is absolutely necessary to us in Koločava. Perhaps it might be possible to examine her now without holding her. We have only two people who know of Šuhaj's whereabouts: her and Derbák Derbačok, and Derbák is powerless now. A dreadful village, sir, and a horrible region!"

Thus Eržika again took the geese to the brook in the mornings, hoed the garden, and milked the cow, and twice a week went to the pasture for milk, watched by a gendarme over every kilometer of the way to see if perhaps she would not leave the road. She knew from experience how simple it would be to slip past them but did not do so. She proceeded calmly, the double sack with the milk buckets over her shoulder.

Making no sign that she was aware of anything, she would think, "He is hidden around here somewhere." And, after another quarter of an hour, "He is probably watching me from this thicket here." There was no reason to run. She had not heard anything from Nikola, and when she asked Ihnat Sopko and Danilo Jasinko about him, they knew nothing either. Evidently he and Juraj were far away somewhere, and perhaps it was true, as people were saying, that he had been seen near the Romanian border, on horseback, riding along the boundary commission and watching the parades of Czechoslovak and Romanian gendarmes and officials as the transfer of the community government was being ceremoniously affected.

At home, the atmosphere was gloomy. Since her return from Chust, her brother had not spoken to her. Sometimes at night he would quietly open the door of her room to glance inside, and on the beams in the hall he kept a gun, all loaded and ready for use.

Sergeant Svozil saw Eržika at times. He saw her more often than did the other gendarmes because he passed the Dráč cabin more frequently. Whenever he caught a glimpse of her in the yard or the garden, he was determined to pass her silently and in righteous anger, frowning and without salutation. She, however, was always bowed over her garden plot or looking elsewhere as she carried her bucket of water; either she never noticed him at all, or else she was only pretending not to notice him. And the latter alternative, too, was unbearable.

Why? The question weighed on his bosom like a piece of steel, and its steady presence never left him. These were days filled with disgrace, humiliation, and shame. He, a good soldier, who had always fought loyally for his cause and had ever been brave, had to witness the cross-examination of Hersh Wolf and Kalman

Leibovich and their entire families over the question of who might have betrayed the secret to Eržika. He had to watch the captain, beside himself with rage and anti-Semitic hatred, yelling at them and shaking his fist in the faces of the weeping women. He had to look calm when they thrashed a thirteen-year-old boy who had been seen to enter the Dráč cabin on the fateful morning. He had to listen to his friends' conjectures and, when asked directly, at least had to shrug his shoulders. The wounded gendarme, who had planned to get married on leaving Koločava, was said to be dying in the hospital in the city. When alone, Sergeant Svozil choked with shame.

The breakup of Austria-Hungary had lowered the concept of "high treason" down to the point of absurdity, but the soldier's vocabulary still contained no word more bitter than "treason," treason against one's comrades, treason against their common interest. The word reeked of the grave and of disgrace for the rest of one's life. Sergeant Svozil had sought to betray a woman. In his soldier's zeal for the common cause and in his desire to settle once and for all with this detested region, he had overestimated his strength. Remembering various escapades in Siberia, he had approached Eržika with deceit in mind. But deceit was alien to his nature, and he could not accomplish his purpose. The tables had turned. It had been she who had been able to accomplish it. She, who was wont to rub her head against him so fondly, who had such a sweet way of half shutting her eyes, had suddenly bitten, and had bitten deeply.

Why? Sergeant Svozil asked himself this question again and again, on his long official tramps through the woods, as well as when, resting on the ground and lighting one cigarette on another, he looked into space. This "Why?" together with Eržika's image troubled his sleep on the straw mattress in the schoolroom. After all that had happened between them, was it possible that she still loved a bandit? Or was it some nefarious nether force of these hills that made her help a man of her own creed as against strangers? Who would answer these questions for him? Even as he was convinced that he would never speak to her again, he caught himself composing long sentences, full of bitterness, which he would say to her when they should meet, urgent questions that he would set her, now crushing her beautiful shoulders with passionate hate, now murmuring to her with loving gentleness. Nobody answered his queries. How could a cat answer, when she was inarticulate and showed nothing of what went on beyond her wide-spaced eyes?

Once he beheld her, a mere arm's length away. She was going to the pasture and it was his duty to watch her. He leaned his forehead against the bark of the tree that hid him, and sighed, "Eržika!" But such bravery can be achieved only once in a lifetime. The next time he came out of his hiding place in the woods and blocked her way. She knew him at once, but did not slow down her steps. She advanced toward him, looking him straight in the face.

"Where are you going, Mrs. Šuhaj?" he asked in a stern official tone, and made an effort to keep his voice steadier than his heart.

"To the pasture," she answered him, as she would have answered anyone, surprised neither by his sudden appearance nor by his form of address.

She wished to walk around him, but he would not let her pass, so they stood facing each other on the green woody path: the giant gendarme and the nineteen-year-old girl wearing bright-colored beads around her neck and a costume that did not reveal her shape, yet was nevertheless only a hempen chemise put on over her bare body. He saw how beautiful she was.

"Eržika . . ."

They gazed in each other's eyes. Something in hers trembled slightly. What was it? A memory? Ridicule? Repentance? His childish soul sobbed a little within him. His voice, too, broke.

"What have you done to me, Eržika?"

He drew closer, palms outstretched. She put her hands in them, naturally, as though she could not do otherwise.

"Little girl, what have you done to me?"

And suddenly he embraced her, boyishly, wildly; she was lost in his bigness. "Sweetheart! The dearest sweetheart in the world!" And not knowing whether he trembled in sorrow or in joy, he kissed her moistly wherever his lips happened to fall.

"I'll buy you beads, I'll buy you a silk shawl, I'll marry you, I'll give up the service and take you home to Bohemia with me."

She did not resist him, not even as much as when he had taken her in his broad arms for the first time. The moment was too short to be wasted on words about what had happened, or on words of any kind. After a shower of kisses on her mouth, hands, and knees (ah, how ridiculous this seemed to Eržika, and, at the same time, how dear!), he told her, "You're late, darling, you must hurry, or else my neighbor will be wondering why you haven't reached him and will come back here to find out whether you've passed me."

She was not surprised. She tied her kerchief, smoothed her apron, and went. He watched her go, wishing that she would turn. But she did not do so. "Was he giving away official secrets again?" he mused. But the sorrow which was trying to weigh him down could not reach his being. He set himself against it in self-defense: "I love her more than I do my comrades. I'm going to marry her."

He cast away the deceit which had gripped his throat so long and had kept him from breathing freely. Confused by the suddenness of his new determination, happy in his newfound love, and somewhat alarmed at the duties he had taken upon himself, he walked to and fro over the forest path, smoking violently. Now and then he would pause. "Yes," he repeated over and over, both in his mind and out loud.

Nikola Šuhaj became from that moment his personal enemy. From thenceforth, Šuhaj would have no enemy more bitter than

Sergeant Svozil, who was out to capture him. What the whole division could not do, he would accomplish single-handedly, even if he had to go to hell to find him. He would get him, and he would get him dead.

The captain of the gendarmes was writing his report to central headquarters. But somehow, his work was not going well. He ran around the room, angrily kicking at objects within the reach of his feet; he bit his fingernails, he drained a glass of cognac, he sat down to write and rose again, only to throw himself down on his cot once more.

The captain was ill. He knew that he should take care of himself. He felt that his nerves were shattered and that he was losing the power of clear judgment. Moreover, he was not the only one; he could notice the same symptoms in his men. If they should have to stay in these thrice-accursed mountains for another six months, they would all go insane, or drink themselves to death, or possibly both. The captain's head ached from the sergeant's loud announcements, he could not stand the voices of several of the gendarmes, every trifle enraged him, and he feared that sometime in a fit of fury like this he would start to laugh or sing crazily. Besides, he was experiencing spells of anti-Semitism. How he hated the Jews! How he hated their countenances, so sadly serious when they were alone, so craftily knowing when they spoke to anyone! How he detested their nervous gestures and their eyes, now frightened, now hard as flint. Ah, to be a dictator here! He would have them hacked to pieces and hanged from the trees! None of them was able to come near him. When he met Abraham Beer, or the venerable priest Hersh Leib Wolf, or any of the others who were worthy of notice, he would stretch out the fingers of both hands and call out roguishly, "*Ai, wai Hast gesehn?* Ah, what have you seen? Phooey!"

The Jews were taking their revenge on him. They wrote anonymous messages to gendarme headquarters, to the state government. They sent articles about him to the city newspapers, even to those in Prague, Budapest, and Vienna, stating that he was absolutely incompetent; that he could not keep Eržika from learning the secret of the expedition against Šuhaj; that everyone was aware that he had her watched when she went to the pasture; that every child in Koločava knew the spot in front of Dráč's cabin where the gendarmes stood guard at night; that Eržika had bribed the gendarme Vlásek with thirty thousand crowns (Let an investigation be made, and it would be seen that Eržika had sold some cattle and received that sum on the very day that Šuhaj had escaped!); that the captain had not succeeded in bringing to justice any of Šuhaj's partners in crime because he had antagonized the entire population, which refused to cooperate with him; that while he did not drink in public he drank cognac at home, ordering it from the city. . . . Eh, the scum! Do away with them! Have pogroms against them! Or chase them all out to Palestine, where they could murder each other at will!

And if the captain did not lose his mind because of this breed, he should certainly lose it because of national headquarters. Here, for example, was one of its charming dispatches: the message stated that banditry in the district had not abated; why, then, did not the gendarmes at least find and bring to justice Šuhaj's accomplices?! He had to laugh. Accomplices? Had he been asked to find the ones who were not Šuhaj's accomplices, he might, being lenient, have found two or three. Accomplices indeed! Could he arrest the population of two and a half counties, from little children to old women on the brink of the grave?

Here was what had happened three days previously: the captain had received word that Nikola was staying in a certain village, but it had not been known just who was sheltering him. The

Czech foresters made such reports frequently, but were always vague in their information. It had been no pleasant undertaking to make the forty kilometers to this village, to proceed with thirty men, mainly through forests, so as not to be seen by anybody, and to reach their destination after nightfall. They should have prayed for better weather before they had set out. When they arrived, it was raining cats and dogs, and they were soaked to the skin. Once there, they had been unable to do anything. He had scattered the men through the cabins; he himself, with six others, had gone to the mayor's. He and the sergeant had occupied the family bed; the others had lain down on the unbearable malodorous hay that the mayor had spread for them over the clay floor. What a night, lying in such a foul hole, tickled by the crawling of fleas over their bodies! In the morning, when it had seemed that the rain was subsiding a bit, they had started for home again. On the way, they had met a Czech forester, who had heard some woodcutters say that Šuhaj had spent this night at the mayor's. What? Why yes, at the mayor's! Back again, to see the mayor.

"You rogue, you beast, you dumb creature, speak!" It was true! About an hour after they had gone to sleep, Šuhaj had arrived.

"Give me lodging!"

"Nikolka, run for your life, I have seven gendarmes in the house!"

"Where will I go on such a night? I'll sleep in the loft."

He had actually done so. It seemed that he had had a good night's rest: they downstairs, he upstairs. The captain had thought he would choke the mayor with his own hands. "Why didn't you tell us?" he had thundered. And the mayor? He had caught the captain's sleeve with both hands, beseechingly. Then, his eyes candid, he had asked in good-natured tones, "How could I have treated you so, sir? Surely you have a mother somewhere, and the sergeant a wife, and so, probably, have the other gentlemen. He had a gun and would have shot down the lot of you!" The captain had placed the man under arrest at once and had had him taken away. Horrible! Seven against one! Yet *he* would have shot *them*. People here were crazy. The captain, too, would lose his mind; they all would.

The captain ran to and fro through the room. He felt like laughing. He felt like raging! "No," he shouted like a man possessed, and sent a chair flying against the wall, "it's enough to turn a man's stomach!" Then, gulping two glassfuls of cognac, he sat down at the desk to continue his report.

He forced himself to write soberly.

"When a criminal reaches the virgin forest (and here it can be reached a few paces beyond anybody's door), he is safe, for owing to the inaccessibility and sparse settlement of the region, every systematic persecution is hopeless and the concentrated force depends primarily on chance. Šuhaj's accomplices include more or less the whole citizenry, who, being incited to irredentism by the Jews in the most consistent, schematic, and organized manner, are inimical to Czechoslovak officials. Under these circumstances, I believe that it will be impossible to carry out the original plan, namely, to catch the bandit alive, cross-examine him, and trap all his accomplices; but, rather, that it will be necessary to content ourselves with Šuhaj's removal. I see no other alternative than to place Šuhaj outside the protection of the law and to offer as great a reward as possible for his capture, alive or dead. (Ah, the captain still could not bring himself to set down the Jewish article of faith: 'Lock up Eržika, free his friends!')

"In regard to the anonymous message sent to the national gendarme headquarters, no proof can be found for its contention that the provisional gendarme, George Vlásek, on July nineteenth last, freed Nikola Šuhaj from custody upon the payment of a thirty-thousand-crown bribe. When cross-examined, Eržika Šuhaj, her father Ivan Dráč, and her brother Juraj Dráč all denied any sale of cattle on the above-mentioned date, and nobody in the community knows anything about it.

"We have been unable to question Petr Šuhaj's family, because it has dispersed. I consider this message one of those low, treasonable rumors whereby the local Jewish population, which is pro-Magyar in sympathy, fights the authority of the officials of the Republic. I am having the author of the anonymous messages traced. The provisional gendarme, George Vlásek, is behaving well and has shown zeal. Since in addition to being one of our ablest gendarmes he is well acquainted with this region, I wish to request that pending the outcome of the disciplinary investigation he be permitted to continue in the service."

The captain rose, drank another glassful, and again threw himself on the army cot. "How dreadful!" he thought. When he had arrived here, he had been quite a decent man. And now he drank and stuck out his tongue at old Jews he met in the street.

A horrible race! It should be killed, murdered, rooted out in the ruthless manner of Herod!

Thus more and more people were coming to express the wish first voiced by Abraham Beer—the wish that Šuhaj might die. And Abraham Beer, Derbák Derbačok, Adam Chrepta, Sergeant Svozil, and now the captain of the gendarmes were not the kind of people to stop at a mere wish. Too much depended on Nikola's death: safety and wealth, honor and a career, love, life itself. If the government could be persuaded that it was necessary to set a price on Šuhaj's head, much could be saved that these individuals held particularly dear.

Even Danilo Jasinko and Ihnat Sopko were full of uncertainty when they met Nikola. Due to Derbák Derbačok's charitable silence, they alone of all of Šuhaj's Koločava friends remained at large, and even they were becoming terrified at the powerful net that was closing in on him. For the time being, he alone was in danger and they still safe. It was still in Derbák Derbačok's interest not to speak, nor could Eržika talk as yet. Since Sopko and Jasinko were careful and did not spend their money, nobody else knew anything against them. Abraham Beer was only feeling them out with his crafty questions.

But what had Nikola to hope for? Many a time they said to him, "Nikolka, run away. Go to Galicia, or Romania, or Russia, or America. You have enough money, you will get along well, and Eržika can join you there later!" He did not want to go. Either he laughed, or his eyes flashed, "So you want to get rid of me, eh?"

He was tempting providence. He was meeting his wife in the village, he delighted in overhearing tavern conversations about his exploits, he rode around with commissions and posed as a mountain guide to tourists. He acted as though he were blind and could not see all the power that was surrounding him, as though it were all his own business and did not involve his pals, whose lives depended on his safety. And he would not budge from Koločava. They knew the reason. He was afraid of losing Eržika. This way, Nikola would perish. And if he did not destroy himself, he would be driven to ruin by that wild young cub Juraj.

Should they die with him? There had been a time when they had not asked themselves this question. When they had first come back from the War, their nerves and their blood had still been attuned to death in all its manifold forms. At that time, they had not known what the next day might bring them, and it had made no difference whether a man died of hunger or of a bullet wound. But that time had passed, quietly, unobtrusively, until, all at once, the world looked changed to them. Nikola alone, isolated in his woods, could see no change. Should they link their lives with his? Their situation was different; he could no longer come back, but they, perhaps—possibly—still could. But how could they part with him?

Could they say to him one day, "Pardon us, Nikolka, but we won't bring you any more cornmeal, we won't be back to shave you, tomorrow we won't help you hold up the mail, it doesn't suit our purpose any longer"?

Ah, they knew how it would be. Nikola had never forgiven anybody anything, and his one word would suffice to incriminate them with him, or alone. Neither could they take the same road to safety that had been tried by Derbák Derbačok, for they had much more on their conscience than he had. But could even Derbák return to normal life? Or had they all been caught in an enchanted maze, through which man and beast must wander in vain, without any possibility of escape?

They went into the mountains together, the swarthy old peasant Jasinko and the younger Ihnat Sopko. They carried their axes over their shoulders. Sometimes it was necessary to cut the ax into a tree and hang on to it to clamber up a boulder more easily, sometimes they had to hew their way through the branches of uprooted trees, or chop some firewood, or cut a slanting roof over their heads as protection against the rain and the morning dew. An ax was a weapon as well as a means of livelihood: it was an all-important instrument; God bless him who first gave it to mankind, if indeed, he himself had not been the donor!

They went over the pasture where in the summers grazed the horses from Koločava. Work was beginning again in the woods, the Forest Administration was hiring teams, and Danilo Jasinko was going up after his animals. Ihnat Sopko was going along to help him.

The morning sun burned hot, and they proceeded in silence. Yet it seemed to them that they ought to talk, that an understanding between them was a matter of life itself. They had lived through a great deal together and knew everything about each other. Could they trust one another?

They passed through the narrow valley of the Koločavka and were climbing up the bed of one of its tributaries. The forest towered above them, silent in the heat; only the little rapids were murmuring. It seemed to them that they should stop, look each other in the eye, and say, "Well, Danilo?" and "Well, Ihnat?" But each feared that the other might not have the courage to answer. Probably they saw eye to eye. They had implied agreement several times, by worried visages, grumbling words, a curse against Juraj, or merely by a wave of the hand. But what if each had mistaken the other's meaning? The stakes were too serious and might mean their lives. They climbed up the steep slope with long measured tread, their axes over their shoulders. They neither spoke nor looked at each other. Could they trust one another?

They arrived at the pasture, but had no wish to leave the woods for the hot glare of the sun. They were in no hurry, for they could get home in three hours. Throwing their axes aside, they lay down, their chests against the dry pine needles at the edge of the forest. Out on the pasture were the horses of the whole village. These, too, had sought refuge from the sun on the fringe of the woods and stood in pairs, with each one's head at the other's croup, fanning one another gently with their tails.

Jasinko and Sopko lay side by side, facing one another. They were looking in each other's eyes, fixedly, questioningly, so much as to say, "Speak first, say just one word! You can trust me, I feel just as you do . . . but, am I really right, do I?"

The pine needles were fragrant in the heat.

"Am I really right?" farmer Jasinko wondered, squinting.

"Well, Ihnat?"

"Well, Danilo?"

"It's a bad business, Ihnat."

"It is a bad business, Danilo."

Each was encouraged by the tone in the other's voice, and so, there by the pasture, beneath the noonday sun, they told each other everything. Not in so many words. Perhaps words played a minor role, for in these parts only the Jews were given to talking. But they saw that they held similar opinions, and were conscious of forming a partnership at this moment—a partnership for life and death—quite different from all their preceding ones.

Certainly, they loved Nikola, or rather, they had loved him a great deal and had been willing to risk their own hides for him. They had lived through a great deal with him and had experienced more good than evil. Having joined causes with him, they owed much to his outlaw's luck. Danilo Jasinko was now a well-to-do farmer; Ihnat Sopko owned no land as yet, and was only a day laborer working for strangers, but when the gendarmes should have left and the excitement with Šuhaj should have died down (ah, when would that be?), he might build his own cabin and marry his sweetheart.

But Nikola was stubborn and would not listen to reason. He had changed from the moment that the snapping young pup Juraj had appeared in their midst. He had grown suspicious. To be sure, they had committed a few robberies on their own hook, one disagreeable thing had happened to them, one horrible thing; whenever they thought of it, they had even yet a prickly feeling along their spines. (How could they have guessed the wild American would fire his revolver at them from his cabin?) But they had never sunk so low as willfully to kill a Jew whose only possession was a black hen. And why did Nikola constantly talk about the Volové fair and the three Jews who had been shot there? Why did he pry, and spy, and secretly question each of them about the other, and investigate like a gendarme? Heaven knew that neither of them, nor Derbák Derbačok, nor Adam, knew anything about Volové, and that in this case somebody else must have used Nikola's name. He promised death to the culprits, and in truth, not even Nikola's closest friends were safe from Juraj's gun. What foolhardiness to threaten one's pals! And granting that Derbák Derbačok had been driven to treason, what stupidity to force him to extremes, what folly to drive away friends now that Nikola needed them so badly. And what stubbornness not to flee. . . . Nikola would die.

Ihnat Sopko sat up in his excitement. And Danilo Jasinko turned on his hip and lay with his face to the ground. He gazed into the dried pine needles. An ant painfully dragging some winged insect caught his attention. Then his eyes fastened on the ax he had thrown down. How queer that ax was! And how new it seemed to him! Its handle was in the shade, but the sun streamed down through the trees on its blade. It was sure to be hot, and its sharpened edge gleamed white and sparkled with a thousand diminutive suns.

But what if Nikola did not perish in the woods? Would they get him alive? His friends, imprisoned at Chust, kept still; Derbák Derbačok, too, held his peace; it was in their interest to do so. But would Nikola himself be silent, Nikola the ambitious, who could expect no mercy and would want to be hanged only for what he had really done? And would Juraj be quiet? If not, then what?

Their hearts were heavy within them. The ant dragged his burden over bits of twig, and its single pinion was transparent and resembled a pine seed. The sun beat down on the pasture, the horses stood as though they were lifeless, except for their swishing tails. The closely sharpened ax blade glistened with a strange suggestiveness.

The gendarmes would not succeed in shooting Nikola. Nobody would. He had a charm against bullets. He would not reveal it, he never spoke of it, and if anybody asked him about it, he only smiled or headed them off, but he allowed nobody to joke about it. Not even a bird could have made its way through that hailstorm of bullets that had been fired at him, but he was always safe and only looked where best to aim his own gun. They themselves had been convinced of Nikola's immunity. But was he protected against other means of death . . . for instance, well, for instance . . . and, since the ax cast off to the side was shining with such a provocative glow . . . for instance, against a blow inflicted with an ax?

Jasinko sat up. He, too, was excited.

"What'll we do, Ihnat?"

"What'll we do, Danilo?"

They looked at each other sharply. But neither uttered the words that both felt quivering on their lips.

Koločava reached the decision that Nikola Šuhaj must die. The rest of the region was not aware of this. It felt nothing of the depressing terror that hung—constant, nameless, and gray—over Koločava.

The people continued to love Šuhaj for the magic of his power, for his courage, his affection, and his melancholy reed pipe, as well as because he had taken upon himself to do what they had never dared attempt: because he had terrorized the classes and loved the masses, had taken from the rich and given to the poor and had avenged their misery and the injustices they had suffered. The name Šuhaj held something of the mystery, fragrance, and sounds of Sunday churches, wherein dwelt he who had to be both loved and feared.

Šuhaj! Nikola Šuhaj! Snakes were neglected as topics of conversation, even such snakes as crawl out of the earth on the day of the Annunciation and such as live behind the cabin ovens and bring good luck; forgotten were the human snake-lords, whose incantations and spittle of tobacco juice could cure the effects of any snake's sting, and whose magic flourishings with a sickle could remove from a cow's udder the sore swellings that ensued where some snake out in the pasture had drunk of her milk. Such enchanters were forgotten, even though by merely whistling they could call together all the snakes of the neighborhood and cause them to crawl through the sleeves of a coat flung down over a tree stump. They spoke no more of wicked sorceresses and kindhearted fairies, of pixies, of nymphs, and of witches, who, standing over three cow tracks, cast their evil spells and sent disease down on mankind and caused hail to ruin the hemp, and who, at nightfall, transformed themselves into huge toads. For where was an end to the recitals about Nikola, so hard on the wicked and so kind to the good? And what day would not bring something new about him?

In a village near the Polish frontier lived a Jewish girl, Rose Grunberg, who was greatly respected by her friends, for she was acquainted with Nikola Šuhaj. Toward the close of the War, after a shrapnel had killed her father, she and her mother had moved away from Koločava to live with an uncle who had given them a means of livelihood. When she and Nikola had been children, he had come to their yard to play, and they had played at "digging the well" and other children's games, and, in turn, she and her sister had gone to Suchar to fetch berries. Everybody in her new home knew all this about her. And on the Sabbath—the only day when it was possible to visit—she would sit with her friends on the bench in front of her uncle's house and with each new report about Šuhaj she would have to tell something of his youth. What color were his eyes? When they had played at "digging the well," had he kissed her? Had her father allowed her to play with him? Had she known Juraj as well? And Rose was proud to know so much.

The preceding day, she had received a large bundle of old clothing from her married sister in America (ah, the fortunate Esther!); in it had been a pair of only slightly used snakeskin slippers and a pair of silk hose that had certainly not been washed more than twice. Rose had fallen in love with the shoes. But before whom could she show off in them? It would certainly not be possible before the afternoon of the Sabbath, when a group of ten Jewish girls and another of eight Jewish boys would stroll back and forth, promenading along the dusty road, playing with smiles and glances at the first timid game of love, strutting in whatever new and handsome clothes they might possess.

She could not part from her slippers, and when she had to take the cow to pasture, she took them along under her arm. The cow grazed and Rose put the shoes on her bare feet and took them off again, over and over, lifting her skirts, turning, pirouetting, until finally with the splendid showcases of city shops in mind, she posed her treasure on the ground with the heels together, as they appear when displayed in shoe stores. She lay down before them and gazed at them so long that the sight made her drowsy. "What's that out yonder in the woods, shining in the sun?" she wondered idly, half asleep. "People can't be carrying scythes, it's too early for hay!" And she slept.

When after a time she suddenly opened her eyes, terror turned her heart to stone within her breast. Nikola Šuhaj stood bending over her. "The cow!" was the first thought to flash through her mind, and right afterward, "The slippers!" A few paces away stood Juraj, and two other men who had their backs turned, obviously to hide their faces from her. All of them had guns slung over their shoulders.

"Hey you!" said Nikola, and she saw that he recognized her at that moment. "Have you seen any gendarmes down in the village?"

"No, I haven't," she managed to get the words out.

"You're not lying, Rosie?"

"Why should I lie to you, Nikolka?"

He looked down at her and smiled as though in reminiscence, and as though, perhaps, he were not feeling very gay.

"You're afraid of me? . . . You, of me, Rosie?"

"Why should I be afraid of you, Nikolka?" Her teeth chattered under her smile. "No, I'm not the least bit afraid of you, Nikolka," and she tried to smile more broadly.

"Kill her! What good is the Jewess?" hissed Juraj.

"May lightning strike you!" Nikola grew angry. "Many a time have I eaten porridge with her out of the same bowl." He turned to Rose. "And how are you? . . . Have you enough to live on? Have you work?"

"Well, you know how it is, Nikolka, a poor person has only his two hands."

Šuhaj turned over the leaves in his notebook. He had some banknotes of a high denomination, then a hundred-crown note and some smaller bills. These last, together with the hundred crowns, he took out and gave to Rose.

"I'd give you more, Rosie, but I haven't any more to spare."

Then they left her, and the guns over their shoulders glistened again. How would Rose keep this colossal secret till sundown? The greatest event that had ever happened in the village since the beginning of time! Yet far and wide there was not a living soul to whom she could impart it. Excited, with flushed cheeks, she counted the money over and over, and repeated to herself every word they had spoken; the snakeskin shoes lost their charm, and she kept glancing impatiently toward the sun, to see when it would finally disappear beyond the treetops.

When at last the sun descended from the sky and hid behind the forest, she hurried home, her shoes under her arm, driving the cow with a willow whip. She blurted out her news to the first comer, a youth she met at the crossroads; he joined her, and they trotted toward the village together, with the cow in the lead. Proud of her importance, Rose talked and he, with his mouth half open, devoured the words which would shortly cause such a sensation in the village.

At home, she expounded anew, savoring her great adventure and relishing her uncle's astonishment and the anxiety in the mother's dilated eyes. And after she had told almost everything, keeping back only a little, she ran to the nearest Jewish cabin and repeated her news, word for word, with the same exception she had made at home: without mention of the money. For it was a vast sum that had fallen into her lap this happy day, and it would buy her many of the beautiful things that she desired so much: she could not endanger her means of acquiring them. She would tell her mother that night, after they were in bed. But meanwhile, there came to the village the announcement that showed to Rose the true significance of the day's meeting: that afternoon, two city merchants had been held up nearby as they were returning with the money they had received for a shipment of lumber.

These events happened on a Friday. The first three stars which would shortly appear in the sky would mark the beginning of the Sabbath. The Jewish women had scrubbed clean the cabin floors and had washed the windows, through which, shining into the gloom of the road, could be seen the white cloths that covered the Sabbath wheat loaves laid out on the tables and many burning candles. Some of these were placed in candlesticks and others merely stuck in empty sardine cans: a candle for each member of the family, both living and dead. At night, after everybody was in bed, the candles would burn themselves out, for this was the day of Jehovah, when all work was a sin, and blowing out a candle was work.

The men, dressed in their best, met in a neighbor's cabin for an hour of prayer. But that one hour sufficed for all ten Jewish girls to collect in Rose's yard and crowd around her in the darkness on a bench under the illuminated window. Oi, oi! Only one in a thousand would have the opportunity of seeing him, and that one only once in a lifetime! Oi, how handsome he was! Tanned like a tree in the woods, but with a mouth that was small and as red as a cherry! His eyebrows were arched, and his eyes shone like the Sabbath window beneath which they were sitting. And Juraj? The cruel Juraj? Oi, he was still a lad, but, if anything, even handsomer.

The following day—the Christian Saturday—a disturbance occurred at the other end of the province, at Chust, near the Hungarian frontier. The workers employed on the Tisza River regulation project started an argument with the paymaster as they were being paid. They were unable to find the entrepreneur himself, and so, after a stormy scene and many threats to the higher-paid employees, they went on strike. They marched to the town in an angered procession and carried a paper banner on which they had written in large letters:

LONG LIVE NIKOLA ŠUHAJ! HE WILL LEAD US!

The eve of that fateful day, Nikola and Juraj, bound for a friend's cabin, were walking along the road that ran through the Terebla valley. They were planning to stay overnight with him. The night was clear, and high above the narrow valley of the murmuring Terebla there flowed another narrow river: a river of stars. The men walked with their guns over their shoulders and felt safe, for they were far from Koločava, and were they to have met a patrol, they would have been two against two.

Hearing a wagon as it rumbled over the highway, they hid in a thicket. Who was it? Nikola strained his eyes. Ah! It was—yes, it really was! Juraj Dráč, stepping calmly beside his wagon.

The blood stirred in Nikola's body. Hot, ardent, it throbbed in his veins—not out of hatred for Juraj Dráč, but out of desire for Eržika. In the wagon, two barrels had been set down in straw and fastened with willow twigs: Juraj Dráč was going to fetch salt water; Juraj Dráč would not be back home for two days. Eržika would be alone with her father. The image of Eržika's lap flashed through Nikola's mind.

They allowed the vehicle to pass and then stepped out in the road. Nikola's long steps were so hurried, that he almost ran and Juraj could barely keep up with him. When they reached their friend's cabin, Nikola said, "I don't need to see him. You stay here by yourself, and tomorrow afternoon expect me up yonder by that pasture!"

Juraj frowned.

Nikola made the thirty kilometers to Kaločava that night. When he arrived, before four o'clock, it was already broad daylight. At the first cabins that he had to pass, the women had already risen, and one of them turned at her door to stare after him in astonishment. He turned off from the road and made for the river, from where he wound his way over stiles and through gardens to the back of Dráč's cabin.

"Eržika!"

He found her in the door that led to the yard.

"Eržika! Sweetheart!" He caught her in his arms and pushed her back into the house.

In the hall he threw his gun down in the corner, and made haste to fasten both the doors—to the street and to the yard.

"Where is your father?" he whispered.

"I'm all alone at home, Nikolka." Her voice laughed.

"My little darling!" He pushed her before him in a crushing embrace over the threshold of the room, to the bed (so drags the bear his prey into the copse!). She was looking him full in the face, her eyes and mouth smiling.

Then somebody knocked on the back door. "Eržika!" said a voice from without.

He did not hear. But women are wiser, and keep their wits about them even in moments when men lose theirs.

"Wait . . . wait . . ." she whispered, and pushed him away.

"Be quiet!" he ordered.

But she pushed his chin away from her with all her strength. The knocking was repeated. "Eržika!"

Now he, too, heard. "Who is it?" he hissed, full of hatred.

She paled. "The gendarmes! Run!"

A single, clear, burning thought flashed through the confusion of his mind. He leaped into the dark hall and reached for the gun he had previously laid aside there. Eržika unlatched the door and opened it a little. In the narrow crack a gendarme appeared, fully armed. Šuhaj clutched his gun. Eržika wanted to slip out, but the gendarme leaned against the door and forced her back in.

"I'm on my way home from duty. I got lonesome, so I've come to see you."

What was this? Somewhere in the depths of Nikola's being, wild whirlpools formed, dark, yet clear, which ruffled the surface of his consciousness as the pools of the Terebla stir its rapids. This was not the way gendarmes usually spoke to Koločava women!

As Eržika anxiously ran from the gendarme, he followed her into the room. She stopped in the corner on the same side of the room as held the door, which he had not closed behind him. She pressed herself against the wall like a partridge that has been shot in the wing and is being attacked by a hound. And when he came toward her, wishing to embrace her, she clasped her hands and held them right in front of his face, held them so tightly that the knuckles cracked. Sergeant Svozil saw for the first time in his life that her eyes could speak, that they could shout and moan.

"What's the matter with you?"

She dug her nails into his face, and her lips whispered in his ear, "Be still, for Christ's sake!"

But suddenly he understood. "Šuhaj is here!" he called out loud.

"No," she whispered, and her knees gave way under her.

"He's here! . . . Where is he?" he thundered. The gendarme had waked up within the man.

"He's not home," she screamed, and wanted to kill and be killed, and wanted at once to deny and to admit her guilt with that shrill cry. "He's not!"

The sergeant searched the room with a single sweeping glance: nobody was hidden here. The lock of his carbine rang out metallically. The sergeant ran through the hall and out the door, but had no time to retrace his steps, for Šuhaj stood at the corner of the cabin.

Eržika heard the thundering shot outside. A shot fired between the walls of houses always sounds loud. The blow hit Eržika full in the nerves. She heard a gun striking against stones and the fall of a large body. The witch of Majdan!

The figures of a few running gendarmes flashed outside the window. A crowd gathered behind them. From the other side somebody cried excitedly, "He jumped back of the shed!" A shot resounded from that direction.

"In the shed! In the shed!" shouted a desperate Jewish voice. Shots were fired from the street. Looking through the window to the gardens, Eržika caught a glimpse of Nikola among the bean-poles; she saw him leap over a stile, run, and disappear. She closed her eyes and took several deep breaths. Now that she had seen him get away, she wanted to sit down and rest her head on the table.

Outside, the firing went on, the valley roaring with echoes; somebody called out some orders, and again the shooting was resumed, but to Eržika it all seemed to lose its meaning and become as vague as though it came from another world and as though it no longer concerned her. She wanted to close her eyes, lay her head down on the table, and go to sleep.

The dead gendarme was laid out on the camp cot in the school. Every glance at his pierced head gave his comrades a stifled impulse to sob and brought a renewed attack of fury, which they made no attempt to curb. They continued to patrol the quiet village, walking around insanely, chasing everybody off the street with blows, penetrating the cabins, and beating up the occupants. "We'll kill them all! . . . We'll burn up the whole village!" When they entered the Jewish shops to make inquiries, they held their guns in their hands and shouted and behaved as though they wished to assassinate the whole family.

The captain, pale as death, was pacing up and down the gendarme barracks. Another murder! And again, all had been in vain: they had not wormed a word out of the prisoners. Not a word after all those blows? How many times had they tried? Finally he himself had ordered them to stop the inquisition of the Dráč family, to cease knocking the Dráčs' heads against the ground and hitting the soles of their feet. He could stand it no longer, and the screams of the woman next door were simply unbearable. Jesus, Mary! And was it true about Vlásek? The captain could feel his strength ebbing and his senses leaving him, he felt that insanity was his inevitable lot. Then he grew angry: how had those fellows been shooting, anyway? Or was the brute really invulnerable? He shouted for the old sergeant.

The sergeant came. The captain roared some senseless questions in his face and made reproaches, his hand constantly fingering the revolver at his side. There really seemed to be danger lest he go raving mad. The sergeant stood at attention and at first answered only in the austere manner of the military subordinate: "I do not know, sir. Yes, sir. No, sir." Then he listened indifferently to the captain's outbursts and only took care not to shrug his shoulders visibly.

"They must tell where he's hiding! They must! Do you hear, Sergeant, they must! If they don't talk, kill them! Kill them all! On my responsibility! At my order! Do you hear? I command you! And destroy the Jews! It is they who are the cause of everything. Have a pogrom against them! Set the population on them! Beat them, shoot them, hang them!" It seemed to the sergeant that at any moment, the captain would start foaming at the mouth.

The sergeant did not know whether to treat this raving as the unwise commands of a superior officer, which for his own security he should ask to be issued to him in writing, or as the outbursts of a half-demented individual.

"Have you heard me, Sergeant?"

"Yes, sir."

He left, his forehead wrinkled, his hand gently waving to and fro. Should he inform national headquarters? Or would everything be all right again on the morrow, the captain having forgotten all about it?

This was one of those horrible days of which Koločava had already experienced so many. In the yard next door to the Dráčs, Eržika lay on her back, next to old Ivan Dráč and his thirteen-year-old, Josef, who had been arrested as they were coming home from the pasture that morning. Next to them lay the neighbors, arrested for reasons unknown, perhaps because in his flight Nikola had first leaped over the fence to their garden. All of them were black and blue, with swollen faces, black eyes, and bloody clothing. Even then, in the afternoon, when the hottest sun rays had ceased beating down on their faces, the gendarmes were still coming over to look at them. Tired though the gendarmes were with all the excitement, they were nevertheless still strong enough to kick one of the prisoners or to stick the point of a bayonet against his chest and ask, "Where shall I pierce you, you beast?" And it required much self-restraint not to bear down in fact.

Eržika's motionless body alone was left in peace. That morning, as they had dragged her around by the hair, struck her face with their fists, and kicked her, she had beheld Vlásek among her tormentors. She had shouted, taking out on him her revenge on them all, "To this man here I gave thirty thousand!"

He struck her in the mouth, punishing the insult she had flung at him in the hearing of his comrades. He had continued to hit her in the face in a furious desire to silence her. But between blows she had shrieked: "You took . . . thirty thousand. . . . You let Nikola go . . . a year ago." He had beaten her the harder, she had fallen, and he, towering over her, had choked her with trembling hands, "You're a liar! You're a liar!" But whenever he had loosed his hold a bit, she had turned her bleeding head and fixed him with her furious eyes and hissed, "You took . . . thirty thousand . . . from me. . . . You let Nikola go. . . . You untied his bonds!" And her revelations had been cut short anew by blows.

The other gendarmes had stood back in amazement, until only the two had been left in the field: she, passionately attacking, he, frantically defending himself. The gendarmes had had the impression of a mad cat that scratched and bit and clawed for her life.

Vlásek? After all, Vlásek? Vlásek responsible for so many human lives? They repeated these questions to themselves, astonished. An old gendarme had stepped up to Vlásek, had lifted him by the collar and, holding him at arm's length, had given him a scorching glance. He had seen a look of desperation creep into Vlásek's eyes.

"Let her go," he had cried, and had thrust Vlásek away from him against the picket fence.

Who could bear the excitement of such a day?

In the dusk, the Dráč cabin went up in flames. The gendarmes circulated through the desolate village, determined to hit anybody who might venture to thrust his head out of his door. But the village was dreary and deserted. Nobody dared even to light a lamp, and the Jewish shops closed at noon.

The Dráč cabin burned with large, perpendicular, smokeless flames. It burned into the quiet night as though it were the dead gendarme's funeral pyre and the village fire bell his death knell.

That evening, Nikola found himself in the mountains at the fork of two rivers, the Terebla and the Rika, over the familiar clearing with the sulfur springs, where, more than two years before, he had come upon the boys in their game of make-believe, pretending to be Nikola Šuhaj. "Šuhaj, lend us your bough!" they had called after him, cupping their hands to their lips, and this memory now flashed through his mind.

He was descending the slopes of the Rika valley in an effort to escape. He did not realize clearly from whom he was fleeing, but for the first time in his life his movement could be described as flight. He did not even know where he was going, but only had the dull, heavy consciousness of whence he was coming. If he could only go on and on, where there were no people, not even Juraj!

He caught sight of two or three lights down below in the village, but did not wish to go there; he turned into the forest to avoid it. He could see that he was in a small copse opposite a gamekeeper's lodge. Below murmured the river, and the building with its tall roof and two red-lighted windows stood on the other shore. As the crow flies, it was not over three hundred yards away.

Nikola stood still. The moon floated in the clouds over the hills, and the surrounding trees cast sharp blue shadows. The whole valley was in a strange, ghastly blue light, and the two windows were like blinking red eyes that stared indifferently into the evening and bore witness to heaven knew what murky filth and foul disease that lurked behind them.

Suddenly, Nikola roared, "Heigh-ho!" He did not know how it had come about, and his own voice surprised him.

"Heigh-ho!" the forest magnified his call in manifold echoes. "Heigh-ho! Here is Šuhaj!"

"Nikola Šuhaj!" It seemed to him that this name, his name, outgrew the treetops and filled the whole valley all the way up to the clouds.

"Do you hear—I, Nikola Šuhaj!"

But nobody answered him. A deep silence hung over the gamekeeper's lodge and over the village. Silence in the woods is good: there it bespeaks safety to man. But in the proximity of human beings it is dreadful.

Bang! Bang! The forest shrieked as a shot was fired, the bullet struck the roof of the lodge, the confused brain of that turbid house.

Bang! Bang! Bang!

"Heigh-ho!" roared the valley and the woods.

"Šuhaj! . . . Nikola Šuhaj! . . . The Invulnerable! . . . Whom no missile can touch! . . ."

He sent one bullet after another at the lodge, at its poor disturbed head. Both its lights were extinguished, as were those that had glimmered in the village. Over and over Nikola emptied the magazine of his rifle, the shots crashed, and the countryside roared with their echoes. Nikola knew that when he stopped, everything would be frightfully, unbearably quiet again.

The people below, hiding in the darkness, jumped down from their beds and groped their way to the best-protected places in their cabins and cowsheds. Mothers dragged their children after them and clapped their hands over mouths about to cry.

A storm raged over the village: the powerful Šuhaj was angry, and, in his wrath, he was horrible.

Friends

"Tsk!" the Jews clucked their tongues and shrugged their right shoulders when they learned from Chust that in the near future all the real and supposed accomplices of Šuhaj were to be freed. This "Tsk!" uttered with such scorn, meant, "They needed a year for that! And have you any idea how many lives might have been preserved, and how much money saved?!" Since Svozil's death, Eržika had finally been kept under lock and key. Perhaps the new officer was going to do a little better than the others, after all.

Moreover, the Šuhaj affair was losing its attraction for the members of the Jewish younger set. Their interest was now turned to an old feud that had flared up again between the Wolfs and the Beers, this time in competition over a tobacco vendor's license (the sale of tobacco being a state monopoly). The young people were aroused by all the gossip, stratagems, and rivalries connected with this contest. Then even this began to bore them, and their attention came to be focused on the pending appointment of a cantor in the Chust synagogue and the ensuing rivalry among the applicants, who represented both Orthodox Jews and Zionists.

The young Jewry was nonetheless considerably excited when, shortly afterward, they saw placards in the Czech, Ruthenian, and Hungarian languages posted on the walls of the Wolf and the Leibovich taverns:

Reward Offered

One Nikola Šuhaj, robber and murderer, and his band, have for some time past been active in the Chust, Volové, and neighboring districts. This band, and particularly its leader, Nikola Šuhaj, is responsible for several murders and robberies, carried out with extraordinary insolence and brutality. To date, the members of this band, having supporters among the general population, have succeeded in evading the arm of the law.

In the interest of all law-abiding citizens, we bid everyone who is able to furnish any information whatsoever concerning the members of this band to do so at once at the nearest gendarme headquarters or police station.

The Civil Administration of Carpathian Ruthenia in Uzhgorod hereby offers a reward of 3,000 (three thousand) crowns to the person or persons responsible for the capture of the leader of this band, the aforementioned Nikola Šuhaj. The reward may be claimed at the nearest federal office.

Signed,

Bláha, Chief of the Civil
Administration

Next to this placard another bill was posted, small and inconspicuous, stating that the Jewish congregations of the Chust and the Volové districts were offering a reward of thirty thousand crowns for Šuhaj's capture.

"Well, at last."

Now, Jews, heads together! For no important work had ever been done with the hands; the head alone counted for everything. The decisive moment had arrived.

But the notary had done a malicious thing. He had not had the bills posted until Saturday morning, and thus the old Jews had to walk past them in dignity, without reading them, and to let others, less pious, tell what was in them, without even asking for the information.

It cost them much effort to keep their minds pinned on the Eternal and free of secular matters, to preserve their brows calm and unclouded, their gaits slow and decorous. Their bodies were continually tempted to hurry along, their faces to pucker in concentrated thought, and their souls to leave their meditation about Jehovah and the heavenly Sabbath, and turn to temporal affairs and to Šuhaj. Fortunately, a little goodwill and a bit of experience in intercourse with the Almighty made it possible to compromise and to think of both: the cause of Jehovah's people always came out on top in the end, and even when it took ages, God always helped. Ah, but how long would it be in human terms before he recalled that his people were oppressed by their enemies, of whom Šuhaj was not the least? What should be done about him? How could they take counsel? Would the Wolfs not be stubborn? Oi, oi! Did they really mean business, and did they intend to pay the reward? (Such thoughts were permissible.)

On Saturday evening, as soon as three stars had appeared in the sky, recalling the Princess Sabbath to the starry throne of the Almighty, the older Jews assembled behind the drawn shades of the patriarch Hersh Leib Wolf's little room. Their hands did no work, for their heads were to accomplish everything, and if, indeed, hands should be necessary, these could be found. The men immediately formed debating groups and shouted their various reactions and plans, each of which was more ingenious than the preceding one, and any of which might have worked. The dispute between the house of Wolf and that of Beer and their respective supporters, while not forgotten, was postponed for the moment. Let Šuhaj's comrades be called before the captain, let him promise them jobs in the woods and on the roads, let him promise them heaven and earth! Divide them, arouse mutual jealousies among them, start a competitive struggle! . . . Thirty-three thousand was a great deal of money, a shocking sum, really! . . . Nobody would dare shoot at Šuhaj, everybody really believed that a bullet would bounce off him and hit back. But didn't they have axes? And were there not enough clubs growing out in the woods? And how about the various brews that old Mrs. Derbák knew how to prepare?

Everything was clear, absolutely clear!

But was it? No, everything was not clear, as they discovered after they established themselves on the sofa, the chairs, the bed, and the window ledges, when Bernard Wolf (of course! Mr. Bernard Wolf always had to find something extra special!) suggested a new problem. He raised it in the form of a simple question about the interpretation of the words of the bill: "the person or persons *responsible* for the *capture*" of Nikola. What was meant by the term *capture?* Did *capture* mean just taken, and not killed? Was one to be allowed only to furnish information leading to his capture and not to capture him oneself? And was it forbidden to kill Šuhaj? Or did the notice say one thing and mean another?

The feud between the houses of Wolf and Beer flared up anew and culminated in the introduction of entirely irrelevant issues, such as the very complex questions about what was permitted by Jewish usage and what exceeded the bounds of orthodoxy. This new argument presented many opportunities to demonstrate one's familiarity with the canon and to repulse one's enemies by the use of logic, dialectic, and citations from the highest rabbinic authorities, as well as by references to the Koločava tobacco shop and the position of cantor at Chust.

The arguers continually jumped up from their places, flinging out brittle accusations against one another and bursting into sarcastic laughter. With reddened faces and gesticulating hands they mocked each other and quarreled man to man. "So you're going to teach me to know the Talmud, you, of all people, you, Mr. Josef Wolf, who sells whiskey on the sly on the Sabbath!" "And who is asking you about the Talmud, you immigrant Polish Jew, we're Chasidins here! And if you must know something: all your girls get themselves baptized to please the army officers at Chust! And now you can go ahead and blow up for all we care!"

The brawl finally became so passionate and the shouts so dangerous that the white-bearded, eighty-year-old Hersh Leib Wolf had to establish his authority. The sage, who hitherto had not moved an eyelash or spoken one word, rose slowly from the greasy sofa. At once everybody grew silent. He spread his hands slightly, as does a cantor before the Torah, and turning his eyes upward, spoke with the measured dignity of a prophet, "Do you have Šuhaj? Is Šuhaj a louse, or is he a flea?"

Having spoken these words, he slowly sat down again.

The gathering kept respectfully quiet.

What wisdom! The patriarch was right, as ever, and truly nothing could clear up a problem as well as a homely simile that everyone could grasp. Their passions subsided, their brains cleared, and their thoughts turned into the only correct channels: it was not permissible to kill a louse on the Sabbath, for it would still be there on the morrow, but it was permissible to kill a flea, for a flea would not wait until Sunday. They really did not have Šuhaj as yet, and it would still cost a great deal of effort before he would be rendered harmless. No, Nikola was not a louse, for which they could reach anytime; in Šuhaj's case it was impossible to preserve the letter of the law, to spare him on the Sabbath. Furthermore, could any day be holier than was the Sabbath? Well, then, if a course of action was permitted on that day, could it not be followed with impunity on any other day as well? Wisdom had spoken; the dispute was finished.

Abraham Beer had taken no part in the debate, but he was frightfully excited.

On the following day (Sunday afternoon), the newly arrived captain called a meeting of the citizenry, to be held at Leibovich's tavern. For a week the division of gendarmes concentrated in Koločava had had a new leader. Nobody knew him, and since he had politely excused himself to the Jewish delegation on the grounds of too much work, nobody knew what to expect of him. Curiosity concerning him was, therefore, general.

About three hundred people assembled under the maples in front of Leibovich's tavern. They grouped themselves in small clusters, sat down on the steps and beside the wall, and leaned against the fence. Only a few of the most respected citizens ventured inside to the trestle tables. The others waited for the gendarme to arrive and tell them what he wanted; not until then would they file over the threshold and push into the room. The Leibovich shop was filled with waiting Jews. Four gendarmes circulated through the crowd, but they were unarmed, and they behaved in a neighborly manner, smiling and engaging the farmers in conversation about cattle prices and carters' wages, just as though they had always lived on the friendliest of terms with the people. What was going on?

The waiting crowd included almost all of Šuhaj's friends, both the convicted and the unconvicted; some of them were out on parole, others had been discharged after questioning. All of them were there, even the one who had helped Nikola take the bucket of sheep's milk cheese at Douhé Gruny, and the one who had been recognized by his torn trouser leg and a belt with army buttons as having taken part in holding up the mails. Even Vasyl Derbák Derbačok and his natural son, Adam Chrepta, and the mildly excited Ihnat Sopko were present. Only Eržika and old Dráč were still in custody at Chust, and Danilo Jasinko was absent.

Jasinko was right not to have come, for a dangerous conversation took place. When Derbák Derbačok saw Ihnat Sopko leaning against a fence, he walked up to him and, striking his own chest with his fist, cried, "I've spared Nikola's pals long enough! Heaven knows it's been long enough!"

Ihnat Sopko strove to look him in the eyes without nervousness. "And why tell me about it?" he demanded.

Derbák Derbačok pretended not to hear him, but continued, "What did my pals do for me after my house burned down? And, for that matter, what did they do for me before it burned?" His fists, thumping his chest, produced hollow rumbling sounds. A crowd gathered around the two men as Derbák Derbačok ran on, "But enough! *I'm* going to kill Nikola! *I* shall find him. I'm not afraid of him any longer. And if I can't find him myself, *you*, Ihnat, shall find him for me."

"Why *I*, particularly?"

But Derbák Derbačok, full of anger, of bitterness, and doubtless of greed for the thirty-three thousand, shot out his forefinger at Sopko: "You, Ihnat, yes, you, particularly!"

The new commanding officer approached swiftly and somehow gaily. A young man. The crowd parted and heads were bared. He saluted with a smile, looked people in the eyes with a friendly air. What was happening?

At the threshold of the tavern he turned. "Well, come in, come in, neighbors!" and he motioned with the palm of his hand, as though he were driving a flock of geese.

He led the people forward into the room and saw that they were comfortably settled. He joked and laughed, and then he swung himself boyishly onto a bench and commenced his address to the packed tavern.

Unfortunately (he told them), the mutual relations between the citizenry and the gendarmes had not developed along cordial lines so far. Misunderstandings on both sides were to blame. The gendarmes had not appreciated the feelings of the population and the difficulties the people had encountered in adapting themselves to new and entirely different circumstances. The people, on the other hand, had not comprehended how difficult and how dangerous was the duty that the gendarmes had to perform here; they did not understand the exasperation, nay, the anger experienced by the gendarmes when so many of their good comrades lost their lives at the hands of the treacherous assassin, whom, they believed, had been abetted by the general population. (This belief, heaven be praised, had, of course, been unfounded.)

Such mutual misunderstandings had to cease. The government would do all in its power to remedy them. Already it had given the gendarmes new orders and made an example of the provisional gendarme Vlásek, punishing him because complaints against him had come in from the ranks of the people. ("Why are you lying?" wondered the farmers, "as though we did not know what Eržika shouted before the fire!" "A mistake," the old Jews said to themselves. "Muddler!" the Jewish youths muttered half audibly as they stood on the counters and crates in the store and looked into the tavern over other people's heads, directly at the speaker.)

It was up to the people of Koločava to forget the past and to start regarding the gendarmes, who were their true friends, in a different light, continued the captain. The War, that horrible scourge of mankind, was over, and the wounds it had caused were slowly healing. Everywhere, its horrors had been replaced by order, which went hand in hand with a regard for law, cooperation, and prosperity. Only here, in this one corner of the globe, war (or, rather, a sort of an outgrowth of war) persisted, here was carried on the most obdurate struggle of all—the struggle against crime.

Somehow the speech was lasting too long. The speaker's soft accent and his language, which was neither the Koločava dialect nor Ukranian nor Russian nor Czech but a mixture of all of these, had put his audience in a merry mood, but this gradually wore off as the people became accustomed to his diction. They began to get bored. And as the orator went on to describe the social ravages wrought by Šuhaj, the farmers thought, "Well, talk on if it gives you pleasure, blah, blah, it won't hurt us to sit for a while and smoke a pipeful of tobacco!"

But suddenly they pricked up their ears: "Not one of you can feel safe from him" ("Oh yes, we can," said the peasants to themselves) "whether you be rich or poor, Jews or Christians! You know how many lives he has destroyed here, you know that he set fire to his own father's house in order that the officers of justice might not find the loot concealed there; you are aware that he burned neighbor Derbák's house to get revenge and that he set fire to the house belonging to his father-in-law Dráč because the two had quarreled over the division of their plunder."

"Ah, so that's your tune, is it, you greenhorn? To the devil with you!" flashed through the peasants' minds. "So you've come to try and fool us, have you?! Imagine that! Well, young fellow, you've chosen the wrong men to fool!" But they sat motionless and continued to look up at the speaker with serious and respectful intentness. The old Jews wriggled in their seats while the Jewish youths on the counters, ready to break a cane over the orator's head, flapped their hands and uttered "Oh, oh!"

"We need to join hands in our labor, for only thus can we render this criminal harmless. The gendarmes alone cannot get him, that is certain by this time." ("Oi, oioioi, he shouldn't have said that!" the older Jews all protested in their minds.) "He can recognize a man in uniform at a great distance, and a lone gendarme disguised as one of the local people depends on a not-too-likely chance.

"But the citizenry is in touch with him. You see him against your will, in the pastures and forests, where he extorts information from you." ("What are you lying about now? What's that he extorts? He extorts nothing, but rather he gives.") "He visits you in your cabins to spend the night when the weather is inclement. I shall not speak of the offered reward"; ("Oho!") "I do not wish to speak of it," ("Oho!") "but I appeal to your honor as citizens: render Nikola Šuhaj harmless! If he comes to you, send one of your children to fetch us. And go about armed, my friends. The government is well aware that there are many weapons scattered over the countryside, that in practically every cabin there is a gun or a revolver. Well, out with them, citizens!" ("Yes, so you can take them away easily!") "The law allows you the greatest lassitude. In this case, because of the necessity for self-defense, there can be no talk of murder or manslaughter, or even of any infringement of the law, for each encounter with Šuhaj is a menace to life, as we have learned to our sorrow in so many cases. If you render him harmless, no matter where or when, you shall have acted out of necessity and legally permissible self-defense. Shoot him, wherever you may find him!"

"Ah the clumsy bear!" and now the audience could barely refrain from open laughter. "He thinks that Nikola can be shot!"

"We have freed Šuhaj's accomplices, since we are convinced that they are not as much to blame as was thought at first and that they acted under the influence of a postwar psychosis rather than with criminal intent. But, to be sure, we expect them to appreciate our leniency and to wipe out their guilt by helping us to apprehend the murderer. We are offering a reward, as you have read. We guarantee you your safety, and what is more, we promise a government position to anyone who shall have actively aided in the bandit's capture. Given sufficient intelligence, a citizen who deserves any credit for this capture may even become a white-collar man. But as I have already said, I do not wish to dwell upon rewards, for these are secondary to you as well as to me. Our common motive is entirely different." And here the captain raised his voice: "It is Public Duty and regard for Law and Order."

The orator concluded with a warm appeal, possibly a bit too long winded, which nevertheless awoke in his listeners the hope that, thank heaven, the end of the meeting was in sight.

It was late in the afternoon when the gathering finally broke up and the Koločava citizens went to their homes. "*Chazerkopf*," said the Jews, and this single Yiddish word into which they rolled their judgment means "pig head."

And at the very moment when the captain, smiling as he reposed in his little room, felt extremely self-satisfied with his diplomatic speech, the farmers, now at home, were taking off their Sunday coats of white sheep's wool and telling their inquisitive wives about the meeting: "He lied to beat the band!"

"But what did he say?"

"He begged us very nicely to catch Nikolka for him, that he doesn't know how to do it himself."

Then they thought of something else: "And whoever catches him will get an office job. A damned fool, the captain!"

"And what about the thirty-three thousand?"

"He said he wouldn't talk about that. Must be some sort of catch in it."

"Ihnat Sopko?" wondered Abraham Beer, even before the meeting was out, having already been informed of the scene between Derbák Derbačok and Ihnat. That inconspicuous lad? Just imagine! How blind a person could be for all he thought he could see through everybody as though they were made of glass! He searched his memory for some telling incidents that may have escaped his notice, but he found nothing.

After the meeting he himself did not wish to shadow Sopko, for it was still broad daylight, so he sent a little Jewish boy. When the child should have ascertained where Ihnat went, he was to stop at the store for some candy.

The boy soon came around with the desired information: "Sopko went to Danilo Jasinko's house."

Oho! Jasinko, old braggart and ruffian, that was a different matter! Last fall he had wiped out his entire debt several times, and Abraham Beer had been suspicious of him for a long time.

Abraham Beer was vastly excited again. Red spots appeared in the exposed patches of skin between his eyes and his beard, his heart beat violently, and his brain worked feverishly, fitting together facts and probabilities. Only this much appeared certain: if Nikola did not get killed during the next few days, he would not get killed at all. The new captain was a fool who did not know what to make of his splendid opportunities and would waste his great capital. He, Abraham Beer, would have to step into the matter himself. . . . Jasinko . . . Jasinko! . . . Could Jasinko really be the man for the job? . . . Were his the proper hands to do it?

Outside, it began to rain. So much the better. At least Sopko would still be there. He waited for about two hours to give the friends time to talk over their business, then he prayed for the success of his undertaking, took an umbrella, and set out.

He found the two friends alone at Jasinko's house. Outside in the rain it was already dusk, which made the room quite dim.

Could Jasinko deliver him about four wagonloads of wood?

Why not?

The following day?

All right.

This preamble disposed of, Abraham Beer sat down on the bench in the corner of the room.

"It's raining."

"Yes, it's raining."

Abraham Beer's excitement waned as he spoke the first words. His heart grew calm and his nerves steady. He waited, watchful. Here was a game he knew how to play, and the stakes were high.

"Well," he turned to them, "how did you like the new officer?"
No answer. "Um," Ihnat Sopko grunted at last.

They were silent, therefore they were on the defensive. Silence
was a typical old weapon in such cases. If they were on the defensive, they felt that they were being threatened. By whom? By him?
How they misunderstood him! He had not come to harm them, he
had come to encourage, to inspire, to underscore the points that the
captain had utilized so poorly; he only wanted to help them hatch
the plan that had long been developing within them.

"Nikola is a wicked man, but now that his end is near, one cannot help feeling sorry for him," he said slowly, emphasizing every
word. How glad Abraham Beer would have been to hear the sound
of their voices in this expectant pause, how he should have liked
to see their faces! They, however, kept still, and their faces were
only blurred red blotches in the darkness. But Abraham Beer could
feel very distinctly that fear was present in this room.

"Nikola is going to get caught," he said.

They did not question him, they were determined not to question him. Their Sunday shirts of white linen, the only objects
visible in the dusk, were motionless, as though they were merely
the wash hung up to dry on the fence on a calm day. Not even a
sleeve fluttered.

"And he'll get caught alive . . . which will be the worst of all."

He could feel them hanging on every word, he could almost
see it.

"Just now, after the meeting, we Jews saw the captain and
talked to him."

He rose, moved to the window, and, bending over the pots of
sweet basil, leaned against the pane as though he were vastly interested in the rain outside. Even as he passed very close to them,
he could not see their faces.

"It's raining." And because the sound of his words evoked no echo, he repeated them, as he slowly returned to his bench in the corner: "It's raining."

Then he began to talk, slowly and cautiously, as though he were unwinding a tangled ball of thread. His were no ordinary lies, but rather a correction of the captain's psychological blunders; they were an experiment to show what he, Abraham Beer, should have done with the given facts, had they been entrusted to him. This imaginary experiment, however, became in Abraham's mind the most genuine sort of reality.

"The captain didn't tell everything he knew. It is not true that he thinks the gendarmes unaided cannot get Nikola. Nor did he really mean seriously that everybody should shoot him on sight. What he really wants is to get Nikola alive. He wants Nikola to talk, to tell all he knows. And he will get him, too. He has made an agreement with two of Nikola's pals who have been released. I don't know which ones they might be. He has worked out a plan with them. I heard they would catch Šuhaj within the next few days. This captain is a different sort of person than was that other one. He has a list of the names of all the people who shelter Nikola at night, and he's been in touch with them as well. If the two can't succeed, the farmers will tie Nikola up with ropes and bring him down from the mountains next winter. Unless, of course, Derbák Derbačok rakes in that thirty-three thousand first. I've heard that he made threats against Nikola before the meeting. He knows it's a life-and-death matter: either Nikola's life or his own. . . . No, Nikola won't come out with a whole skin. Not anymore. . . . He can't. . . ."

The two white shirts seemed to remain hanging in space, motionless.

"It's a great deal of money. Oi, oioi, a whole fortune! Things are different now from what they used to be during the War, when one cow cost thousands. For this much money a brother would sell a brother, and a son his own father."

In the darkness, Abraham Beer stretched out the palm of his left hand and pressed his right thumb against his left little finger. "In the first place, thirty thousand from the Jewish congregation, cash, right away, no waiting. The captain has the money ready in his safe." And now he pressed the thumb against the ring finger. "Second, three thousand government money." The middle finger followed. "Then there is the thirty thousand in special taxes assessed against Koločava. When Nikola is taken, this tax will be canceled, and, naturally, the community will have to reward the persons responsible." Abraham Beer arrived at the forefinger. "As for the state position that the captain mentioned, matters stand something like this: whoever wants to be a forester will be a forester, whoever wants to be a road warden will be a road warden, and whoever wants no other work for the rest of his life other than to fetch the officials' beer and bologna, such a one may become porter in some city office. And besides, all of them will get pensions. . . . Fie, it's a lot of money!"

Abraham continued to sit for a time. Then he looked out at the rain once more, remarked something about wood and wagonloads, and left.

The room remained still. The air within was close, and outside the rain continued to fall. One of the white shirts moved as though to rise, but thought better of it. "They'll get Nikola, Danilo!"

And only after a long pause a voice answered, muffled and choked: "They'll get him, Ihnat!"

"Nikola murdered Derbák Derbačok!" cried a young girl in a red kerchief, dashing down from the mountains into the community. She called out her news to everyone she met, until she reached Derbák's sister's cabin.

"Where? Where?" asked the passersby, stopping.

"On the pasture on Čerenýn."

Derbák Derbačok's wife and sister began to scream. People ran out of the neighboring cabins.

Adam Chrepta, his stepmother, and his aunt set out for Čerenýn Mountain. Derbák's younger children and their playmates ran with them, determined not to miss anything. The dead man's mother, the witch, stood in her doorway, sucking on the short pipe between her thin lips. The other women were weeping, but her eyes, with which she followed the departing group, were dry and evil.

The message was more than likely to be true. The haying season had arrived, as it was August. That morning, Derbák Derbačok had left for the pasture on Čerenýn to mow the parcel of meadowland he had rented up there. If a trace of hope remained in his hurrying family, it was only that the shots had not killed him, that a spark of life might still be found in his body.

The cowherds had already arrived at the pasture. They formed a semicircle around the dead man. They stood where the grass had been cut in order to avoid trampling down the part not yet mown. Their expressions were serious and they respected the wailing of the women. Derbák Derbačok had probably been dead for several hours. He lay on his back across a row of fresh hay, and his glassy eyes were turned upward. Beside him the scythe lay where it had fallen; the horn with the whetstone was sticking in the ground close by. One shot had wounded his arm and another had lodged in his belly. The sleeve over his elbow was damp with blood.

Soon the captain and the gendarmes arrived. He stormed at the people for having destroyed all the clues. "What clues did he need?" the cowherds wondered crossly as they drew back. Couldn't he see that the man was dead? And didn't he know who had shot him? What more did he want?

When Koločava heard how Derbák had been killed, the whole community realized that what the girl had called out (and what the captain probably still believed) was not true: Nikola had not shot Derbák Derbačok. Nikola did not have to shoot twice at the same man. Juraj had done that.

Ihnat Sopko, his face deathly pale, came running to Jasinko's cabin. He summoned Danilo. "Have you talked to Nikola since the meeting?" he whispered as soon as he saw him.

"No."

"Things are bad, Danilo. And he drew Jasinko away, through the gardens to the river.

"So Nikola does not know of Derbák's threats?" Fear was written all over Ihnat's face.

"I don't know, Ihnat. I'm to see him the day after tomorrow. He wants flour and cheese. Haven't you talked to him either?"

"Yes. I met him and Juraj yesterday morning, as I was going up to turn the hay on the pasture by the brook. They were probably expecting me. But the strange part of it is—they didn't want anything."

"You didn't tell him about Derbák's threats?"

"No. That's the worst of it."

Through Sopko's terrified mind there flashed the image of Nikola's suspicious gaze of the preceding day, his nonchalant question about what Derbák Derbačok was doing these days and whether he was still in touch with the gendarmes, even after the burning of his cabin should have warned him to desist. Sopko also remembered that as Nikola had been speaking, Juraj had grinned wickedly.

"Why didn't you tell him?" Jasinko asked.

"I was afraid to, because Derbák had told me to find Nikola for him."

They stood on the pebbled shore of the Koločavka, looking at the current and the overhanging rocks, over which fell a narrow white cascade that looked like a thread.

"Things are bad, Danilo. Nikola is in touch with some of his old pals." Surely, that must have been it.

"Danilo, Juraj will shoot the lot of us." Yes, he would murder them all.

"Let's kill them, Danilo." The dreadful words that neither of them had dared to utter that hot day in the woods near the pasture were out.

"Let's kill them, Ihnat." Their hearts began to beat fast. And Danilo Jasinko saw in his mind's eye the edge of the ax as it had appeared in the woods that day—silvery, scintillating.

"When, Danilo?"

"The day after tomorrow. Monday."

At that very moment Adam Chrepta was at Sopko's house for the third time. He was looking for Ihnat, furiously looking for him everywhere. Full of bitterness and unshed tears, he ran through the gardens and stopped at cabins. The image of his dead father, lying glassy-eyed over a row of hay, was frightfully real to him, and his heart was filled with revenge. He would kill the assassin! Though all the powers of hell were on the murderer's side, and all the magic potions in the world protected him, still he, Adam, would kill him. And Ihnat would have to help. And if Ihnat should hesitate, then Adam would tell the whole world who had killed the American's family and who had committed a whole series of robberies that spring, when Nikola had lain ill. He would give himself up and demand only one condition of the captain: time for vengeance. And he would perform his vengeful deed, as surely as there was a God in heaven!

Adam was looking for Ihnat Sopko. His fury mounted hourly, he flew out at people instead of questioning them decently, but they forgave him, for once making allowances. Then, near the church, somebody had told him that he had seen Sopko and Jasinko going toward the river together. Adam went there and found them. He made directly for Sopko; resolved to threaten and fight, he shouted, "My daddy asked you for something before he died."

"I know," Sopko answered mildly.

"He wanted you to find Nikola."

"Yes."

"Now it's I who want you to find him."

"Yes."

"What do you mean, 'Yes'?" Adam screamed, clenching his fists.

"I mean, yes, I'll find Nikola for you." As Ihnat faced Adam, his eyes, too, sparkled.

"You . . . will find Nikola . . . for me?"

"Yes."

"When?"

"The day after tomorrow. Monday."

The following day, Sunday, brought three carriageloads of gentlemen from Volové: the district commander, the district judge with the court clerk and the scribe, the district health officer, a porter, and some tourists from Prague who longed to see the notorious village.

The dead man was undressed and laid out on a table in the yard behind Leibovich's tavern, where there was a plot of grass. The gentlemen chatted in groups. To keep out the villagers, the gendarmes were lined up both within and without the yard alongside the fence, over which the black-eyed Susans were nodding on their tall stems.

The district health officer, who was also the coroner, donned a white smock, took scalpels, forceps, saw, and probe out of his bag, ranged them beside him on a board, threw a bichloride of mercury tablet into the washbasin, washed his hands, wiped them on his towel, and rubbed Vaseline on them.

"How many autopsies had he already performed in this accursed village!" he reflected, and his conscience pricked him a little. The thought of a dark room with a clay floor and a medieval loom, of his trips through the melting snow, of Šuhaj's feverish eyes and powerful chest. The place had been called Zvorec, he believed. Why had he not sent the gendarmes out after him then? Out of romantic gallantry! Oh nonsense, what kind of gallantry was it, when he had been threatened from the start! Out of cowardice! He had allowed the name Nikola Šuhaj to dazzle him, just as it dazzled all these other fools. Šuhaj was the real cavalier, not to have told anyone of the doctor's visits and to have been able to persuade the others who knew of them to hold their peace. But—and again the physician had the unpleasant idea that had already traced a new line on his brow—someday Šuhaj's gallantry would no longer permit him to tolerate the accusation that he had committed all the hideous crimes of the previous spring, of which he was innocent. In that case, Šuhaj would ask the doctor to prove his alibi. What then? Fie! The physician would even prefer facing him here on the autopsy table to facing him across the courtroom at Chust.

The doctor, using the probe, examined the wound.

"These robbers around here really have splendid physiques," remarked the clerk.

"Yes, they have," the doctor nodded, but in his mind he remembered that poor big Svozil had a finer one.

"Tell us, Doctor, in Romanian, doesn't *hucul* stand for 'robber'?"

"The country around here isn't Romanian, and there aren't any Huculs here. These people belong to the tribe of the Bojkové."

"Well, maybe they aren't Huculs, but anyhow they're robbers. In any event, the word *Bojkové* is likely to be derived from *bojovati,* 'to fight,' and so they are apt to be fighters. And how many Derbáks have you here?"

"I don't know. But probably one out of every five is a Derbák."

The doctor dissected the body. He opened the abdominal cavity with his scalpel.

"A nice mess in his belly," he said, "blood and excrement."

He examined the inside of the wound. It contained linen threads from Derbačok's shirt; he had, therefore, been shot from a distance.

"A bullet wound in the jejunum. Perforation of the intestines. Internal hemorrhage into the abdominal cavity," he reported.

The captain of the gendarmes was one of the audience at the autopsy. He had seen hundreds of wounded in Galicia and in Siberia, but the expert examination of the dead man's organs was most unpleasant to him, perhaps because the green garden, the yellow flowers, and the naked corpse recalled to him the terror he had felt as a child when near a little chapel in the woods. Then too, this affair affected him too intimately, he felt that he was responsible for Derbačok's death. "You won't accomplish a thing here. You'll go crazy!" his predecessor had prophesied in turning over his force, and, truly, after a year in this village, the man himself had been ripe for a sanitarium for nervous disorders.

"Is the bullet lodged in the body?" he asked the doctor.

"No, no," the doctor replied, and raised the intestines with his hands, "it went out his back, somewhere near the first lumbar vertebra. But it was obviously inflicted with a rifle of the Austrian infantry, as in the cases of Svozil and the other gendarmes. . . . Well, of course, the descending aorta was involved, too. That's why there was so much blood. At least the poor devil didn't suffer long."

"Of course," thought the captain. Šuhaj aimed at the jejunum, and his chief concern was to involve the descending aorta! Why all this cutting up of a body after death? The captain felt the same sort of hostility toward the physician as on the preceding day the cowherds on the pasture had felt toward him. The issue was clear: all those learned terms together only meant death. And everything else was clear, too. It could have been nobody other than one of Šuhaj's comrades who had divulged Derbačok's threats, made just before the meeting had taken place a week ago. And how did they expect, by looking at Derbačok's intestines, to find who had betrayed him when they could not even find the bullet there?

The responsibility was beginning to make the captain apprehensive. Perhaps it had really been madness to have locked up Eržika, the only human bait upon which Šuhaj might have been caught, and to have secured the release of that whole band of ruffians. (How difficult it had been!) Now they were loafing in the village, lounging in the taverns, holding forth, seeing Šuhaj, and probably plotting new crimes with him. They had no intention of catching him. And the Jews were to blame for the whole situation. His predecessor had been right: a dreadful breed, these Koločava Jews! They considered him their man, they ran after him, not giving him a moment's peace, they kept buzzing their notions in his ears, they would torment him to death. They were the ones to unearth that old mystic nonsense about people not dying through the good in them but rather through the evil in them, and had pestered him so long, until he had believed it himself. And a horrible people, these Bojkové of Koločava! You could threaten them, torture them, pamper them like children, address them in honeyed tones—it all made no difference, you could not move them. And if you hacked them into small pieces, Nikola still had his magic bough and old Mrs. Derbák would still be practicing witchcraft. . . . Well, anyway, her sorcery had not helped her son here!

The doctor finished his work. He was washing his hands in the tin basin.

"Get ready, we'll write it down," he told the court scribe.

At that moment, a pale face appeared over the fence, above the black-eyed Susans, and a clenched fist was raised.

The assembled gentlemen gave one start and stiffened. They lived through the sort of split second that ruling heads experience when five yards away from their carriage a fist is raised to throw a bomb. No bomb, however, flew out of the fist above the blossoms. Its owner merely waved it to and fro as he shouted, "Today you're cutting up my daddy, but within three days you'll be cutting up Šuhaj!"

The district commander came to his senses. "Who is that?" he called frantically. The gendarmes pulled the man away from the fence. "Who is it?" repeated the district commander. Now he was screaming at the top of his lungs.

"The murdered man's son," said the captain and he motioned to the gendarmes to let Adam go.

"This damned village!" thought the district commander. "To give a man such a fright!"

The following morning, Monday, Ihnat Sopko and Adam Chrepta went forth to kill Nikola Šuhaj.

Adam stopped for Ihnat, who, paling, went to fetch his ax from the storeroom; there, in the dim light, he made the triple sign of the cross over the blade; then, straightening up and looking skyward, he crossed himself three times. There was no longer any turning back. "Help me, O Lord!" Ihnat prayed.

They went. The morning was overcast.

Two men with axes over their shoulders were in no way conspicuous, for men did not go to the woods otherwise than with axes; moreover, these two had work in the Suchar Woods, on the pasture by the brook. Sopko's father had rented a piece of grassland up there, about an hour and a half's walk from the village, on a slope above the Koločavka, where it wound its course through the underbrush. The spot where Šuhaj was to meet Jasinko this day was close by. The plan had been well conceived: Ihnat had already been working on the meadow for several days, and the fact that his friend Adam was going to help him could arouse no suspicion. Jasinko was to meet them toward noon.

The haystacks had been built, and the two young men were putting up wickerwork fences around them in order that the cattle grazing there in the fall might not pull out the hay. They trimmed their stakes, drove them into the ground around the haystacks, and interwove them with branches that they had brought from the woods.

The day continued gloomy. Even before they had arrived at their destination it had begun to rain, really to drizzle, making their coats heavy and laying a blanket of sparkling drops over the hay. Adam Chrepta found it difficult to work in silence and to force himself not to tremble at the thought of how much his nerves should have to bear. He would put down his ax at short intervals, and walk up to Ihnat. In his need to hear somebody's voice, he would ask Ihnat questions, the answers to which Ihnat would or would not know, any more than he himself. But Ihnat was more prudent. "Talk if you must," he cautioned Adam, "but don't walk up to me. Keep working as you talk; perhaps he's watching us from the woods somewhere."

He was right. The Šuhaj brothers were observing them from a distance of about four hundred paces. Nikola was looking at his friend, his former friend, whose father Juraj had killed two days before. A traitor, to be sure. But Nikola knew how fond the father and son had been of each other.

Juraj had a gun over his knees. Why wouldn't Nikola let him approach them from the lower side of the slope and shoot them when they were both together so conveniently? Nothing good would come of those two, so what was the sense of sparing them? Adam was the enemy who together with his father had been betraying them to the gendarmes and who would never forgive them for his father's death. And Ihnat, too, was a traitor. Even at their last meeting he had shielded Derbák Derbačok and had not said a word about his threats. Why not, then, put them where they could do no harm? Had he been alone, he would not have hesitated for an instant.

"What do those two want here?" he asked for the second time that day.

Nikola gave him a sidelong glance. "Put down that gun! You

can see: they are fencing in the haystacks. And you yourself know very well that Ihnat has been coming here for almost a week."

"And Adam?"

"You can see. He's helping."

"Watch out, Nikola! They've come to kill you."

"Oh hush," Nikola waved a hand.

Below, Adam Chrepta and Ihnat Sopko, weaving fine branches between their upright stakes, had no inkling of the nearness of Juraj's gun and of his finger on the trigger.

After an hour's time, at about eleven o'clock, Danilo Jasinko could be seen walking through the mist on the pasture. He leaned on his ax as though it were a cane and carried two sacks tied over his shoulder, one hanging over his back, the other over his chest—obviously, supplies for Nikola, who sat watching him through his binoculars. Jasinko walked to the haystack and talked for a time to Adam and Ihnat. Then, picking up their axes, they all crossed the pasture and headed for the woods.

Nikola rose that he might go to meet them.

"Don't go, Nikola!"

"Leave me alone, Juraj!"

"Nikola, don't go!" cried Juraj beseechingly.

"But that's nonsense, Juraj! Why, we have our guns, haven't we?"

He went. Juraj followed. They descended through the edge of the woods along the pasture, and when they came out into the open they were only fifty paces away from the three others.

Adam Chrepta's heart started to pound fiercely. They met. Nikola shook hands with Jasinko and Sopko. He took no notice of Adam. Through Adam's mind flashed a scene of the preceding day—the garden back of Leibovich's tavern, his father, undressed and with his belly ripped open, the gentlemen all around, and he, Adam, looking over the fence, shaking his fist, and, later, roughed up by the gendarmes.

Nikola was talking to Jasinko. Juraj had remained standing a few paces away, ready to fire his gun, watching the three axes and their every motion.

"What's new in the village?"

Jasinko told about the gentlemen's visit on the previous day and poked fun at the new captain of the gendarmes.

"Don't stay here, Nikola!" Juraj almost shouted.

Nikola surveyed the pasture and compared it to a piece of woodland behind them.

"You're right, Juraj, we'll hide from the rain."

They went into the depths of the forest: first Nikola, then Jasinko, Sopko next, then Adam, and finally, no less than four paces behind them, with his weapon by his side, Juraj.

Jasinko turned to look over the situation, and, as he saw the frowning Juraj, he laughed: "Well, Juraj, what's the idea? Why, you're driving us just like an armed gendarme!"

Nikola stopped and turned. He looked gaily at his brother, and then his gaze swept over his friends' faces. He tossed his head in the direction of Adam. "What does that one want here?" he asked.

Adam could feel himself turning pale. Juraj grasped his gun even more firmly and gave Nikola a questioning look.

"He's been helping me fence in the haystacks, so he's coming with me," explained Ihnat.

Nikola's merry eyes, his smile, and the barely visible shake of his head answered Juraj, "Don't be a fool, Juraj!"

The strange procession, really resembling a chain of convicts being driven forward, again took up its silent advance. It made for a slope covered with hazel trees. There in a grassy spot it stopped. The fine misty rain still continued, although the noonday sun was trying to pierce it.

Here the men sat down in a semicircle: Nikola to the right, then Ihnat, Jasinko, and Adam, Juraj, again a few paces apart from the rest, on the left end. The two brothers could see each other's faces. The ground was covered with many rustling leaves and dry twigs so that anyone who might have wished to approach would perforce have betrayed himself by the sound of his footsteps.

Nikola was calm. Not so Juraj, who had an evil premonition. He was almost as sure of his instinct as he had been that time the spring before, when the god of the forests had guided his steps directly to his sick brother's side. He could scent danger. It was in the air and touched every inch of his body, and if Nikola could not get wind of it as he breathed, if he did not notice it in the atmosphere and feel it in the pit of his stomach, all the responsibility of watchfulness devolved upon Juraj himself. His eyes and nerves were constantly on guard. Ah, that he might only last out and not relax. After they should leave, it would be possible to rest. Tomorrow! All the rest of his life perhaps, only not this day!

Jasinko and Ihnat again held forth about the meeting and the new captain, about the people's reaction to his foolish suggestions, about the released prisoners and their tales. They talked about everything, excepting Derbák Derbačok. But Nikola, as though this were the one subject he wanted to discuss, suddenly interrupted their conversation by turning to Adam: "Are you sorry for your daddy, Adam?"

The youth grew frightened. "You know I'm sorry for him."

Nikola gave him a long look. "Well, it can't be helped." And after a time he continued, "I hear you want to get married."

"Yes."

"Come up, I'll give you money for the wedding."

"You aren't going to give me a thing, anymore, ever," thought Adam to himself.

Then Ihnat fetched some water in a mug and started to shave Nikola. Juraj's watchful tension strained to the breaking point. He saw only the streaks of white lather disappearing progressively from his brother's face under the motions of Ihnat's hand. The gun on his knee became a living thing and he was acutely conscious of the feel of the cold trigger against his fingers.

"Should I? Now?" Ihnat was saying to himself as he drew the razor over Nikola's throat. "We agreed on a different plan, to be sure, but will another such opportunity present itself again today?"

But when he squinted at Juraj and saw the boy's sharp eyes, and the muzzle of Juraj's gun aimed at him as though by chance, he finished his task with a steady hand. Nikola's lathered face beamed on Juraj in a brotherly, reassuring manner. "Heavens," thought Adam, "how the time was flying! Ihnat had not dared! Would this day dissolve into nothingness?"

Juraj's nerves could not bear such prolonged tension. "Nikola, Nikolka, come on, let's go away!" He spoke in the wheedling, impatient voice of a willful child. His eyes were fixed on his brother.

But Jasinko opened his two sacks and took out the supplies: cheese, onions, Jewish wheat bread, and a bottle of spirits. There had been a purpose for this choice: if one ate soft white bread and drank it down with alcohol, one would soon get drunk.

They drew out their clasp knives, ate, and sipped from the bottle. With the distribution of the food they shifted their positions somewhat. Jasinko and Adam drew closer to Juraj, Ihnat Sopko was now half a pace behind Nikola. The handle of his ax lay against the sloping earth beside him, and he sat on the blade.

That was when it happened.

As Nikola bent over for the bottle of spirits at his feet, Ihnat Sopko gradually rose, grasped the ax, and stretched slowly. Yawning, "Eh, how my back hurts me today!" he poised the weapon for a blow. Then, suddenly, it swung down full force and its blade stuck in Nikola's exposed head.

Juraj fired. He sprang up. Adam caught him by the shoulders from behind. Jasinko swung his ax at the boy's head. But as Juraj straightened up and leaned back in his struggle to free himself from Adam's grip, the blade did not reach his head. Merely glancing his forehead, it struck his abdomen and ripped it open, exposing his entrails. Juraj fired once more. He wrenched himself free and tried to run away in spite of his wound. Jasinko stooped for his gun and shot him in the back at six paces. Juraj fell. He tossed for a time, clawing at the rocks and biting the earth.

They turned to Nikola, ready to give him a finishing blow should he show any signs of life. But when they turned him on his back they could see that his eyes were already growing dim.

"It's all over. . . . This is the end!" was the refrain that ran through their minds. The air had the bitter odor of decaying leaves. Everything was very still. The mist continued to fall. Adam felt the blood pounding wildly in his temples.

After a time they went through the dead men's pockets. Nikola had a gold watch and twenty-six thousand six hundred crowns in his billfold. On Juraj's person they found two gold chains, with a pocketknife suspended from one of them. All of these things they took.

Not wishing to meet or to talk to anybody, they stayed in the woods until sundown. They roamed over winding paths to recover from their horrid work; they examined their clothing and washed their axes in a stream. They sat under an old beech tree for a long time. At first they were silent, but then they deliberated about what to say and how much of Šuhaj's money to acknowledge.

Late in the afternoon, when it had cleared up and the air glowed yellow, they returned to the pasture by the brook to finish the fences around the haystacks. They were glad to have hit upon this work, which at least soothed their nerves even if it did not take their thoughts away from the two they had killed. These lay in the clearing by the hazel grove, wet from the rain-drenched grass and leaves.

The friends stayed in the pasture until after dark. Then, walking over the log that lay across the Koločavka, they took the path that ran down alongside the stream. They walked slowly in order to get home after the village should already be asleep. Adam was sent to Koločava-Horb to hide twenty thousand crowns at his stepsister's house, they having decided to report six thousand six hundred crowns to the gendarmes. Ihnat Sopko and Danilo Jasinko went to Leibovich's tavern. Adam was to follow them there later.

At the tavern, they seated themselves at a trestle table under a dim petroleum lamp. The taproom was empty, and nobody heard them enter. But they did not object to the poor service. They were grateful for this opportunity to collect themselves.

The door to Kalman Leibovich's private chamber was wide open. Inside, on a table with an embroidered spread, a lamp was burning brightly. A merry, loud company was assembled there: gendarmes, revenue collectors, Leibovich, and his seventeen-year-old daughter. The revenue collectors had talked a novice in their group into offering Leibovich some of his wine. The green youth coaxed, Leibovich made excuses that he did not drink wine, the daughter smiled. The young man, insistent and offended by turns, created a situation that caused the others much merriment. They knew that the Jew would never taste any wine that had been touched by a Gentile who had had a chance to perform ritualistic magic with it.

Clouds of cigarette smoke floated in the bright lamplight. Jasinko and Ihnat sat in the semidarkness, looking at the well-illuminated scene in the smaller room as though it were on a stage.

Finally, Leibovich peered into the taproom. He had to shield his eyes with the palm of his hand to see them. They ordered a bottle of beer. As the Jew was setting it down on the table, Jasinko said, "We should like to tell you something, Leibovich!"

"Well, what is it?" he demanded impatiently, for he was in a hurry to get back to the other room, where he had to keep an eye on his daughter.

"Sit down!"

"I haven't time now."

"This is very important."

The words were spoken in so decisive a voice that Leibovich looked first at Jasinko and then at Sopko; he went to the threshold of the little room and called out: "Faigele! Mama is calling you. She needs you in the kitchen!"

Closing the door behind her, he sat down beside the two under the dim lamp.

"Well, now what is it?"

Jasinko, looking into the Jew's eyes, waited a few seconds before he spoke: "How would it be, Leibovich, if the Šuhajs were dead?"

"What?" Leibovich whispered, not daring to comprehend the idea all at once.

"They are dead," Jasinko told him. "We killed them."

"What?" Kalman Leibovich laid all ten fingers on his forehead. But his temperament got the better of him immediately. "When? How? Where? Both of them?" he blurted out, seizing Jasinko's arm and pressing it with both hands.

His questions were answered briefly.

"Go and tell the sergeant about it, Leibovich!"

The Jew sprang up. At the door he turned, as though to come back. But he opened it into the smoke and the glare.

"Come on out!" he motioned to the sergeant. They went out the back door and into the yard together.

"Both the Šuhajs are dead. Jasinko and Sopko hacked them to death with their axes."

The sergeant whistled. Instantly grasping the situation, he laid a finger on his lips: "Not a word to anybody, Kalman!"

Leibovich wanted to expound on something, but the sergeant became completely the gendarme. He ordered, "Send the other sergeant out here!" And in a very threatening tone he repeated, "Remember, Kalman, not a word to anybody! Not even to your wife!"

For over a year they had lived with no other thought than to remove Šuhaj, for over a year they had pursued him and awaited this moment. Now that it had arrived, the sergeant found no joy in fulfillment; it was as though life had suddenly lost its purpose. Somebody else had killed his rare game. The longer he stood there in the darkness of the backyard, the greater the weight that the news assumed. Thirty-three thousand. The good opinion of his superiors. His career as a gendarme. Glory. Newspaper columns with his full name given. The debt he had run up at Leibovich's tavern. All was lost. . . . Or was there still a chance?

The other sergeant arrived. They deliberated, walking to and fro in the yard or sitting on the lumber. Then they ordered three gendarmes to stay with them and asked the remainder of the assembled guests to disperse. All five put on their leather belts and went to sit with Sopko and Jasinko and with Adam, who had arrived in the meanwhile. The sergeant had some bottles of beer brought in, and then he drove away Leibovich, who was still bustling around them, not even allowing him to trim the lamp.

"Drink, boys, it's on me!"

After they had touched glasses, he asked in a friendly tone, "Now how did it happen?"

Jasinko began the account on which they had agreed, and which he had already outlined to the tavern keeper. Ihnat Sopko, he said, had requested Adam Chrepta to help him fence in the haystacks; he, Danilo Jasinko, had chanced to be on the pasture, too; the Šuhaj brothers had come out of the woods and engaged them in conversation. They had bidden them to the hazel grove. Once there, the Šuhajs had acted suspiciously, had winked at each other as though to harm them, and when Juraj had raised his gun, the three of them had thrown themselves on the brothers and had beaten them to death.

The gendarmes tried to register statement after statement in their memories.

"We-e-e-ell!" drawled the sergeant, stroking his mustache. He had experience in such matters and grasped immediately that Jasinko was dwelling somewhat too long on how they had made the fences and passing somewhat too hurriedly over the leading event itself. Moreover, the great fear that Jasinko pretended they had all felt before the Šuhajs somehow reeked too much of the captain's speech of a few days before.

The sergeant questioned them and in his mind he tried to reconstruct what had actually happened. To be sure, he did not need to be friendly any longer: he had enough information to turn up the lamp suddenly and, drawing himself up in his full dignity, to thunder at them. But the situation was such that it was better to stay calm and to strike the strategic blow safely at the right moment. He was preparing for it.

"We-e-e-ell!" he said once more. Jasinko, Sopko, and Chrepta immediately sensed a snare. "It happened rather differently, boys."

Their attention quickened.

"It happened this way. You didn't just chance to meet Nikola. You, least of all, Chrepta!" the sergeant sneered. "When Chrepta here promised us only yesterday that we would be doing an autopsy on Šuhaj within three days! You all met Šuhaj to talk over some new skullduggery. But you got a hankering for the thirty-three thousand, and you were afraid lest Nikola would tell on you when we got him alive! And then I believe he had some money on his person, eh? That's the way it was, boys! You see, we have been keeping track of you a little longer and know a little more about you than you realize . . . but never mind that for the present. . . . It was your duty to catch Šuhaj and bring him to us, or, if you hadn't the nerve for that, to get us and we would have known how to fetch him down here ourselves. To me, this whole damned affair smacks of premeditated murder, if not of murder with robbery as the chief motive. Isn't that right, eh? It's really my duty to arrest the three of you!"

Having pronounced these ugly words, the sergeant lapsed into silence. Stroking his mustache and his chin, he turned from one to the other of them, looking straight in their eyes. "We-e-e-ell. But drink your beer in peace, boys. . . . I shan't do it . . . that is, perhaps I shan't. . . . But nothing will come of the thirty-three thousand, I can tell you that right now. Understand?"

Fear gripped the hearts of the three under cross-examination. Jasinko took six thousand six hundred crowns out of his pocket and laid the bills on the table. Ihnat Sopko saw again in his mind's eye the two corpses in the hazel grove, all of Šuhaj's glory now drenched in the drizzle. Should they have held back after all?

"Who else knows about it?"

"Nobody, only Leibovich."

"Who else?" asked the sergeant sternly.

"Nobody."

"Listen, Chrepta, you came in later than the others. Where were you and whom did you see?"

"Nobody. I had a headache and so I went for a swim in the river."

This was not improbable. The youth was deathly pale.

The sergeant took one of the gendarmes aside to a dim corner of the tavern and for a long time they considered ways and means. Then they returned.

"Do you know how to hold your tongues, you three?" The sergeant spoke severely.

"We do," replied Jasinko.

"All right. Tit for tat. We shall not arrest you. We're the ones who got Šuhaj. Is that clear? As for the reward, we shall share it with you."

"We understand."

Everything was not yet entirely clear to them, but perhaps it would be better this way. Petr Šuhaj, the old bear, was still around, and Nikola's brothers were growing up. It would certainly be of some advantage if they never learned who had killed Nikola. The three conspirators again began to breathe more freely. The reward, it is true, shrank out of sight, because the gendarmes would cheat them out of it all, but Adam had probably hidden the twenty thousand securely, and that in itself was a great deal of money! The thought of the outlaw, dead in the grove, was losing its terror: his invulnerability had been overcome with an ax, and his lips were sealed.

"And now, boys, don't worry about anything and have a drink!"

They drank until late in the night.

After midnight, the gendarmes threw their carbines over their shoulders and set out. The three peasants went along to lead the way. The moon was bright. They advanced through the soundly sleeping village, crossed the meadows, and, finding their way with the aid of flashlights, they took the rocky path up the Koločavka valley. Walking over the log to cross the stream, they mounted the slope. Jasinko led now, just as he had done at noon. They pushed through the underbrush of young hazel shrubs. "Over there!" said Jasinko, pointing.

On a grassy plot about ten paces ahead of them two black shadows could be distinguished on the ground. Five flashlight bulbs turned on them and threw the two corpses into sharp relief against the greenness of the wet grass and growing hazel leaves. They lay on their backs and their outstretched limbs were stiff.

The sergeant's flashlight circled the plot and penetrated the thicket, illuminating its recesses. The sergeant was looking for a vantage point. Finding it, he led his men behind the shrubbery, whence he had them fire at the corpses. They shot at Nikola and at Juraj, as though they wished to make up for all the shots they had been firing all year in vain. They fired pell-mell into the darkness, volley after volley, riddling the bodies with bullets, until the first clear streaks of approaching dawn appeared over the hazel grove. Then one of the gendarmes was sent down to the village to fetch a wagon. The rest lay down in the deep woods and wrapped themselves up in their cloaks to doze a bit after their long night.

Jasinko, Chrepta, and Sopko now understood perfectly. Yes, perhaps it was really better this way. Now, after the official consecration of their deed, it seemed to them that the two corpses in the grass belonged to strangers, that the Šuhaj brothers had ceased to exist long ago, and that if they three had ever had anything in common with them, they had now achieved complete absolution, of which the gendarmes' fire had been the outward sign. They felt at ease.

It was already fairly light when the Jew arrived with the wagon. He drove up the riverbed to the upper slope of the mountain. The three friends had disappeared in the woods before his arrival, that he might not see them here. The gendarmes dragged the corpses down the slope and threw them into the wagon. They came to Koločava in broad daylight.

That Tuesday, the Jews strutted very contentedly over the pebbles of the Koločava street. They were in a Sabbath-day mood. The members of the younger generation forgot the quarrels within the Jewish community: the struggle waged between the houses of Beer and Wolf over the tobacco vendor's concession, their secret Zionism, and their careful undermining of the Chust rabbi's authority. Once again, they felt like one big family, at peace with their elders. The Jewish maidens donned hose and were wearing their best blouses. They strolled in twos, stopping near the groups of boys and responding with gracious smiles to the gendarmes' greetings. The old Jews held forth outside the doors of their shops. Among them was Adam Beer, whose mild smile had never been as benevolent as

on this day. And when the happy captain hurried by, the Jews'
bright greetings were full of friendly familiarity. He was, they felt,
a fool, but their man nonetheless; he had performed his work well
because he had taken their advice. They were the ones who had
come upon the eternal truth that a man does not die by what is good
in him, but rather, by what is evil in him. They were the ones who
had reduced this abstract wisdom to a practical motto "Lock up
Eržika, free his friends!" For could anyone deny that the death of
the Šuhajs was causally connected with Eržika's arrest and with the
release of his friends? Could anybody wish to shut his eyes to the
result? And what fool would dare claim that he comprehended cause
and effect and understood the intentions of the Almighty, whose
eternal name be praised?!

The gladdened captain, hero of the hour, the man who came, saw,
and conquered, rushed to the Forest Administration at Koločava-
Horb and borrowed a camera from the director. For on the grass of
the garden back of the gendarme station lay two corpses. They lay
with their heads in opposite directions, like trophies of the chase.
Nikola's feet lay over his brother's abdomen, possibly to hide Juraj's
horrible wound, or perhaps because this arrangement was necessary
in order that both might be included in the same picture in an effec-
tive pose. Two carbines were laid crosswise over the dead men's
chests, and between them was hung a blackboard, inscribed with
fancy lettering in chalk:

ŠUHAJ'S END

AUGUST 16, 1921

» » » Epilogue « « «

Thus ends the story of Nikola Šuhaj. Or is there anything further to be added?

Now, after the lapse of so many years, the author of this narrative has no desire to assemble and verify the historical crumbs that the great outlaw of the Carpathians left behind him. Nor is it of any particular interest to learn that Eržika has married again and that her husband is Ilka Derbák Dička (another of the numerous Derbáks of Koločava!); nor that after Šuhaj's death she bore a daughter, Anča, at the Chust jail; nor that in the hope of helping her cause, she testified that she had had the child by Sergeant Svozil, but that one has to smile at this lie when one looks at the beautiful little girl with the arched forehead and small chin, so characteristic of all the Šuhajs. The child might be described in the same colors that Rosie Grunberg once applied to the father: she is as tanned as a tree in the forest, with lips as red as a cherry, with arched eyebrows and black eyes that sparkle like a window on the Sabbath.

It is unnecessary to add that the district health officer from Volové, doing an autopsy on the Šuhaj brothers—"You, too, at last, Nikolka!" he had thought, secretly ashamed—had to see at first glance that neither rifles nor bayonets could have inflicted the horrible wound in Nikola's head or could have ripped Juraj's abdomen.

It goes without saying that the proffered prize was not awarded. ("Oi, oioioi," said the Jews, "what a lot of fuss and quarreling there would have been in the synagogue if we had really had to dig down and collect thirty thousand!") And there is no point in reporting the tedious proceedings of the district court in the trials of the provisional gendarme Vlásek and many others, accused, among other offenses, of arson. In the end, such researches tell us nothing for we cannot find out how matters were finally settled.

And it would be quite useless to tell of the numerous requests, entreaties, and accusations made by Ivan Dráč, who wants to get compensation for the property damage suffered through the burning of his house and barn, with the incidental loss of cattle. He has even pestered the chief justice in person. The old man is stubborn as a mule and completely deaf (perhaps from the many blows he has received in his lifetime), and his case cannot end otherwise than with an eight-month sentence to prison on the grounds of libel and contempt of court.

It would be worse than boring to try to decipher the atrocious handwriting of the examining magistrate of the district court at Chust and his report on the hearings of Adam Chrepta, Danilo Jasinko, and Ihnat Sopko, who were held in custody for almost nine months and accused of premeditated murder. They defended themselves on the ground of self-defense and were finally acquitted, for while murder is murder, Šuhaj was, after all, Šuhaj.

What is the use of praising the government for having kept its promise of rewarding with government jobs those who should remove Šuhaj? Why report that Adam Chrepta has become a provisional employee in the Forest and Estates Administration and that he would be completely content if only he might be transferred from Koločava, where he has to be too careful of his hide? Or that Ihnat Sopko is a road warden in the Volové district? Or that Danilo Jasinko alone of the three conspirators has preferred independent enterprise to civil service and, having sold his property in Koločava, has bought a farm in another part of the mountains, where, unfortunately, his buildings have already been razed by fire on two separate occasions?

Should we satisfy the curiosity of the thoroughgoing, systematic reader by reporting that a study of the land register at Volové and an examination of the relevant deeds and abstracts verify that Abraham Beer is not only the registered owner of the meadow on the banks of the Koločavka, but also its actual holder?

The author of the narrative about Nikola Šuhaj, the outlaw, considers all these facts of little significance. Certainly nothing could be plainer than the lesson they teach, namely, that no matter how illustrious the head that may be struck down with an ax in the Suchar Woods, the event changes neither the flow of the Koločavka nor the movement of the clouds in the sky between two mountain ridges nor the course of days and nights, which continue to come and go, each bringing its own new burdens. The author would, rather, ascribe importance to another point.

The mountains that tower above the narrow valley of the Koločavka and bring morning so late and evening so early and admit spring only after a long delay, these mountains, changing unceasingly, have during this whole period moved too little for human perception. On their slopes and precipices, in their caverns and glens, grow virgin forests, which are dark and sad and which reek of decay. Should the wayfarer reach down for a fallen limb to be trimmed for a staff, it will fall to pieces, having lain there for decades, untouched by man or beast. The great dead trees, whether they perished in windstorms, by lightning, or of old age, consider it a point of honor not to relinquish their places after their lives are ended; they prohibit the free development of the multitude of small living trees that struggle with their lifeless glory, push up to the sun through their dried branches, spread greedy roots over their gnarled ones, and climb to their crowns in curiosity and impatience to learn which ones are fated to live and which to decay with the dead giants. The forest is astonishingly still: there are no songbirds or small game here. Except for the utterly insignificant living things, such as insects, fungi, and molds, whose lives are too unimportant to be noticed, only such can survive here as carry powerful weapons and are eternally ready to strike—with beak or talons, with trunk, fang, or claw, or with horns, which last are the most horrible weapons of all, because the deer, their owner, has no longing to kill.

High up in the mountains, above the timberline and close to the clouds, are located the sunbathed expanses of pastureland. Here the gentians, white crowfoots, yellow violets, pansies, hawk-weeds, daisies, and blood-red geraniums grow, profuse and bright, but the grass, grazed by herds of cattle, is meager.

God still lives in these mountains, the ancient god of the earth. With his icy blasts and spring torrents he destroys all weaklings and lavishes his love upon the strong things that have found favor in his sight: trees, swift streams, beasts, men, and rocks. He loves all these alike: capriciously, cruelly, and generously, like a medieval monarch. In the heat of noonday, he bends over streams to drink out of the palm of his hand and reposes in the crowns of old maples; he plays with bears in the thickets, fondles the calves run away from their herd, and gazes with pleasure upon children who have fallen asleep on the shaded moss. An ancient pagan god. God of the earth, master of forests and flocks.

This alone is of importance.

Another matter: people live in the narrow valley, on the slopes where the woods have relinquished a little space to the meadows, or up on the pasture. They live in cabins that resemble groups of mush-rooms under the birches. The men spend their days out in the fresh air, and the women emit the odor of the smoky indoor fires. These people are shepherds and woodcutters, for they have not yet arrived to the level of agriculture, and in these parts the plow has not yet been invented. They are descended from nomads who fled from the Ukrainian plains, driven to the impassable mountains by the Tartar hordes. They are the great-grandsons of rebellious serfs who ran from the horsewhips and the gallows of Josef Potocký's Cossack hirelings. Their grandfathers revolted against the exploitation of Romanian warlords, Turkish pashas, and Magyar magnates. Their fathers, brothers, and sons were killed in the slaughterhouse of the Austrian Emperor's army. They themselves have been tormented by Jewish usurers and by the new masters. All of them, without exception, are outlaws at heart, for living outside the law is the only form of defense that they know. It is the only defense that works: for a week, a month, a year; in the case of Nikola Šuhaj, for two years; in that of Oleksa Dovbuš, for seven. What matter if it comes high, costing no less than life itself? Is life indeed eternal? Man is born but once, he can die but once!

Their minds are filled with vague memories of past wrongs and a burning consciousness of present wrongs, while a wild longing for freedom is in their hearts. Dovbuš had this same longing. So did Šuhaj. The people love them for it.

Near the first houses of Koločava, right by the road and not very far from the forks of the Koločavka and the Terebla, is a steep, rocky, cone-shaped hillock, like a cast-off scrap from the mountains that rise behind it. It contains neither trees nor shrubs, and only a little grass can grow in its rock debris. The cows that roam over it, jingling the bells around their necks as they pass from one grassy valley to another, have but little occasion to stop and bite off any morsels here. This place is the Koločava cemetery. One does not pass through a gate or over a fence to enter it, and will realize its identity only as one clambers up the slope and sees a few crosses, all alike, stuck among the stones. The crosses are invariably made of two boards nailed together and stand not more than two feet high; others have fallen or been knocked to the ground by the cattle and lie in rotting fragments.

In these parts, tender memories of the dead are unknown. "Come, Brethren, let us kiss the dead for the last time!" Thus speaks the priest as he sprinkles holy water over the corpse and the deacon chants, "Oh Lord, give peace to this thy departed servant!" These ceremonies end everything. All is over for you, dead man; now live somewhere else, do not come back to K=Koločava, do not haunt or harm us, you have nothing further to seek here!

Side by side, in this cemetery, are buried the bones of the brothers Šuhaj. But neither the inhabitants of the cabins on the highway below nor any of the members of the Šuhaj family will point out their resting place. Even Eržika Derbák Dička has to look around for a time before she stops in front of a mass of gravel, long since leveled to the ground. She stands for half a minute, silent and motionless, then sighs a little and goes her way.

But Nikola Šuhaj's glory lives on. In Koločava, where people knew him and where a new generation, come after his time, has only recently passed the age of adolescence, here, beneath Šuhaj's outlaw fame, his human likeness may still be discerned. Outside Koločava, however, he has become a mysterious personage. His actions and shooting ability have been celebrated in song. His green bough and his treasures, which would dazzle the world if they could be unearthed, have become the awe-inspiring subjects for tales to be told on winter evenings, when it is snowing outside and the beech logs are crackling in the oven. Nikola Šuhaj has become a legend. He has become a symbol of the struggle for freedom because he was the friend of the downtrodden and the enemy of the ruling classes. Were he living today, they believe, there would not be so much misery in the world. Ah, that the narrators of his exploits could take from the rich and give to the poor! That they, too, might avenge injustice! Ah, that they had his green bough and his treasures!

When the stars overhead are like glacial pools in the blue-black night, and the will-o'-the-wisp dance in the primeval forest, shepherds overcome their fears. Blessing themselves with the triple sign of the cross, they venture into the sylvan depths to mark the spots whence the mysterious lights issue in order that they might know on the morrow where to dig for Šuhaj's buried treasure. At twilight, having supped on corn porridge, they sit by the open fire in front of their shelters and take their reed pipes from their bosoms. Alternately singing a stanza and playing it on their pipes, they send forth their song into the thickening darkness:

> The cuckoo bird sang so plaintively
> From his tree in the forest green:
> "Nikola Šuhaj! Please tell me why
> You are no more to be seen."

This closes the story of Nikola Šuhaj.

Let us return but for a moment to the beginning of this account, to the shelter on Holatýn. And let us recall that in his heart Šuhaj was always aware of his oneness with these mountains, their forests and brooks, their bears, herds, and people, clouds and streams, with everything here, including even the planted hemp seeds and the melancholy tone of the reed pipe and the thoughts with which people fall asleep. Šuhaj's instinct did not err when he felt that he would not die. Nikola Šuhaj lives on in these mountains and within them, and shall continue to live, let us not say "forever"—for today we comprehend the meaning of this word even less than did our pious forbears—let us say, rather, "for a long time."

Thus, when Nikola felt immortal, he was as right in his way as the shepherds who told his story were in theirs. Having in mind only his personal individual existence, they had to limit the conception of his invincibility to mere immunity from bullets in order to leave a way for death to slip through his defenses and take his body, even as his spirit remains in his native mountains.

»»» CHARACTERS AND PLACES «««

Balassagyarmat   home of a Hungarian regiment.

Bela, Lenard   a gendarme sergeant intent on capturing Nikola Šuhaj.

Bláha   a Czech official.

Bojkové   an ancient tribe that settled in Ruthenia.

Brázy   a mountain in the Carpathians; associated with the activities of the outlaw Oleksa Dovbuš.

Burkalo, Fedor   one of Nikola's accomplices.

Čerenýn   a mountain in the Carpathians.

Chemčuk, Kalyna   a young girl in Koločava.

Chrepta, Adam   a young peasant and the son of Derbačok; one of Šuhaj's accomplices.

Chust   a town near Koločava.

Derbák   a family name very common in Koločava. Members of the Derbák family mentioned in the work:

  Ilka Derbák Dička, a Koločava peasant.

  Marijka, Derbačok's wife.

  Miša Derbák (Miška, diminutive), a soldier.

  Olena Derbák, Derbák Derbačok's mother.

  Vasyl Derbák Derbačok, a peasant; Šuhaj's accomplice.

Douhé Gruny   a mountain in the Carpathians.

Dovbuš, Oleksa   (Dovbušík and Oleksík, diminutives) a celebrated outlaw of the past.

Dráč   a family name. Members of the Dráč family mentioned in the work:

    Eržika Dráč, the heroine; Nikola Šuhaj's wife.

    Ivan Dráč, Eržika's father.

    Josef Dráč, Eržika's younger brother.

    Juraj Dráč, Eržika's older brother.

Drahov   a village.

Dzvinka   the family name of Dovbuš's mistress.

    Štefan Dzvinka, her husband.

Holatýn   a mountain in the Carpathians.

Hucul   a Romanian tribe.

Hurdzan, Hafa   a young girl of Koločava.

Ivanyš, Marijka   a peasant woman.

Jasinko, Danilo   a peasant of Koločava; Šuhaj's accomplice.

Jevka   a girl's given name; the Russian witch's daughter.

Koločava   a village in the Carpathians, where the story is set. The village is made up of three regions: Horb, Lazy, and Negrovec.

Koločavka   a river that runs past Koločava.

Kosmače   a village; the home of Dovbuš's mistress.

Krásná   a mountain where Lenard Bela tried to ambush Nikola Šuhaj.

Kraśnik   the scene of one of Šuhaj's engagements during the War.

Lugoš, Juraj   military commander elected by the peasants.

Majdan   a village in the Carpathians.
Molnár   the notary.

Rika   a river in Ruthenia.

Sopko, Ihnat   a peasant; one of Šuhaj's accomplices.
Stokhod   the scene of one of Šuhaj's engagements during the War.
Subota, Hafa   a young girl of Koločava.
Suchar   a mountain in the Carpathians.
Šuhaj   a Ruthenian family name meaning "young man." Members of the Šuhaj family appearing in the work:
   Anča Šuhaj, Nikola's sister; also, Nikola's daughter.
   Juraj Šuhaj, Nikola's brother.
   Nikola Šuhaj (Nikolka, diminutive), the hero, an outlaw in the Carpathians. Miklos is the Hungarian form of Nikola.
   Petr Šuhaj, Nikola's father.
Svozil   a Czech gendarme.

Terebla   a river in Ruthenia.
Tisová   a mountain in the Carpathians.
Tisza   a river in Ruthenia.
Točka   a village in the Carpathians.

Uzhgorod   the capital city of Ruthenia.

Vasia   a girl's given name; the Russian witch's daughter.

Verchovina   a name meaning "hill country" that is applied to the region in which the plot is set.

Verecký   a Carpathian village.

Vlásek, George   a gendarme.

Volové   a Ruthenian town.

Vorobec, Jevka   a peasant woman.

Vratislaw   a Polish town.

Vučkov   a small town in Ruthenia.

Ziatykov, Ivan   a young peasant of Koločava.

Zvorec   a Carpathian village.

Ivan Olbracht was born in the Czech town of Semily in 1882. After studying law and history in Berlin and Prague and serving two years in the Austrian army, he became a journalist and later edited *Rudé Právo*, the leading Czech communist paper. Olbracht wrote several novels and shorter works and translated Arnold Zweig, Thomas Mann, and others into Czech. He is best known for *Nikola the Outlaw* and the story collection *The Sorrowful Eyes of Hannah Karajich*. He died in Prague in 1952.